Praise for *K*

Blin...

"A jaded television reporter and a ... y bond in Walsh's delightful conten ... urn romance is a nuanced exploration ... trust, desire, and negotiating boundaries, without a hint of schmaltz or pity. The sex scenes are sizzling hot, but it's the slow burn that really allows Walsh to shine."—*Publishers Weekly*

"Karis Walsh always comes up with charming Traditional Romances with interesting characters who have slightly unusual quirks."—*Curve Magazine*

Sea Glass Inn

"Karis Walsh's third book, excellently written and paced as always, takes us on a gentle but determined journey through two womens' awakening...The story is well paced, with just enough tension to keep you turning the pages but without an overdramatic melodrama."—*Lesbian Reading Room*

Improvisation

"Walsh tells this story in achingly beautiful words, phrases and paragraphs, building a tension that is bittersweet. The main characters are skillfully drawn, as is Jan's dad, the distinctly loveable and wise Glen Carroll. As the two women interact, there is always an undercurrent of sensuality buzzing around the edges of the pages, even while they exchange sometimes snappy, sometimes comic dialogue. Improvisation is a true romantic tale, Walsh's fourth book, and she's evolving into a master romantic storyteller."—*Lambda Literary*

Wingspan

"As with All Karis Walsh's wonderful books the characters are the story. Multifaceted, layered and beautifully drawn, Ken and Bailey hold our attention from the start...The pace is gentle, the writing is beautifully crafted and the story a wonderful exploration of how childhood events can shape our lives. The challenge is to outgrow the childhood fears and find the freedom to start living."—*Lesbian Reading Room*

By the Author

Harmony

Worth the Risk

Sea Glass Inn

Improvisation

Mounting Danger

Wingspan

Blindsided

Mounting Evidence

Love on Tap

Tales from Sea Glass Inn

TALES FROM
SEA GLASS INN

TALES FROM SEA GLASS INN

by

Karis Walsh

2016

TALES FROM SEA GLASS INN
© 2016 BY KARIS WALSH. ALL RIGHTS RESERVED.

ISBN 13: 978-1-62639-643-2

THIS TRADE PAPERBACK ORIGINAL IS PUBLISHED BY
BOLD STROKES BOOKS, INC.
P.O. BOX 249
VALLEY FALLS, NY 12185

FIRST EDITION: JULY 2016

CREDITS
EDITOR: RUTH STERNGLANTZ
PRODUCTION DESIGN: STACIA SEAMAN
COVER DESIGN BY SHERI (GRAPHICARTIST2020@HOTMAIL.COM)

PROLOGUE

The smell of cinnamon lured Pam Whitford out from under her soft burgundy comforter. She grabbed the pair of jeans and sweatshirt she'd draped over a chair near the bed and pulled them on before leaving the room she shared with Mel Andrews. She'd long since learned not to venture upstairs without being reasonably dressed since the people staying at the Sea Glass Inn could appear in the common areas at any time, day or evening. On one particularly embarrassing night, an older guest had turned on the kitchen light and discovered her sitting in a wash of moonlight at the breakfast table, finishing the leftover pizza from the fridge and wearing nothing more than a sports bra and underwear. He'd apologized and left the kitchen with an empty glass, one he had presumably been about to refill with water, and she had escaped into the downstairs suite with the pizza box. They'd both avoided eye contact during breakfast the next morning, and Pam had never again left her and Mel's room without the minimum requirements for decency.

She took the steps two at a time and inhaled deeply as the scent of Mel's baking grew stronger. Pam was a private person, happiest when she was alone in her art studio or snuggled with Mel. She should hate the intrusion of the inn's constant stream of guests in her life, the need to be fully dressed before she entered her own kitchen, and the effort to make small talk with the strangers who shared meals with them. But she didn't. Because of Mel. Pam came through the door and paused for a moment as she watched Mel rolling out a batch of dough on the counter. She felt like a goofy teenager with a crush every time she saw her partner and lover. Her heartbeat skewed off course and she couldn't keep the silly grin off her face if she tried.

Mel had changed her life in unexpected ways. Loner Pam now met new people every week. She ate meals and took walks on the beach with them. If one of them stopped in the backyard to look through the studio's large windows and watch her paint, she waved and smiled. Sometimes she kept working, and other times she actually invited the guests in and showed them around. The old Pam would have covered the windows with blackout curtains and hidden inside. Not the new Pam. She'd seen how willing Mel was to open her home and heart to complete strangers, and she'd personally experienced the healing effects of Mel's warmth and love. Because of her, Pam was more open, too, and she'd made friends from all over the world. In turn, those friends, with their stories and secrets, gave her plenty of inspiration for her art.

She crossed the kitchen and stood directly behind Mel, wrapping her arms around Mel's waist. She kissed the side of Mel's neck and felt her insides melt when Mel leaned into her.

"Mmm." Pam nuzzled the hollow between Mel's neck and collarbone. The dough combined with Mel's shampoo to make an intoxicating blend. "Cinnamon and vanilla and roses. I could eat you up."

She opened her mouth wide and took a pretend chomp out of Mel's neck. Mel laughed and ducked out of reach, holding her floury hands in front of her. "Let me finish these rolls first, and then you can nibble all you want."

Pam braved the threat of a flour dusting and leaned forward for a kiss. Mel's lips felt warm and soft against Pam's. Despite her protests, Mel was the one who slipped her tongue into Pam's mouth and deepened the kiss into the kind that made Pam see stars when she shut her eyes. The contact from thigh to breast charged Pam's nerve endings so much she thought it had to be visible. She must be glowing like a firefly. At the same time, Mel's touch brought her a now-familiar sense of peace. The peace of being *home*.

Mel pulled away. Her throat was pink and her eyes looked

hungry, but she pointed toward the back door. "Go paint or... something. Walk the dog, watch the sunrise. If you don't, we'll be trying to pass off frozen pizza as a gourmet breakfast and our reputation will plummet."

Pam grinned. If it weren't for hungry guests, she and Mel would be back in their bedroom already. Or maybe right here on the kitchen floor...

"Later," Mel said, as if reading Pam's mind.

"Most definitely." Pam waggled her eyebrows and made Mel laugh. "Come on, Piper. We've been banished."

Pam's small brown-and-white spaniel jumped off her bed in the corner of the kitchen and trotted to the door, her entire back half wagging in anticipation of a morning seagull chase. Pam gave Mel one more quick kiss—heroically resisting the urge to press her against the kitchen counter—and went outside. She and Piper navigated the path through the backyard without needing more than the predawn glimmer. The summer air felt warm and damp against her skin, but Pam shivered with anticipation. She and Mel would have the entire afternoon together. They could wander through the town of Cannon Beach or explore a new trail in Ecola State Park. Or maybe just lock their bedroom door and stay inside all day.

Pam inhaled deeply and coughed the exhale. She wrinkled her nose at the putrid hint in the air. Had something washed ashore during the night? "Just a quick walk today, Piper," she said, reaching down to scratch the dog between the ears. Pam would keep a close eye on her this morning, and then later, when the sun was up, she'd come out here alone and do whatever cleanup was needed on the beach. Their property only extended to the beach access cliff, but Pam considered all of Cannon Beach to be her responsibility as much as anyone else's.

She hesitated at the top of the staircase leading to the beach and Piper scampered down, a few steps ahead of her. Pam couldn't count how many mornings she'd begun this same way, with a walk on the beach. She'd never tire of it, even if she had a hundred lifetimes. She heard the relentless waves and felt each one crash and ebb inside her. The air reeked today, but normally the fresh taste of salt tingled in her nose and throat, and the familiar memory was enough to make the faint hint of something rotten fade into the background for a moment.

The beach was still bathed in darkness, and Pam could barely see more than an outline of Haystack Rock. The ocean glowed an iridescent black, except for the occasional whitecap peeking through the early-morning gloom. Pam shivered. She'd been on the beach in the deep dark of moonless nights before and she'd never felt anything but at home and welcome there. Why was today different?

She heard a faint whine and walked down a few steps before she saw Piper standing on the lowest stair. Her white fur stood in stark relief against the backdrop of glistening black sand, and Pam spun around and looked over her shoulder. A bright half-moon hung in the east, high enough to illuminate Piper. Pam turned around again and fought down a wave of nausea as she realized what she was seeing.

The beach was *black*. Not shadowed, not reflecting the night. Black.

"Piper, come." The dog immediately followed her command and ran to Pam's side, leaving smudged footprints on the wooden steps. Pam knelt when Piper reached her and picked up one of her paws. It was coated with a thick sludge, and when Pam held her trembling hand in front of her face, her mind finally registered what she had been seeing all along.

Oil.

Pam told Piper to stay and she walked the rest of the way to the beach by herself. Everything was covered in a thick coat of oil, as far as she could see in either direction along the beach. Even the sea in front of her. A thick rope of terror coiled around her heart as she fought for breath. The smell—what was it? Animals? Birds? How many were trapped out here? How would they ever clean this off the sand?

A flash of white—startling movement against the still shadows—caught her attention. The flailing motion broke her out of her frozen state and she ran up the steps, grabbing Piper on the way.

She raced across the backyard with her dog clutched to her chest and slammed open the back door.

"Mel. The beach. Oil." She spoke between gasps. When had she started crying? "A bird. I need to save it."

Mel swiveled away from the pan of cinnamon rolls and stared at her with an expression as horrified as the one Pam felt must be on her own face. A long moment passed as if Mel was processing the information and the bedraggled and oily state of Pam and Piper, but then she snapped into action.

"The dog crate is in our closet downstairs," Mel said. She took Piper from Pam and cradled her against her white shirt with one arm while she reached for the phone with the other. "Take some of the towels from the bathroom."

Pam heard the distinctive beeps of Mel dialing 9-1-1 as she flew down the stairs. By the time she had wrestled the rarely used crate out of the back of the closet, stuffed a few towels in it, and run back upstairs, Mel had hung up the phone. Pam paused and looked at Mel hopefully. It couldn't be as bad as she'd first thought. A barrel of oil, and no more, had crashed ashore in the night, just below the inn. The damage was limited.

Mel shook her head silently in answer to Pam's unspoken hope, and rested her cheek against Piper's head. Tears rolled down and onto the dog's fur.

"What's wrong?" Jack, one of their guests, stood in the kitchen doorway still wearing his robe. His partner Trevor was behind him, in jeans but barefoot. "Did something happen?"

"An oil spill," Mel said in a choked voice. "The beach is covered for miles."

"What can we do?" Trevor asked, resting his hand on Jack's shoulder.

"Can you help me empty out some cardboard boxes in the garage?" Mel asked. "They've already opened the convention center as a refuge. We can take birds and animals there, but we'll need…"

Pam left Mel and the guests to gather more boxes and she retraced her steps to the beach. She waded through the oily sand that threatened to suck her light sneakers right off her feet, staring into the darkness for some sign of the bird she'd seen. The entire beach was still, too still, and she nearly stepped on the seagull before it feebly lurched to its feet and fell over again.

Pam knelt in the muck and opened the door to the crate. She gathered the struggling bird as gently as she could, folding its wings and nestling it on a pile of towels before she closed it in. She stood up and lifted the heavy burden while thick globs of oil plopped off the crate's bottom and the knees of her pants. The smell of Mel and the kitchen, the warmth of the inn and the promise of an afternoon of idleness, and the rejuvenating joy of a morning walk on the beach receded from her world like they'd been sucked down a drain. The sun was beginning to reveal the shore's secrets now, and Pam saw flashes of movement here and there as creatures struggled to move, to survive.

She had one bird, and Mel was collecting boxes for more. But how would they ever save them all? Would her world ever heal from this?

LOW TIDE

Jenny Colbert pushed a loose strand of unwashed hair behind her ear and squinted against the harsh fluorescent lights as she counted the makeshift animal pens filling the vast convention hall. She had arrived at Cannon Beach two days ago, refreshed after a two-week stay in Puerto Vallarta and clean after a long shower in her temporary Los Angeles apartment. She hadn't showered, eaten, or stopped to catch her breath since.

A woman holding a clipboard came over to her. She was wearing cutoff jeans that showed her slender, athletic calves and an inside-out faded yellow T-shirt. She looked as weary and grubby as Jenny felt. Jenny forced her tired mind—usually quick to remember details—to recall her name. Pam? Yes. Pamela Whitford. An artist of some sort, and one of the owners of the Sea Glass Inn where Jenny would be staying while she was here. Not that she'd be spending much time in her room there, away from this convention-center-turned-wildlife-hospital.

"Hey, Jenny," Pam said. Her shaky voice and red eyes were proof she'd been crying not long ago. She cleared her throat and blinked a few times before continuing with a more composed tone. "The entrance hall is almost filled with the donations we've been getting all night. Home Depot has sent three truckloads of plywood, trash bags, and plastic tubs for the washroom. The local paper brought stacks of old newsprint, and they published the list of items we need, so people have been stopping by with things like blankets and gloves. Workers from the PetSmart in Tillamook are having a drive to collect crates and dog runs, and they'll start bringing what they've got so far to us tomorrow morning. My friend Tia has set up a phone line, and we're getting calls from people all over the Northwest who want to volunteer."

Jenny watched Pam tick off each item on her clipboard as she shared the information. Jenny had been doing this work long enough—traveling to cities after disasters and helping the animals and birds involved—that she could easily spot the few key people she'd need as cornerstones on her team. Pam and Melinda Andrews had been immediate choices, and Jenny's instincts had been spot-on. The two hadn't paused since Jenny had walked into their damaged town and started directing the rescue efforts. Mel—Pam's partner and owner of the Sea Glass Inn—was in charge of the main room where the birds would live until they were able to return to the beaches. Pam was in charge of what Jenny thought of as the infrastructure. Crates and pens, workers, tables and chairs. All the equipment they'd be using over the next few weeks. She was organized and persuasive, relentless in her desperate desire to take care of her home after the disastrous oil spill. She'd already plowed through Jenny's hastily written list of necessities.

"Thanks, Pam," Jenny said when Pam seemed to run out of things to say. She put her hand on Pam's shoulder and gave her a squeeze. Years of living a nomadic lifestyle had helped Jenny hone her talent for bonding quickly with strangers, even though those relationships she made never turned into anything deeper than an occasional postcard that found its way to her next temporary home. The friendships she formed were transitory, but important. They helped her assess people and connect with them during a crisis, when the most vital action was forming a team to handle the problem at hand. She cherished the shared sense of purpose she felt, for a short time, at least, with the people whose lives had been affected by a disaster, the people who were willing to devote their time and energy to help her heal the local wildlife. Once the danger was over, she would pack up her scarce belongings and move on.

Letting go of relationships when it was time for her to leave was as necessary in her chosen profession as forging them immediately upon arrival. Still, despite her parents' warnings about getting too close to people she'd eventually leave, and her own self-protective instincts, Jenny occasionally met people like Pam and Mel who made her wonder what it would be like to know them better. To just hang out with them on a normal day, without a life-or-death mission attached to their friendship. She didn't let her thoughts linger there too long, though. She gave Pam another pat on the shoulder and dropped her hand to her side. "You've done an amazing job so far. Try to take a little break. Get something to eat or some sleep, if you can."

Pam nodded before she walked away, but Jenny doubted she'd take her advice. Pam wasn't any more likely than she was to stop right now, to sit and put her feet up and sip some tea. Those small normal acts didn't belong in this damaged world. Jenny sighed. Someday Pam and Mel would sit in their backyard, on the top step of the stairs leading to the ocean, and relax with a glass of wine or morning cup of coffee. Someday. But not now.

Jenny froze in place when she saw another woman intercept Pam before she got to the large bank of doors leading into the foyer. She was a stranger to Jenny—a new volunteer? She was dressed simply in jeans and a long-sleeved, light green sweater, with her tawny hair pulled back in a ponytail and a basket over one arm.

Jenny had a million-item list in her head: Make sure the people from the water company were installing the right number of spigots at the proper height. Double-check the charts for in-processing the oil-covered avian patients. Greet each volunteer and start collecting their names and skills before she assigned them to jobs.

Later, though. She'd cross every item off the list before she allowed herself to take even a small catnap, but for the next few seconds she'd let herself stand idle while she watched the interchange between Pam and the woman who was giving her a hug and handing her something wrapped in paper. After exchanging a few words with Pam, she moved on to the next volunteer and repeated the same gestures. A hug, a short chat. Handing over a wrapped bundle from her basket.

Jenny needed to get on with her own work. She'd delegated

volunteer training and recruitment to Pam and Tia. But Jenny ignored her carefully structured system for once and walked across the cavernous room toward the newcomer. She was surprised by her own movement, and even more so by her fervent wish that she'd been able to shower and change in the recent past. Since when did she care how she looked, especially when there was more important work to be done?

"Are you here to volunteer?" she asked. The woman spun around to face her, looking startled at the words. She looked as clean and rested as Jenny felt bedraggled and weary. Just standing next to her was refreshing, and Jenny felt some of the stress she had been carrying inside since her arrival dissipate, only to be replaced by a new kind of tension. Attraction. Jenny allowed her energy to be buoyed by the feeling, but she wouldn't let herself linger here any longer than she had when imagining a lasting friendship with Pam and Mel. "Tia is in the lobby, and she'll assign you to a work station."

"Oh…sure. Of course I'll be glad to volunteer. I'm Helen Reiser, by the way."

"I'm Jenny Colbert." She shook Helen's hand, surprised by the firmness of her grip. Helen had a softness about her, accentuated by the tantalizing aroma of yeast and butter that seemed to linger in the air around her, but her strong fingers and direct gaze showed she was anything but weak. Jenny was reading too much into a handshake, but it was part of her job to come to quick judgments about a volunteer's character. Just as quickly, she discovered the unexpected way her body responded to Helen's touch.

"Nice to meet you, Jenny."

Helen smiled and a few fine lines appeared near the corners of her big blue eyes. Jenny had first thought Helen was in her early twenties, but the lines made Jenny add a decade to her estimate. Helen had a youthful grin, but something in her expression showed she had lived through tougher times than these. And she was beautiful. Understated, but with something sharp beneath the calm exterior. Jenny shook her head. She was here for one purpose only—to return the shore and its inhabitants to their clean, pre-spill condition. She needed to know enough about her volunteers to be able to do that job well, and nothing more. Maybe she should put some distance between her and Helen until she had more sleep and was her usual efficient and detached self.

"Yes, well, nice to meet you, too. Be sure to check in with Tia and she'll assign you to a work station." Had she said that before? She was having trouble concentrating.

"I saw her and fed her," Helen said with the rueful look of someone who had listened to one of Tia's breathless monologues. Jenny had only been here two days, and already she'd heard more words from the one woman than she herself had spoken in the past month. "I'll ask her what she needs me to do as soon as I've delivered these croissants. I figured no one here has bothered to eat much today."

Helen reached into her basket and handed Jenny a parchment paper cone. Jenny paused before accepting the warm package. "I really shouldn't. I have too much to do, and—"

Helen waved off Jenny's words. "Nonsense. It's small and portable and you need food to have enough energy for this job."

Helen walked away before Jenny could protest anymore. Not that she wanted to. She couldn't even remember the last thing she'd eaten, but she was damned sure it hadn't been as good as whatever Helen had given her smelled. She opened the top flap of the parchment and took a bite of the small, perfectly moon-shaped croissant. A thick slice of ham and some gooey, melty cheese were folded inside. Jenny finished the pastry in two more bites and crumpled the paper as she watched Helen talking to Mel on the other side of the room. She shook her head. Helen intrigued her mind and aroused her body. Now Jenny's stomach had joined the fight against her concentration. She'd better stop drooling like an enamored and hungry puppy and get back to work.

Jenny tossed the paper into a trash can and turned away from temptation. The convention center's floor was crisscrossed with channels, so segments of walls could be pulled out, separating the main floor into several smaller conference rooms. She had arranged for most of the space to remain open, but a corner of the room was enclosed on three sides. This quieter area would soon be filled with waist-high sinks where volunteers would clean the seabirds, washing every last drop of oil off their delicate feathers. Now, though, it was empty of both people and equipment. The perfect place for Jenny to regroup.

She pulled a small pad and pen out of her back pocket and flipped through several pages of names. She added Helen to the list, feeling a small tingle of secret pleasure, as if she was writing her name with a heart around it in a school notebook. She rubbed her eyes. Helen's effect on her was a symptom of sleep deprivation. Nothing more.

Jenny added a star next to Helen's name. Even though Tia was technically in charge of volunteers, Jenny kept careful track of them during the early stages whenever she organized a new rescue center. She noticed the leaders, like Pam and Mel. She watched for aggressive recruiters, like Tia, because the rescue effort would desperately need bodies to help, and most people would have a difficult time saying no to her. She also identified groups of friends who would be more inclined to remain interested if they were on the buddy system. Helen was definitely a leader. Jenny had noticed the way the other volunteers responded to her. She brightened their expressions, and not just because she was handing out heavenly pastries.

What was it about these coastal towns? Jenny had witnessed it time and again—all communities drew together after disasters, but ocean side towns seemed to transcend the temporary closeness of other places. They were a family.

Helen was the embodiment of the community's intimacy. She was feeding the people, nurturing them, with her personality and not only her food. Jenny would be a part of this place for a short while, welcomed inside because of her knowledge of this type of tragedy, but then she would move on to the next place where she was needed. She was a catalyst. She'd handle details, train volunteers, put a system in place. Assign duties and tasks, and then stand back and let the community do the work.

She'd always been an outsider, moving from disaster to disaster, just as she'd done throughout her childhood with her doctor parents. She had the experience needed to run this rescue effort, but without the people from the community nothing would be done. People like Mel and Pam. Helen. They had the heart and the drive to heal their home. Jenny gave them the tools and resources they needed and then she moved on. Sometimes she felt a twinge of longing when she left, but nothing she couldn't handle. Because by then she had performed her role—the one her parents had instilled in her from childhood.

So why did it feel different this time? Why did Helen make her feel a small but persistent urge to see what the view was like from the inside? Just once, just for a moment? Whatever the reason, Jenny didn't have time to dwell on it right now.

She saw some weary-looking, grime-covered officers from the Department of Fish and Wildlife carrying crates through the back door of the center, and she stuffed the notepad into her pocket again and rushed over to help. Tonight, she would concentrate on getting as many frightened birds and animals as possible into the safe, yet artificial world of the event center. Tomorrow, they would begin washing and treating them. Hopefully in the not too distant future, they'd be releasing them back into the wild, and Jenny would be released as well.

❖

Helen felt the lingering weight of Jenny's gaze as she walked away. She figured it had more to do with the basket she was carrying than with her as a person, but she let herself bask in the electricity she had felt between them. The center was full of exhausted and hungry workers—of course they were going to respond favorably to anyone offering fresh-baked food. Especially her famous ham and Gruyère croissants. She could look like the Incredible Hulk, and she'd still expect to be on the receiving end of salivating glances in this crowd.

She delivered several more pastries on her way over to Mel. Everyone responded with ravenous gratitude, but something about the look Jenny had given her made a deeper impression. Tia had mentioned Jenny as soon as Helen walked through the door, carrying on a monologue about Jenny's brilliance and her organizational skills. Between surprisingly short pauses to take huge bites of croissant, Tia had delivered a barrage of facts about Jenny's competence and her gorgeous looks. She had sounded like a fantasy woman, and Helen had expected her to have some mysterious aura, visible from across the room. In reality, Jenny had looked as zombielike as all the other sleep- and food-deprived people in the room.

And in reality, Jenny had been one of the most glamorous and regal women Helen had ever seen. A quick swipe of a washcloth and a catnap, and Jenny would be fit for a stroll down Rodeo Drive, although she looked too down-to-earth and principled to be interested in anything as inconsequential as fashion. Tall and slender, she made even the ratty tan coveralls she was wearing look elegant. Her blond hair was streaked with platinum, more likely due to time spent in the sun than in a hair salon, if Helen was right in her assessment of Jenny's personality. And the green eyes Tia had rhapsodized about? They were as reflective and bright as a tide pool that hid an entire mysterious and varied ecosystem in its depths.

Damn those eyes. Helen finally reached Mel, who was standing in the center of an empty plywood pen. Helen had planned on coming here with an offering of food and nothing more. Actually, she hadn't even meant to do that much. Not because she didn't care, but because she couldn't afford to give away even a tiny croissant. She had maybe two months' buffer between this moment and bankruptcy, and given the state of the beaches, crowds of tourists weren't likely to be flocking to her bakery and buying dozens of muffins anytime soon.

"Hi, Mel." Helen hesitated next to the wood panels. She didn't doubt her abilities as a baker, but she still felt a little reluctant to offer her food to Mel. People raved about the breakfasts at the Sea Glass Inn, and Helen wasn't sure how her pastries would compare.

"Helen, it's good to see you here," Mel said, stepping over the barrier and giving Helen a quick hug. She broke away and peered into the basket. "What smells so delicious? I'm not above begging if you don't offer me whatever it is you have in there."

Helen laughed and handed Mel a croissant. She'd remained distant from the locals so far, preferring to keep to herself, but Mel's implied approval seemed significant to her. In the three months Helen had been in town, she'd already seen several stores open and then fail. Businesses were started on a whim because of the appeal of living and working in the laid-back and naturally beautiful coastal community. Too few of the owners—and Helen lumped her naive self of three months ago in with them—actually realized what it took to succeed. She didn't blame the longtime proprietors for waiting until new arrivals were established before considering them part of the family.

"I'm supposed to ask Tia where she needs me to work, but do you mind if I help you here for a while?" Helen was skipping steps in the process, but she hoped Jenny wouldn't mind. Functioning bodies were most likely in demand, no matter what job they were doing, and Helen had made a tenuous connection with Mel. She wasn't ready to be thrust into the midst of a group of locals who were still strangers to her.

Mel's sigh of relief made her glad she had offered to stay, not just for herself, but for Mel and the cause.

"I'd love to have help. Volunteers seem to prefer to move on quickly to one of the more glamorous, hands-on jobs, so I've been doing this alone." Mel rubbed her temple and left a black smear across her pale, tired-looking skin. "Not that any of this is glamorous, of course. I didn't mean that. What I should say is—"

Helen stopped her with a quick squeeze on the shoulder. "I get it," she said. And she was pretty sure she did. She'd spent enough time in the foster system to understand the myriad reasons behind people's motivation to help others. Still, help was help, no matter what the reason behind its offer. She'd prefer to stay out of the crowded areas here. Get dirty and do her part, but keep some distance. "Although maybe I should ask what's all over your hands before I commit to anything."

Mel smiled and held out both hands, palms up. "The local news." She gestured toward the empty pen behind her. "We're using balled-up newspapers as bedding for the birds. Jenny said it's good cushioning for them, and it's easy to clean out the soiled papers. Be prepared for hand cramps."

Helen interlaced her fingers and flexed them in front of her. "Finally, those hours spent kneading bread will pay off. I knew I was training for *something.*"

She stepped over the side plank of the pen and picked up a stack of newspapers. Mel followed, and they began to separate sheets of paper and scrunch them into balls. They worked in silence for several minutes, until Helen's hands were blackened and silky-feeling from the residual ink. "Are you afraid?" she asked quietly, finally giving voice to the fear in her own mind.

"Of ink poisoning?" Mel asked. She laughed without humor and shook her head. "I know what you mean. About our livelihoods. I will be, but not now. I'm trying to focus on what needs to be done, and what I can do to save these beautiful creatures. Deep down, all of us are afraid of what will happen to our businesses and our homes here. We're coming together now to do what we can to save the beach. Later on, we'll work together to survive without a strong tourist season."

Helen had no doubt the core of locals would band together and weather this storm, but where would she fit in? Her bakery was new. She'd barely gotten started before this disaster, and she hadn't been convinced she'd be able to make her business last. Now, at the height of tourist season, when she should be making enough to keep herself in flour and eggs, her store was empty. Apparently even *she* wouldn't be in the store much over the upcoming weeks, given the amount of work to be done at the center and the number of people here to do it.

"Your inn is established." Helen admitted her fears after a brief internal struggle. She usually would keep her concerns to herself, but something about this place made her want to talk. People and emotions were laid bare here. "You have a reputation, customers who will return once the beaches are clean. I don't know if I'll make it that long, and even if I do, who will remember to come to my shop?"

Helen felt the beginning of a panic attack coming on. She wasn't prone to them, but they'd been fairly regular since she'd taken on the stress of starting a business of her own. They'd become even more persistent over the past few days, ever since the tide of oil had slicked across Cannon Beach. She found some comfort in the rhythm of pulling sheets of paper off the stack and forming them into balls. Slide and scrunch. Slide and scrunch. Breathe.

"We've only been open for a little less than two years, so I'll be looking for creative ways to attract customers, just like you will. It only took me two hours to drive to Cannon Beach from my old home in Salem, but the real journey to get to this place was a long and hard one. I'll do whatever it takes to stay here. I'm sure you feel the same."

Helen nodded without looking up from the strange little sculptures she was forming with her hands. Mel didn't know her past, but Helen figured most people in this isolated town had complex reasons for being here. The anonymity of tourist season, when the streets would be crowded with strangers. The hibernation of the off-season. The very reasons Helen had chosen to come here. To find some peace at last.

"Besides, you've made a loyal following already with those croissants of yours." Mel tossed a wad of paper onto the growing mound of them. "I figure a few more days of this work, and you'll be exhausted and numb enough to give me your secret recipe."

Helen grinned, feeling a small release in the tension she had been carrying in her chest. "Not a chance. I'd have to be—" She paused abruptly and pointed across the room where four coveralled people were carrying dog crates through a side entrance. "What's going on over there?"

"They found more birds," Mel said quietly. "We should go help them."

Helen saw Jenny moving quickly toward the newcomers. Almost before Mel had finished speaking, Helen had hopped over the side plank and was jogging over to her. Something about the way Jenny was carrying herself gave Helen a sense of urgency, but she slowed to a walk as she got closer. The men set the dog crates down and went back outside, presumably for more. Without a need for words, Helen stepped to one side of a crate and gently helped Jenny lift it.

Jenny smiled a weary but clear thank-you and gestured with her head toward one of the pens already filled with newspaper balls. Helen felt the weight of the crate shift as the birds inside jostled each other. She tried to make the short walk as smooth as possible, and her fingers hurt from gripping the cage tightly so she wouldn't drop it.

"Let's cover this end of the pen before we turn them loose," Jenny said once they had deposited the crate in the four-by-eight enclosure. Helen helped her place a large piece of plywood over one half of the pen, making a small cave. Jenny opened the crate and tipped it slightly, sending four oil-covered birds scurrying into the darkened side.

Helen followed Jenny's lead and quickly placed a second plank over the other end of the pen, completely enclosing the birds. She was as bewildered and surprised by the tears running down her cheeks as the birds seemed to be by their new prison.

"What kind are they?" she asked with a tremble in her voice.

Jenny looked up from where she was kneeling by the crate and pulling out dirty newspapers. She stood and came over to Helen, putting an arm across her shoulders. "They're murres. Are you going to be okay?"

Helen leaned into Jenny's embrace, surprised yet again by her own willingness to be touched. Usually she was the one doing the holding—holding herself at a distance from everyone else.

"Yes," she said, drawing strength from Jenny's combination of detachment and caring. Obviously this work meant a great deal to Jenny, or she wouldn't be doing it. But at the same time, she seemed to have a shield in place. Do the job without the tears. They wouldn't offer help anyway, neither for the birds nor for Helen's future here in oil-soaked Cannon Beach. "They just seem so frightened. I hate that this happened to them."

"I agree. They'll be scared for a while, and then they'll adapt. We'll do our best to make captivity easy for them until their release. But remember, these are the lucky ones, the ones who get to come here and be scared. They're safe now and will be clean soon."

Helen nodded and picked up her end of the empty crate. They'd take it back to the people who would soon fill it with more birds for her to help heal.

As she worked side by side with Jenny into the night, Helen's eyes remained dry. She had been thinking about herself earlier tonight. What it meant for her to be at risk of losing her bakery so soon after opening it. The loss in income, the guilt-driven need to volunteer. She'd learned as a child to put herself first, because she'd never had anyone else to take care of her. The sight of those four birds, burdened with oil and helpless in their cage, had finally driven her focus off her own problems and onto the small creatures huddled in corners.

❖

Jenny sat on a wooden bench at the top of a staircase and stared at the beach below. She had witnessed scenes like this on countless occasions, but the discrepancy between normalcy and disaster always unsettled her. The timeless sound of waves thundering to shore from deep ocean origins was unchanged, unhindered by the spill. Rugged Haystack Rock looming in the foreground looked the same as it did on the numerous postcards sold at every store in town.

Contrasted with these were the lingering stench of oil and the volunteers spreading across the beach as the sun rose. They made slow but steady progress as they scooped blackened sand into trash bags. The sight of them made Jenny feel guilty for not being at the center doing her part to help, but Mel had practically carried her back to the inn for a few hours of rest.

Jenny stretched and yawned. The short nap had been good for her. She had been getting punchy with lack of sleep, and she needed to be clearheaded enough to make good decisions for the animals and birds temporarily in her care. Plus, she had organized the rescue effort well enough for it to run without her for two or three hours. Shifts of volunteers had been working around the clock for five days, but starting tonight, Jenny would shut down the operation during the night except for a small staff of people to keep watch over the full pens. Both the workers and the frightened sea creatures would benefit from the dark, quiet hours. Time to heal and rest.

Although she usually moved on as soon as life was returning to normal at a disaster site, she thought she might stay here at Cannon Beach for a little longer. She could imagine the area in full glory, with white-and-gray gulls dotting the shore and sky. The waves would be blue green and splashed with foam, not rainbow slick with oil. Tide pools would be full of life and not merely dead, greasy puddles. Like the mosaic hanging over her bed in the inn, with Pam's signature scrawled across the bottom corner. The painting showed a slab of basalt, lit by the sun and darkened by shadows, standing watch over a pool of clear, glistening water. Starfish shimmered with embedded pink sea glass. Anemones and mussels adhered to the rock's surface, giving a sense of permanence and solidity.

Jenny rarely stayed in one place long enough to see the stable, real world reappear. She only saw the veneer of disaster covering the familiar, and the steady progress of those laboring to remove it. Surprisingly, she wanted to be here long enough to see Mel welcoming guests to the inn, and to stare through the studio window as Pam painted. To see Tia opening her gallery once again and gabbing the ears off every tourist who strolled in.

Most of all, though, Jenny wanted to see Helen in her bakery, covered with a film of flour and chatting with customers, the worry lines around her eyes and creasing her forehead gone for good. Jenny sighed deeply and coughed at the smell of oil, feeling as if it was coating the inside of her mouth and lungs. She had spent long hours in the same room as Helen over the past couple of days. They had talked a little, but only about the work they were doing. They had never been alone like they had been when they first met, but instead had always been surrounded by crowds of volunteers. Still, Jenny had felt a connection and she couldn't shake the desire to know

Helen better. To know who she was when she wasn't functioning in disaster mode.

A cool, wet nose gently nuzzled her hand where it was resting on the edge of the bench. Jenny smiled, relieved to have a distraction from thoughts of Helen, and reached down to pet the inn's resident spaniel.

A young man's voice called, "Piper! Piper, where are...oh, there you are." Danny, Mel's son, came around the corner of the garden path and halted when he saw Jenny. "I should have known she'd find you, Jenny."

He sat on the bench next to her, over six feet of gangly college sophomore. He and some friends had driven from Corvallis to help with the rescue efforts, and the sight of the six rested and ready-to-work young people had nearly made Jenny cry. She and the other volunteers had been dragging with exhaustion after the first heavy wave of birds came into the center, and the reinforcements had been more than welcome. Jenny saw Mel in her son's face and eyes and in his friendly, easygoing manner. But even though Jenny knew they weren't related by blood, she saw Pam in him, too. He was sensitive and artistic, with a deep connection to nature and animals. He took to the job of washing the fragile, oil-covered birds as if he'd been born to do it.

"I've been trying to clean her ears, but she hates it," Danny said, holding up a tube of ointment and a gauze pad. "She's been tilting her head and fussing at her right ear, and we think she got some oil on her paws and then got it inside her ear when she scratched it. She'll let us do anything with her, except this."

"She's probably hurting," Jenny said. Piper was sitting at her feet, gazing at the beach with a forlorn expression. She didn't move beyond the yellow tape marking the shore as off-limits, though, treating it like a solid barrier. Jenny slid off the bench and gathered the small brown-and-white dog against her. She wrapped one arm around Piper's chest and used the other hand to gently raise the outer flap of her ear.

"She has some inflammation, but it looks like you caught the problem early enough." She reached for the ointment and gauze, and then read the label before awkwardly smearing some of the tube's contents on a clean pad with one hand. "This stuff should clear up the problem in a week or so. See how I'm holding her against me? She's confined, but she's also comforted by the pressure and closeness."

Jenny swabbed Piper's ear while she quietly explained everything she was doing to Danny, who had come to kneel beside her. "You should clean both ears, even if she's just showing symptoms in this one," she said, releasing Piper and getting a new gauze pad out of its wrapper. "Why don't you try doing her left ear?"

After a short struggle, Danny got the hang of holding Piper still while he treated her ear.

"Good job," Jenny said when he let the dog go with a pat.

"Thank you. You make it look so easy, but by the end of the week, I'm sure I'll be better. I've thought about trying to get into the vet school at OSU, so any practice or advice I can get will help."

Jenny had met quite a lot of aspiring veterinarians doing the work she did. Some were discouraged by the manual labor and heartbreak involved, but others seemed to thrive on the work at her temporary rescue centers. Had any of them gone on to finish school? Would she ever know if Danny made the choice to follow that dream or not? Most likely she wouldn't. By the time he made any serious plans for his future, she'd be in a different state, or even country.

"I'll make sure you get a chance to work with some of the injured animals and birds while I'm here," she said. She could trust him to be gentle and to listen to her. "You'll be helping them, and it will be an interesting experience to add to your application, if you decide to pursue your degree."

"That'd be fantastic. Thank you," Danny said. He stood and called Piper to his side. "Thank you for everything you're doing here, not just this chance to help you."

He looked back at the inn for a few moments before meeting her eyes again. "And for my mom. This place means so much to her. If she lost too much business, or ever had to close..." He shook his head. "And for Pam, too. She cares about the sea life, and I know it's killing her to see any creature suffering. You're doing something really good for all of us."

Jenny blinked away the unexpected and unpleasant heat of tears. She felt proud of what Danny was saying to her, and she'd enjoyed the small interaction with a pet and its owner. She hadn't had a chance to do simple vet work since her earliest internships and clinic work. She had been raised by parents who gave up everything to practice medicine abroad, and—except for following her heart to vet school instead of medical school—she had tried to follow in their footsteps. Danny's appreciation touched her on a personal level. She'd heard similar words before, but she'd never felt them so keenly.

She shrugged, creating some emotional distance with the casual gesture. "It's just what I do. But you're welcome."

Danny nodded and turned away. Jenny figured he was as uncomfortable with the emotions this rescue project was bringing to the surface, in him and in his mom and Pam. Jenny knew it was better to focus on the details and not the feelings involved. Build pens, assign volunteers to tasks. Deal with the facts on the clipboard, not the emotions in her heart.

Unfortunately, the cause of too many disconcerting emotions was standing on the path watching them. Danny nearly bumped into Helen in his haste to get back to the house.

"Oh, sorry, Helen, I didn't see you there," he said. "Is breakfast ready? Whatever you and Mom were baking smelled awesome."

"There's quiche and banana bread on the table." Helen smiled at him, and then turned her attention to Jenny. "Are you coming? You really should eat something before you get back to work."

"In a minute," Jenny said, hoping Helen would stay with her instead of disappearing into the inn. She breathed a silent thank you when Helen sat on the bench next to her as if in response to Jenny's unvoiced request.

Helen was silent for a few moments, apparently unaware of the turmoil she was causing in Jenny's mind. The two of them had worked together for days, but they hadn't yet been alone together outside the center. Jenny had been trying to keep her perspective clear, seeing Helen as merely one of her volunteers. An attractive and tempting one, to be sure, but in reality no different from the hundreds of other people Jenny worked with at every job site. Sitting here, close enough for their thighs to touch, was something altogether new. Jenny felt them connected to each other and held apart from the rescue effort. This was one of those moments they might share if there was no spill, no need to rush back to the center, if Jenny was just a regular member of this community. Sitting on a bench together and watching the ocean waves—so normal, yet so out of reach. Jenny tucked her hands under her legs to keep from touching Helen, who looked beautiful with her cheeks slightly reddened from working in the kitchen. The scent of vanilla seemed to enrobe the two of them in a homey and safe bubble.

"Danny is right, you know." Helen finally spoke, in a quiet voice and as if choosing her words with care. "You're doing something amazing here. With the birds and animals, of course—their care is the most important—but for the community, too. You're healing this town, in a way. People would suffer if their businesses had to close because the beach stayed toxic. But it's even more than the money. It's this community. The people here are close and care about this place, but you come here as a stranger and work alongside us like you belong. You seem very selfless."

Jenny shrugged again, as conscious of her need to deflect Helen's praise as she'd been when Danny had thanked her. "I appreciate the way everyone has made me feel like part of the community. This is a special place with very generous people who give more of themselves than I do. Look at what you've done here. When you aren't working at the center, you're feeding the volunteers. I've chosen to live as a nomad, but I sort of envy the way you belong."

Helen gave a short, humorless laugh. "I don't know about belonging." She stared out toward the ocean, but Jenny wondered what she was really seeing. "I was so excited when I found the perfect spot for my bakery, but before renting, I should have asked how many people had tried and failed to run a successful business in that very spot. When I first got here, everyone was very polite and friendly, but I used to wonder if they were secretly making bets about how long I'd last. I'm certainly not the first person to come to the ocean with big dreams and little business sense."

Helen looked at Jenny again, her intense gaze direct and almost sharp. "And to be even more honest, I wasn't planning on volunteering when I walked into the center. I'd spent the day trying to figure out how to get out of my lease because of the spill. When I worry, I bake, so I ended up with several dozen croissants. I thought I'd drop them off and get the hell out of there."

Jenny laughed. She kept her hands under her thighs but used her shoulder to bump Helen's softly. Instead of moving away again, she leaned into Helen and felt her respond in kind. She meant the gesture to reassure Helen, but Jenny felt more electric and recharged from their contact than she ever did after a good meal or decent sleep. "Whatever your initial motivation, you jumped right in with everyone else. Like it or not, you're as much a part of this town as anyone who's been here for decades."

Helen shook her head with a rueful expression. "I always thought a community was where other people lived, something out of reach for me. I never expected to have one of my own, and now I probably won't...Well, never mind."

Jenny wanted to question Helen. Find out what was going on behind her troubled expression and offer comfort. But she wasn't here to get involved more than necessary. Her attraction to Helen was obvious to her, but she couldn't even imagine a way to act on it. She couldn't picture a future that didn't have her leaving town and Helen staying. Her parents had always warned her about attachment because they never knew where their next assignment would be or when they'd need to pack up and leave. Jenny had become very good at being on her own, making friends quickly and letting them go just as fast, and she used the skills her parents taught her in the career she'd chosen. Most people had a few friends they knew for years, her mom had told her. She said Jenny was lucky to have hundreds of friendships, even if they only lasted a brief time.

The argument hadn't made much sense to five-year-old Jenny, but she'd taken it to heart and lived by it for years. Sitting here next to Helen, wanting to wrap those loose tendrils of Helen's dark gold hair around her fingers, somehow the argument seemed as foolish and hurtful as it had when she was a child.

She stood and held out her hand to Helen. "I always thought community meant a place where I'd visit for a while and then leave. It's the way I grew up." She tugged Helen to a standing position. "Right now, this community needs us, and we can't let it down. First, though, I want to have some of this banana bread Danny's been raving about."

❖

Helen kneaded a large mound of soft dough on the marble countertop in her bakery's kitchen. Over the past five days, she hadn't been open for business more than three hours each morning, and even then she'd had a limited supply of pastries for sale. She'd been baking more than she had when she was in culinary school, though, as she helped Mel feed practically an entire town of volunteers every day.

The slow beach cleanup and the continuing flow of birds into the rescue center were clear signs that this summer wouldn't be the heavy tourist season she'd been hoping for. She'd had dreams of selling dozens of muffins and cupcakes every day—enough to support her through the long winter months when customers would be sparse. Instead, she was giving away more than she put in her display cases.

Helen punched the dough with a tight fist and felt a mist of flour puff into her face. She braced her hands against the edge of the counter and stood quietly, her head bowed while she struggled for control. No need to punish the dough for her foul mood. She had a pile of bills in her office and itemized lists of her projected expenses. She'd written dozens of budgets, trying to find a way to keep her business going without a significant summer income, but she felt trapped in a maze with no possible way out. So what did she do? She left her bakery door shut while she made another large tray of food for the center's volunteers. Foolish.

Helen heard a rapid series of knocks on the front door and she pushed past the blue plaid curtain that separated the kitchen from the sales floor. Not that the word *sales* seemed appropriate since the large display cases held only a few dozen cookies and some chocolate cupcakes. She sighed when she saw Tia standing next to the closed sign and waving at her. Not a hungry horde wanting to buy her scraps for exorbitant prices, but someone who was probably looking for more donated snacks. Given the way Tia talked and Helen's apparent inability to say no, Tia would most likely leave the store with full boxes. Leaving Helen with empty display cases and a similarly empty cash register.

She unlocked the door with a resigned click. The cookies and cupcakes had been made this morning, anyway, and Helen wouldn't have kept them much longer—they might as well be put to good use.

Tia came through the door in midconversation. "And I said I'd bring something from my favorite bakery for our snack. You don't think it's wrong of us to meet, do you? I don't want to be disrespectful, but I also believe it's important to maintain a sense of normalcy. Not to let this tragedy destroy the life we've built here. Right?"

Helen was too busy wondering how she had become Tia's favorite bakery, when the woman had never been here before, to grasp the full meaning of her words. "What meeting?"

"Our book club, at the Beachcomber," Tia said. She wandered over to the sparse display cases and peered inside. "You should join. Most of the locals are members. We meet at seven on the first Thursday of every month."

Helen, ashamed of the scanty offerings in her cases, was happy to keep off the subject of baked goods. She was flattered by Tia's reference to her as a local, even though Tia hadn't seemed to consider her one until after the oil spill. "I have to volunteer tonight, but maybe I'll come next month," she said. If she still owned the bakery and was in town, she added silently.

"Please do." Tia frowned and tapped a long, red-painted nail on the glass. "We were thinking of canceling because of the spill, but Jocelyn and I decided to go ahead with the meeting. Were we wrong to plan something fun during a tragedy? Jocelyn said we should continue to function as a community, that the meeting would give all of us a chance to get together and talk. To share our pain. What do you think, dear?"

Helen had been in the bookstore twice since arriving in Cannon Beach, but she easily recalled the owner, Jocelyn. She and Helen had spoken for a few minutes, and then Jocelyn had moved around her store gathering an armload of exactly right books for Helen. New books by her favorite mystery authors, two titles Helen never would have chosen for herself but ended up adoring, and a book of poetry. She had devoured the books and had gone back for more, and this time Jocelyn had a stack waiting behind the counter with her name on it.

"I think you two are right," she said. "Everyone is working hard, and the days have been long and sad. You'll probably end up comforting each other and talking about the spill more than books, but that's how it should be." Comforting each other and gathering together in a familiar and beloved routine. Helen understood the appeal even though she wouldn't accept Tia's offer to join them. She'd be the outsider.

"Should I go with the muffins or the cookies?" Tia asked, interrupting Helen's reverie. "They both look delicious."

Helen was still thinking about the book club, and she took a moment to switch gears mentally. "I have some sand dollars in the back room," she said. "I'll go get a couple dozen for you."

"Wonderful!" Tia smiled with a remarkable amount of energy and enthusiasm, given that she'd been working as volunteer coordinator nearly nonstop for the past two weeks. She seemed indefatigable, and Helen envied her ability to keep moving and talking without rest. Helen wasn't as resilient these days, but Tia had the advantage of being a permanent fixture at Cannon Beach—not a newbie baker who wouldn't last the season. Helen would never be as openly extroverted as Tia, no matter what her situation, but she certainly had reason to lack Tia's verve.

Helen layered the soft pastries in a pale pink to-go box. She'd been making a similar dessert since culinary school, but after naming her bakery the Sand Dollar, she'd changed the shape of them. The disks of flaky, buttery Napoleon pastry were filled with different flavors of cream. Grooves and notches were piped on top in vanilla icing to give them the look of sand dollars. The ones she had made today were stuffed with an almond-flavored pastry cream mixed with fresh raspberry coulis. She'd been planning to stop by some local restaurants on the way to the center and try to sell her signature pastries at a discount, willing to take the loss if it meant she could earn some paying customers. A lucrative account supplying desserts to a five-star restaurant would have been great. Instead, she'd donate her pastries to the local book club.

"These are beautiful," Tia said as she peered inside the box. "They'll remind us of what we've lost on our beaches, and what we'll find again under the layers of disgusting oil. How much do I owe you, dear?"

Helen quoted a price that would barely let her break even given the cost of ingredients. She wasn't sure why she was undervaluing the high-end and time-consuming confections. Was she trying to buy her way into the community, or was she doing this as a way to support the people involved in the cleanup effort? Maybe a little of both. Unfortunately, every step she took to belong to this community was another step away from financial success and the chance to really make this her home.

"Nonsense," Tia said, putting double the amount Helen had asked for on the counter. "I'll see you at the rescue center later on this evening. And remember, if you need a break, come by Jocelyn's."

Tia had already pushed out of the door without pausing for breath or to say good-bye, as if she was carrying on a day-long conversation, and Helen happened to be part of it for a few minutes. Helen took the cash off the counter and gratefully put it in the starving cash register, then she closed and locked the door behind Tia. The streets were empty and she wouldn't have any more paying customers tonight. She might as well go to the center and start her shift early. She boxed up the remaining items from her case and set her dough in a cool spot to rise overnight for tomorrow's loaves of bread. Although she specialized in sweet pastries, she had planned from the start to offer some sourdoughs and whole grain breads as well. The more she diversified, the more likely she was to make some cash. Besides, her pastries were indulgences, but fresh breads were staples. She needed to cater to the families living here year-round as much as to the occasional tourist who would come to their oil-covered beach.

Helen hung her blue striped apron on a wooden peg and went into the bathroom to wash her hands and scrub flour off her cheeks. She couldn't do much about the smear of pink pastry cream on her T-shirt or the dribble of chocolate batter on the thigh of her faded jeans without going back to her apartment and changing her entire outfit. She'd rather be a little messy than late for evening feeding at the rescue center, but part of her wanted to look her best, or at least look reasonably clean, when she saw Jenny. She turned away from her reflection with a tired sigh.

She was foolish to think Jenny would care what she was wearing or how presentable she was—Jenny was interested in the birds under her care, not in Helen. Well, Jenny did seem to care about her volunteers but not how they looked. Helen shook her head. She was tired and rambling to herself. She needed to get to the center and get to work before she crawled on her bakery counter and fell asleep. She piled the remaining boxes of sand dollar pastries into her arms and carried them outside, balancing them against her hip while she locked the bakery door.

"Can I help you with those?"

Helen spun around and saw Jenny walking toward her with an armful of pizza boxes. She looked tired and sleep-deprived, as usual these days, but her natural loveliness shone through the veneer of weariness. The drawn expression on her face only emphasized her high cheekbones and curved lips. Her socks were mismatched and her sweatshirt was torn, but if a television crew swooped down right now to interview her for the news, her devotion to this cause and her unyielding goodness would enhance her looks more than makeup or a restful night's sleep could ever do. Helen was sure of it because just last night she had watched Jenny on the evening news, lighting up the screen with inner and outer beauty.

Helen wished she'd kept a change of clothes here at the bakery. "Looks like you've already got your share," Helen said, pulling her focus off Jenny's lips and nodding toward the boxes she carried. "Besides, the heat from the pizzas would melt the pastry cream."

"Please tell me you made more of your sand dollars," Jenny said as they started walking along the sidewalk together. "I don't want to sound like I expect you to bake for me and the other rescue workers every day, but I'm seriously addicted to those things."

Helen laughed. How was Jenny able to relieve all her tension with a few words? The money she was spending on ingredients and the time she spent baking, assets she could barely afford to squander, were worth every stressful moment just to hear Jenny's compliments.

"Yes, these are sand dollars. The filling for this batch is—"

"Don't tell me, let me guess." Jenny shifted the boxes to her left hand and traced a path along Helen's lower ribs with her right index finger. "Strawberry?"

Helen nearly dropped her boxes at Jenny's touch. One finger, a second or two of contact, and a layer of cotton between them. No big deal. Then why did Helen feel as if her ribs had been seared? "What?" she asked, more startled by her response than by the touch. She stopped and faced Jenny.

"You have the remains of something pink on your shirt. I thought it might be a clue to the ingredients you used." Jenny put both forearms under her pizza boxes again.

Helen couldn't read the look in her eyes. She gave up and stared at the pastry boxes. "I would have changed shirts, but I wanted to… well, it was almost feeding time, and…"

Jenny shook her head. "Why bother? We'll be covered with oil and mashed bird food before the night is done. Besides, right now you look good enough to eat."

Jenny cleared her throat and started walking again. Helen swallowed the surge of arousal she felt at the simple statement and hurried to catch up.

"Raspberry," she said.

"What?"

Helen grinned. Jenny seemed as distracted by her company as she was by Jenny's. "The filling is raspberry, not strawberry."

"Even better."

They walked in silence while Helen struggled to find a topic of conversation that wouldn't leave her breathless. "You have good taste," she said. She realized too late that Jenny might think she was referring to her *good enough to eat* comment, and she hurried to explain herself better. "People make pilgrimages from all over the state to get Fontana's pizza."

"I make it a point to sample all the local favorites when I'm in a new place," Jenny said. Helen thought she saw a flush of red under the crew neck of her sweatshirt. "From local restaurants, I mean," she continued in a rush. "Fontana's pizza, Mel's scones, your sand dollars."

Helen liked having her baked goods lumped in with the other Cannon Beach specialties. She'd hoped to make that exact name for herself and her bakery this summer. Too bad she was earning a reputation from donations instead of sales. Money again. Why worry about it when there was so little to be made right now?

"You called yourself a nomad before. Do you travel all the time?"

"Yeah," Jenny said. "It's the only life I've ever known, except for the years when I was in vet school. My parents worked with Doctors Without Borders, and I traveled with them from the time I was only a few months old. I even got my college degree online since I was still a minor."

"Really? What an exciting life you must have led." Helen paused at a street corner and looked both ways before crossing the road even though barely any cars were out. The first weeks of summer had been crazy, with city-sized traffic on small-town streets. Jenny must be bored with the meager offerings of Cannon Beach, especially when she compared them to the grander and more exotic specialties of far-off lands. Helen had moved around far too much as a child—but not with her parents and not for philanthropic reasons. She imagined Jenny running through villages like she belonged in them, playing games with the local children...

"It wasn't as romantic and exciting as people think." The bitter edge to Jenny's voice broke through Helen's daydreams and caught her full attention. "If my parents were called to a specific place, it was because a lot of people were sick there, and I wasn't allowed to mingle with them. Most of my childhood friends were stray animals I'd find when I played outside of towns, and not other kids my age. By the time I'd pick up a little of the local language and get to know a few families or get attached to another pet, we'd be moving on to the next epidemic and leave them all behind."

Helen wasn't sure how to respond. The adult Jenny, who had chosen a lifestyle similar to the one her parents had followed, evaporated before her eyes. In her place was a lonely, isolated young girl who seemed similar to the child Helen had been. But Helen had made different choices, as soon as she was old enough to be on her own. She veered over and walked close enough to Jenny so their arms touched. "Didn't you ever want to settle down in one place, once you could make your own decisions? A place where you could make friends and be part of the lives around you?"

Jenny gave her a rueful smile and leaned in to their contact for a brief moment. "I used to think I would someday, but when I got to vet school, it was months before I adjusted to the idea that I was going to be with these same people long enough to make friends. Forming lasting relationships isn't exactly a skill of mine."

Helen almost tasted the bitterness and hurt in Jenny's voice. "From what I've seen, you are great with relationships. Everyone who works with you here trusts and likes you. Was there someone in particular who made you believe you aren't capable of making lifelong friends?"

Jenny sighed and looked away, although she kept her body close by Helen's side. "I guess. I really had only one serious girlfriend during vet school. I never really thought it would be a forever type of thing, and we had our rough spots, but when she left me I had a really hard time handling it. I was used to being the one who left, and even when our family moves were sudden, they were never unexpected. It was a crazy overreaction, but I almost dropped out of school because of it. But then I was offered a summer internship with a wildlife biologist who was traveling to South America. Travel was familiar to me, and I enjoyed the work, so I focused on finding jobs that kept me moving."

Helen couldn't imagine how she would have felt if she hadn't had any significant interaction with people her own age until she was of age and on her own. In some ways, Jenny must have grown up faster than other kids, and in others she had been left behind. Her parents should have been preparing her for school and life, not keeping her separated from it. Helen heard the dichotomy coming through in Jenny's tone of voice as she went from relating the story of her girlfriend—who must have been insane to let her go—to talking about her present life.

"I can help more animals and birds and communities if I move to where I'm needed," Jenny said. "My mom tried to explain that to me when I would be sad about moving again. She'd say it was selfish of me. I didn't understand her at the time, but I think I do now."

Helen spoke without pausing to think. "Nonsense. They were the selfish ones, not you." She felt a buildup of her old rage. All she could hear was her uncle's voice. *I gave you everything after your parents died. A house, food, clothing. And this is how you repay me?* The cost of his generosity had been much too high for Helen to accept, but she'd been torn by guilt when she heard those words and was too young to know better. She was trapped in her own memories, but the sensation of Jenny moving out of reach and the chilly sound of her voice brought Helen back to the present with a thump.

"I did see more of the world than most people ever will. I was exposed to local food and customs and places, so I learned more than any school-bound class could have taught me. And my parents have saved thousands of lives. I'd never be selfish enough to think that a real house or a sleepover with school friends should have made my parents give up their mission."

"No, I guess not," Helen said, trying to adjust to the quick shift out of her own past as Jenny now defended her parents' lifestyle choice. She guessed that Jenny had wavered between anger and guilt for a lot of years. Helen had been on that particular seesaw often enough to recognize the signs. She wanted to help Jenny banish the guilt forever. "Still, couldn't they have compromised even a little once you were born? There must have been plenty of opportunities to help others in the States or by staying in one place where you could make friends and be safe."

Helen paused at the edge of the rescue center's parking lot when Jenny stopped in the shadows. Beyond them, volunteers were moving in and out of the building.

"I know you mean well," Jenny said. She sounded as if she was speaking through gritted teeth. "But you probably grew up in a traditional home with parents who went to work from nine to five each day. Maybe one of them even stayed home and took care of you full-time. You can't possibly understand the amount of suffering in this world. People who sacrifice their lives to ease it are doing something vital, and if I had to give up the stray dog I'd befriended or the tree fort I'd made, then I was doing what needed to be done."

Helen shifted the awkward boxes in her hands. She was tempted to upend the lot on Jenny's head. "You have no idea what my life was like growing up. I've seen my share of suffering, and I've experienced plenty, too. Just because I'm trying to find a quiet and settled home here doesn't mean it's all I've ever known. It means I've had enough of the opposite to last a lifetime."

Helen walked away without giving Jenny a chance to say anything else. She was worn-out from the amount of work she'd been doing and by the conversation she'd just had, and she was about to lose her business on top of everything. All she wanted to do was go home and curl in a ball, but she pushed through the glass doors and set her boxes on a folding table, where they were quickly attacked by hungry workers who mumbled their thanks around crumbs and pastry cream. This might not be her community or her home for long, but right now she was needed here. She grabbed some long rubber gloves and a handful of trash bags.

Time to clean some cages.

❖

Jenny took her time crossing the parking lot, and by the time she entered the rescue center, Helen was nowhere to be seen. She put her pizzas on the table next to the already-plundered pastry boxes and snagged a couple of sand dollars before they disappeared. She paused in the doorway leading from the large foyer to the open auditorium and leaned against the doorjamb while she ate and watched the scene before her.

The main floor was covered with plywood pens, laid out like houses on city blocks. Jenny knew the inhabitants of each one, even without seeing them. A few Western grebes along the far wall, although luckily many of them had been farther inland during breeding season and were safe from the oil spill. Pens for the murres were clustered on the north side. The gentle and timid loons were tucked in a quiet corner. A dark curtain separated the washing area from the rest of the space. Quiet human voices blended together, creating a background murmur.

Jenny licked a trail of raspberry pastry cream off the side of her palm and thought about her reaction when she had innocently touched the pink stain on Helen's T-shirt. Powerful and unexpected, like everything else about Helen. Jenny had been foolish to make assumptions about Helen's life before they met. She'd seen hints of toughness behind Helen's cheerful smile, as if she'd survived something difficult and had stories to tell about her journey. Jenny had tried to ignore her interest in Helen, had lumped her in with what she thought of as everyone else. Jenny's own life had been so far from the traditional ones she read about in books and saw in movies that she sometimes forgot *everyone* varied from normal in some way. She'd activated her usual response against getting attached to a community and had thought of herself as someone too different from these people to ever truly relate to them. Or care about them.

She'd made a mistake and had made Helen angry. Jenny rarely had long enough relationships to need to worry about apologies or fights, and she wasn't convinced she knew how to handle either of them, but she didn't want to back away right now. She wanted to move closer, if only for a brief time.

She took a huge bite of her second pastry and turned her attention to Helen. She had spotted her immediately, of course, as soon as she had looked into the auditorium, but now she let the rest of the world fade away and saw only her.

Helen was cleaning the grebes' cages with her accustomed grace and efficiency of movement. She gently herded the birds into one end of the pen before she removed the soiled papers from the other. Then she moved them to the clean side and repeated the process. Pen after pen, with a quiet and experienced touch. She had developed a routine, and Jenny loved watching her work. Mostly because she was good at her job and kept the birds calm, of course. The tempting sight of Helen bending over to pick up a dropped glove or tie a full bag shut was only a bonus and *not* the reason Jenny was mesmerized by her.

Jenny wiped her powdered-sugar-covered fingers on her jeans and grabbed a pair of gloves from a supply box. She walked to the pen Helen was cleaning and stepped over the side of it, silently going to work alongside her. Helen didn't acknowledge her verbally or even with a glance, but she subtly altered her rhythm to accommodate Jenny's presence.

From the start, Jenny had recognized her own work ethic in Helen. Helen understood the importance of behind-the-scenes work. She stayed on the grubbier side of the rescue effort, cleaning pens and holding birds while a special food mash was tubed into their stomachs. Because she was such a familiar part of their days, the birds seemed to have adjusted more quickly to temporary captivity here than at other rescue sites Jenny had managed. She took on the role of assistant now, letting Helen move the birds. The elegant black-and-white grebes with razor-sharp, slender beaks waddled silently from one end of the pen to the other as if they'd been following Helen's directions their entire lives. Helen might not realize what a difference she was making, but Jenny did. She'd have to find a way to thank her for taking care of the chore that was usually the least favorite for the volunteers but was one of the most vital to the well-being of the birds. Jenny had a few ideas about how she could thank Helen, but they all involved a more hands-on approach than

Jenny usually took with the people she briefly met in disaster-torn communities. Maybe she'd have to settle for getting her a gift card instead, but the other options seemed much more enticing. She kept her thoughts to herself and wordlessly stuffed paper into garbage bags. Together they finished cleaning the remaining grebe pens and then carried the trash bags to the Dumpster behind the center.

The back lot of the rescue center was quiet in the growing dusk as they lobbed the bags into the huge, rusty container. Helen led the way back to the building, but Jenny put her hand on Helen's arm to keep her from going through the door and returning to the brightly lit, crowded auditorium.

"I'm sorry," she said, picking up the thread of their earlier conversation as if it had just happened. "I shouldn't have implied that you had a boring or easy childhood. And I didn't mean to sound like I thought I was superior because of the way I was raised or because of the way I live now. I'm not. It's just the only way I know how to live."

Helen shook her head and looked off into the distance. The fading colors of the sunset gave her skin a peachy glow and made her eyes glisten. "I'm sorry, too. I shouldn't have insulted your parents or the choices they made. I just heard some echoes of my own loneliness when you were talking about not having many friends, and I wanted to take your side against them. And maybe I was a little jealous because you were such a huge part of their lives and their work."

Jenny realized she still had her hand on Helen. She should move it, let go, step back. Instead, she slid her palm down Helen's arm until she reached her hand. Their fingers interlaced loosely.

"You weren't close to your parents?" Jenny asked. Admittedly, after watching Helen interact with her neighbors in Cannon Beach, Jenny had pictured her growing up in a close-knit family. Learning how to bake in the kitchen with her mom. Experiencing the cozy domesticity Jenny had sometimes longed for.

Helen shook her head. "I never had a chance. We were in a car wreck when I was still a toddler. The truck hit us head-on, and since I was in the backseat, I was the only one to survive."

"I'm so sorry."

"Grieving is abstract when you barely knew someone." Helen leaned against the metal siding of the auditorium, still keeping her hand in Jenny's. "Anyway, my uncle brought me to live with his family, but he was…well, he wasn't a nice man. I don't think he and my father were ever close. As soon as I was old enough to pack a bag, I was running away on a regular basis. I stayed on the street or in foster homes, but then I'd be taken back to his house. We lived in a small town, so the cops got to know me well enough to recognize me and I never got far. Once I turned eighteen and graduated from high school—barely—I got the hell out of there."

Jenny sighed and propped her shoulder on the wall next to Helen. She felt a current of excitement being this close to her, their hands joined and their thighs barely touching, but she put her own responses in the back of her mind. This was a time for a different kind of intimacy, and she didn't want Helen to stop talking. Jenny lived her own story. When she went to disaster sites to work, the focus was always on the present—how to deal with the crisis of the moment. Rarely did she stand still long enough to listen to someone else's life unfold through their words and expressions. Rarely had she ever *wanted* to hear.

"What did you do once you left?"

Helen shrugged and Jenny felt the friction of the movement against her own shoulder. Her fingers tightened on Helen's reflexively, and Helen returned the squeeze.

"I was directionless. For most of my life, I had been straining to get away, but I never had any idea where I was headed *to*. I didn't have the best support system in place. Most of my friends were runaways, too. Ditching school, leaving home, getting into trouble. I managed to stay clear of the worst parts of street life, but I was on a downhill slope. I was crashing with some people I knew and couldn't seem to get a decent job, let alone hold on to one if I managed to get hired."

Jenny shuddered to think of the direction in which Helen's life could have gone. She realized the sharp edge she had seen beneath Helen's surface had been honed by survival. The added dimension made her even more attractive to Jenny, but it scared her, too. She wasn't accustomed to seeing depth—just names and faces that blurred together and faded from her mind once she moved on.

"And now you're a pastry chef and entrepreneur. I'm impressed. What made you turn your life around?"

Helen looked at her with an appreciative smile, as if Jenny's compliment actually meant something to her. "I got a job washing dishes in a diner. Not exactly the dream career for most people, and it didn't pay much, but I got a hot meal every night. It was owned by a huge Italian family, and I loved watching them fight and laugh and run their business together. They were everything a family should be, and nothing like the one I had. At first I figured I'd be there for a month or two and then leave—my usual work pattern—but I stayed. Every once in a while, one of them would give me a little cooking lesson, and eventually I was working on the line. My favorite things to make were breads and desserts. I worked my way through culinary school and saved enough to open a bakery of my own."

Helen spoke the last three sentences with a casual voice and a shrug, as if the journey had been as simple as one-two-three, but Jenny knew better. The effort and discipline required to start from scratch and build a new life were awe-inspiring to her. She felt an inexplicable sense of pride in Helen's accomplishments, and she wasn't sure why. She'd had nothing to do with Helen's life before this, and she had no stake in her future. She didn't understand how an attachment seemed to be forming between her and Helen, but she had to stop it before it got strong enough to threaten her life's work.

And she would stop it. Later.

Right now, though, Jenny gave in to the itchy feeling in her fingers and she reached out to touch Helen's hair, tucking a strand of gold behind Helen's ear. She let her hand linger there, feeling the warmth of flesh and heartbeat.

"You seem to fit here," Jenny said, feeling somewhat sad because she herself didn't fit anywhere. "After accomplishing so much, I'm sure you'll have no trouble making your bakery a success."

Helen gave a bitter laugh. She straightened and pushed away

from the wall, breaking all contact between them. "Thanks, but I'm already on my way out of business. Everything I read told me to have at least six months of living expenses saved before trying to start a new business, but I only had saved enough for maybe three when I found the opportunity to rent here. I thought I'd be okay since the summer season was about to start, but then..."

"But then..." Jenny echoed. The spill. The damaged beaches and wounded animals. Jenny had seen this happen again and again, when lives were ruined by this type of disaster. She did her best to help everywhere she went, but somehow this felt different. She was inside, with the rest of the community. "You've been doing more than your share of work, but we can get by if you need to spend more time at your bakery. And all the donated pastries you bring each night—you really don't need to feel responsible for feeding everyone here. It must be costing you a fortune in ingredients. I'll come to your store with cash when I need my sand dollar fix."

Helen laughed. "I'd much rather be here doing something good than sitting in my empty bakery and watching the empty street. I like bringing food, too. I crunched the numbers, and if I stopped it would only delay the inevitable. I wouldn't save enough to make a real difference. But I can make a difference here. I think I've always felt like it was me against the world, but now I'm part of a team. I don't want to lose that feeling, even if it's only temporary."

"I've always been the team coach," Jenny said with a grin. "But I've never really been part of it, until—"

"Jenny, there you are. I have a surprise for you." Mel's voice broke into their conversation, shattering the intimacy Jenny felt growing between them. Jenny turned to see Mel framed in the open doorway, backlit by the bright fluorescent lights. She didn't have to hear what the surprise was since she recognized the two silhouettes behind Mel.

She sighed and walked toward them, away from Helen. "Hello, Mom. Dad. It's good to see you both. Why didn't you tell me you were coming?"

❖

Jenny opened the door to her room at the inn and dropped her mom's light canvas bag on the floor next to the bed. She shouldn't have been as surprised as she was to see her parents at the center tonight. She knew they were in the States—albeit on the other coast, in Florida—and they often came to see her and help with her rescue efforts whenever they could. She tried to be grateful because they were giving their time, and they worked hard no matter what job they were given, but somehow their visits were more exhausting than the hard work of disaster relief.

"You'll be staying in here and I'll move to the smaller room upstairs," Jenny said. She didn't like leaving what she'd come to think of as *her* room. Now she'd have to share a bathroom with two of Danny's college friends, and she'd miss sleeping in this room with Pam's beautiful painting of the tide pool. She stared at the mosaic whenever she felt despair or weariness settling in her bones. The sun shining through her window and making the sea glass sparkle gave her the lift she needed and the incentive to keep going until the beach returned to the state of Pam's vision. Still, she couldn't begrudge her parents the larger room, and she was glad Mel had space for her somewhere besides the floor in here. She was accustomed to much more primitive conditions than this on most of her job sites, so she wouldn't complain.

"Very glamorous," her father said, as if reading her mind. "I hope you don't forget you're here for work and not a vacation."

"I never forget why I'm here," Jenny said softly, but he had already walked over to the window where her mother was standing. She watched the two of them as they looked out at the dark and looming hulk of Haystack Rock. Eve and Lars Colbert. Dark and light. They looked as young as they had when she first left them to attend vet school in the States. Similar in build and quick in movement, they only showed the passing years in a few lines on their faces. They would be leaving for the Sudan in a few days and stopped here to volunteer along the way. She wondered where they got their energy to keep moving and changing. She was always on the go, too, but the effort was sometimes too much to bear.

"Mel's partner Pam did the paintings for all the rooms," she said when Eve turned away from the window and came over by the bed. "They're spectacular. I can show you the others one of these days."

Her parents both made the right comments when they admired the mosaic, like Jenny had when she'd first seen it. The difference was, Jenny had immediately wanted to buy one like it, impractical as it would be. Mel had told her that almost everyone who stayed at the inn wanted to buy one of the paintings. The cost was prohibitive for most, but Pam had created a line of smaller, more affordable canvases, each with a scattering of sea glass. Jenny had already bought one with a purple- and coral-colored starfish on it. She didn't offer to show it to her parents, though. They would have liked the small oil painting if they'd seen it on display somewhere, but not as a possession. She didn't want to hear the lecture about how impractical it was to purchase souvenirs from all her trips. Mental pictures were easy to pack, her mom liked to say. Anything besides the essentials for living was a waste of space and travel funds.

Jenny said good night and left her parents to unpack and rest after their long cross-country flight. They looked as perky as ever, while she dragged herself up another flight of stairs leading to her new room. They had always been energized by travel and new places and unfamiliar people. Jenny was the opposite. Her day had been filled with nudges out of her comfort zone. Her parents' arrival, her spat with Helen. Most of all, the sensation of closeness she'd felt when she and Helen had talked outside the auditorium. She'd been drawn into Helen's life, and she had been both disappointed and relieved when Mel and her parents had broken the spell.

Jenny opened the door to the rose-colored room and saw what Mel had done to make the place welcoming. Her belongings had been packed and moved here while she was still at the center with her parents. Mel had turned down the bedcovers and had put some bottled water and snacks on a small mahogany table. Jenny stripped down to her underwear and fell onto the bed, pulling the quilt up to her chin. She was thirsty, but even the thought of uncapping a bottle of water seemed to be too much effort.

But there was Helen. Downstairs right now with Mel, preparing breakfast for the small army of volunteers. Jenny was tempted to go see her and to offer some help, just to be around her again. Common sense warred with temptation. Tired as she was, Jenny was about to give in and make the long trek downstairs when someone tapped at her door. Her first instinct was to feign sleep in case it was one of her parents, wanting her to go for a midnight jog or go swim with the whales or something insanely active. But neither of them would have knocked politely and waited for her to answer. The door would be open by now.

"Come in," she called, pulling herself to a sitting position against the headboard.

It was Helen, with her cheeks flushed from the heat of the oven and smears of flour and some sort of orange-y batter on her navy sweatshirt. Much too beautiful to be alone with Jenny in Jenny's room in the middle of the night. Jenny didn't have enough self-control for this.

"I thought you might like some tea." Helen came over to the bed and set a small tray on the bed stand. "Chamomile, to help your mind stop circling and let you sleep. And a piece of pumpkin bread in case you're hungry."

Say thank you and good night. Instead, Jenny patted the mattress next to her hip. See? No self-control. "Thank you for this. Why don't you sit with me for a few minutes. You look like you could use some rest, too."

"I'm all right," Helen said, but she sat on the bed with a groan. "Great. Now I'll never get up."

"Fine with me."

"Stop." Helen laughed and swatted at Jenny's covered legs. She lay down crosswise on the bed, her rib cage draped over Jenny's calves, and propped her head on her hand. "You're tempting enough, saying things like that," she said.

Jenny had been worried about her own response to Helen, afraid to get too close after a lifetime of moving and with more of the same in the foreseeable future. She hadn't stopped to consider whether Helen might feel the same attraction to her, but Helen's words and the deepening red on her neck hinted at her feelings.

Jenny cleared her throat, acutely aware of Helen's breasts and side where they rested on her lower legs.

"Your parents certainly jumped right in to help tonight," Helen said.

Jenny was glad to have a change in topic. Talking about her parents was the mental equivalent of a cold shower. "They always do, no matter what the cause. They seem to have unlimited energy and drive."

A trait Jenny didn't share. She had strength and endurance when it came to her work, but her parents were on another level entirely. The evening with them had been a whirlwind as she showed them around and put them to work helping Helen clean pens. Soon her dad had wanted to try something new, and he had ended the night in the wash area, sudsing and scrubbing the oil from the fragile feathers. Her mom had likewise wanted to be part of every aspect of Jenny's operation, and she had volunteered to examine and treat the recuperating wounded animals and birds in the ICU area of the center. Jenny had been glad for capable extra help, of course, but the difference between being with them and sitting here with Helen was astronomical. Helen stirred her up but centered her at the same time.

"Always looking to do more," Helen said. "Did they expect the same from you when you were small?"

"Not at first." Jenny remembered long, boring, dusty days when she would have done anything to get parental attention. Once they turned it on her full force, she had longed to return to her days of invisibility. Somewhere in the middle would have been nice. "When I was a little kid, I was...let's say unsupervised. Once I was old enough to help at the clinics and was planning my own future, I became more of an object of interest to them."

"They must be very proud of what you do. It's incredible, how many lives and communities you've saved." Helen plucked at the quilt where it lay over Jenny's knees.

Jenny swallowed, distracted by the buffered but electric touch of Helen's restless fingers. "I guess, in a way. But I guarantee they won't be here long before I get The Talk again."

Helen's hand stilled. "The sex talk?" she asked with laughter in her voice. "Aren't you a little old for that?"

Jenny laughed too and jostled Helen with her legs. "No, silly. The *Don't you think it's time you gave up this hobby and went to real medical school?* talk. Although I'm too old for that one, too."

"You're not serious, are you?"

Jenny nodded. "Completely. They believe I'm in a phase. I'll eventually go to med school and we'll travel the globe as a happy family."

"Insane. You're a natural with animals, and you're doing important work. I'd expect you to go the other way if you were planning to make a change. Maybe settle somewhere and have pets of your own. A family. A community. Something you haven't allowed yourself to have before."

"Never," Jenny said with emphasis. The single-word answer was her knee-jerk reaction whenever anyone asked her the question about settling down, but it wasn't the whole story. And Helen wasn't just anyone. She deserved more of an explanation. "I used to imagine having a real home with a yard for animals and friends who lived close enough to see whenever I wanted. I sort of had the life I'd dreamed of in vet school, but it was a transition time for all of us, between college and career. Everyone was looking toward the future, and I didn't feel settled like I'd expected."

"I understand why you couldn't find the home of your dreams when you were young and living with your parents, and even during vet school. But you have options now."

Helen shifted her weight on Jenny's shins. Their skin wasn't touching anywhere, but Jenny felt Helen's movements as friction when the cotton sheets rubbed against her bare legs. The exquisite pressure from Helen's body made Jenny want to stay here forever, but she couldn't let her body and heart make the decisions, could she? "Movement is what I know. I can't let myself feel dissatisfied or second-guess the choices I've made. If I do, then the pain of saying good-bye is too hard to bear. I learned that lesson early."

"Out of necessity. To protect your heart when you were a child. Do you still need those defenses?"

"Do you?" Jenny rubbed her leg against Helen's back as she spoke, using the contact to let Helen know she wasn't trying to insult her with the words. "You told me you kept yourself at a distance from the people here until the spill. Everyone has some armor in place, to protect themselves from being hurt by other people or the circumstances of life."

"True, but I'm changing. I came here believing I didn't need anyone else's help or support. I've realized I need the people around me, and they need me, too. The oil might have drowned my business, but I'll start over again somewhere else, somehow. And next time I won't be so stubborn about opening myself up to friendships and connections."

"Somewhere else. Exactly." Jenny focused on the one thing Helen had said that seemed similar to Jenny's own life, although in her heart she was convinced Helen belonged right where she was. "It's not this town or these specific people. It's the way you feel about them. I'm not even sure a house or piece of land would make me as happy as I imagined when I was little. I was lonely then and thought a home was what I needed. I just pictured home as a building. Now I see home as something else entirely." What was her definition now? A person? Helen? "It can mean a community full of friends, like Cannon Beach, and I can take them with me wherever I go, reaching out to them from wherever I happen to be. I could work more on making lasting friendships, but I'm born to travel, I guess. It must be in my genes."

"I was forced to move around, looking for a home," Helen said. "I'm tired of it."

"Me, too, sometimes," Jenny admitted in a barely audible voice. Helen crawled up the bed and curled up beside her. Jenny wasn't immune to the arousal she felt when Helen got so close, but the awareness of their divergent futures was enough to keep her feelings in check. She wrapped an arm around Helen's waist and pulled her close, taking comfort in this one moment they were able to share.

❖

Jenny had been lonely before. Playing hopscotch by herself on a dusty lane while her parents treated sick children in their clinic. Getting in bed alone on every first night in every new city or village. She thought she was familiar with every facet and nuance of loneliness.

And then she woke up without Helen.

Jenny was up before the sun, but Helen had already slipped away. She lay quietly for a moment, letting the sensation of being without Helen wash through her like a tsunami. Somehow she knew there was a good chance she would feel this way every morning for the rest of her life. She'd gone to bed as a whole person holding another person in her arms. She woke with a missing piece.

At the same time, she felt better rested and more alive than she had for months. She'd slept soundly and with a sense of peace she hadn't known before. Nothing in her reaction to Helen was straightforward. Everything was full of contradictions. Their night had been chaste, but she now felt closer to Helen than anyone else. She had shared with her. Shared the doubts she rarely voiced, and the dreams she never allowed to flourish.

She got out of bed and went through her normal morning routine. Speed shower, put hair in a ponytail, and find the cleanest clothes in the pile on the floor. Within ten minutes of waking up, she was on her way downstairs. She considered stopping by her parents' room, but as early as she'd gotten up and as quickly as she'd gotten ready, she was certain they had beaten her downstairs.

"Good morning, sleepyhead," her dad said when she came into the kitchen. He was sitting at the small breakfast nook with her mom, Mel, and Danny. "We were going to come get you if you didn't wake up soon."

Jenny took a deep breath while she put last night's tea tray in the sink and rinsed her cup. The backyard was still in shadow, but she saw Pam's figure moving past the windows of her art studio. Pam spent a lot of time in there when she wasn't at the rescue center, but Jenny had overheard enough to know Pam wasn't actually painting right now. This oil spill was affecting everyone in its path. Eventually, though, life would find its balance again. Pam would paint, Mel would have a full house of paying guests, and Helen would somehow find a way to run her own business and make it a success. And Jenny? She would move to the next place that needed her. If she'd learned anything from living in one crisis after the other, it was not to believe in the temporary reality a disaster created. She'd fallen for it this time, but soon enough she'd be back to her routine. Her parents—even though they drove her crazy at times—understood her lifestyle more than anyone else.

"I haven't slept through the night in ages," Jenny said as she poured a cup of coffee and added cream and sugar. Might as well keep the peace. "I guess I stayed in bed longer than expected."

"You look rested," Mel said with a subtle wink. "I guess the bonus features of your new room agreed with you."

Jenny couldn't hide her answering grin. Mel must have noticed Helen going into her room and not coming out until morning. Jenny still felt Helen's absence like a wound, but the memory of holding her made her smile. "Yeah," she said. "The bed was very comfortable."

"I'll bet it was."

"What room were you in?" Danny asked, looking back and forth between the two laughing women. "Did you get a new mattress, Mom?"

"We're going to miss you when you go back to school, Danny," Jenny said, changing the subject. "You've been a great help at the center."

"Are you in college?" Lars asked. "What are you studying?"

"What school?" Eve chimed in.

Jenny rolled her eyes. She recognized the eagerness in their voices. They were asking simple questions, but they could become serious medical-profession recruiters at any moment. She sometimes wondered if they got a commission every time they talked a student into pursuing a medical degree.

"I'm on scholarship at Oregon State University." Danny smeared grape jelly on a thick slice of toast made from homemade bread and passed the jar to Jenny. "I haven't picked a major yet."

"I think he'd be a brilliant professor," Mel said, elbowing him in the side. "Maybe literature?"

"Yeah, right," Danny said with a laugh. He looked at Jenny. "Can you see me in a tweed blazer with elbow patches?"

"You probably can wear whatever you want. I don't think there's a required uniform," Jenny joked. She took a bite of her toast. Crunchy outside and soft in the middle. Flecks of whole grains and chopped walnuts gave it good texture and complemented the sweet jam. She'd bet anything Helen had made the bread. Was there anything she couldn't make? Money out of thin air, Jenny supposed. She sighed and tried to get her mind off Helen and back on to the conversation going on around her.

"Yes, Mom, I know Pam wants me to be an art major, but you saw my final project for the drawing class I took last semester. What a disaster." Danny wiped his hands and neatly folded his napkin. "Actually, I've kind of been thinking of vet school. Jenny and I were talking about it, and after working with the animals here at the center, I'm even more convinced I'd like to try."

"Really?" Mel asked with a proud smile on her face. "You haven't mentioned it before, but I can see it being a good fit for you. You've always been great with animals."

"If you're interested in the medical field, you might want to consider working with people instead of animals," Lars said, taking a sip of coffee. "The opportunities for helping others are limitless, and you'd be making a real contribution to the world."

Mel and Danny sent shocked looks Jenny's way, as if they were hoping she hadn't heard the comment. She'd heard it too many times to be bothered by it anymore. She took another slice of toast and coated it with butter and a drizzle of honey. "I think you're a natural, Danny. If you need a letter of recommendation, count on me. Vet school admissions committees love to see this kind of volunteer work on applications."

"Thanks, Jenny," he said. "I just might take you up on that."

Jenny didn't miss the look her parents exchanged. She could already feel them gearing up for The Talk.

❖

Jenny was silent on the way to the center. Her parents had talked nonstop yesterday about Cannon Beach, the beauty of the area, and the work Jenny was doing here. Today, they had already moved on and were focused on their upcoming trip. She wouldn't be surprised if they left as unexpectedly as they'd come. She was sure they'd remember some city or research library or colleague they desperately needed to visit before they left the States. She wouldn't take it personally when it happened. By now she knew they weren't trying to cut their visit with her short but merely shifting ahead to the next stop on their never-ending journey. They couldn't stop their itch to get moving again. It was their nature as a couple and as doctors.

Even as she listened to their chatter, Jenny replayed the scene from breakfast in her mind. Mel obviously had an interest in Danny's future, and she had ideas about what might be good for him. But the moment he mentioned a different choice he was considering, Mel was right there with him. Jenny had no doubt Mel and Pam would encourage and support him no matter what career he picked. Her parents had been thrown into relief against the backdrop of Mel's unconditional acceptance, pushing their agenda as always. Again, Jenny couldn't blame them or get angry. Again, it was their nature.

But was it hers? She knew she'd never go to med school. She couldn't imagine a life without animals—caring for them and protecting them. She'd felt confident in her choice and proud of herself for following her own heart. But had she truly committed to living her own life? She sometimes wondered if her insistence on constant travel was really her own decision, or a way of atoning for her rebellious decision to be a vet. Or maybe she'd taken the easiest path, the one most familiar to her. She treated the patients of her choice, but she mimicked her family's chosen method of doing so.

Jenny pushed the jumble of thoughts out of her mind as they pulled in to the parking lot. Right now, she was more concerned about Helen. Would she be here this morning? Would there be tension between them? They'd done nothing more than sleep in the same bed, but Jenny had a feeling the night had affected Helen just as deeply as it had her. Otherwise, she wouldn't have left without a word.

She got out of the car and her heart jumped when she saw Helen running across the lot toward her. She hesitated for a moment before she recognized the worried expression on Helen's face. Jenny knew trouble when she saw it.

"What's wrong?" she called, sprinting toward Helen. Had something happened to the birds? One of the volunteers? Helen?

Helen stopped, gasping for breath, and grabbed Jenny's sleeve. "Amy Hansen. Her dog. Hit by a car."

"Is she inside?"

Helen nodded. "In the back room. The nearest emergency vet is in Seaside. Too far."

Jenny squeezed her shoulder and took off toward the door to the auditorium. Amy was one of her regular volunteers. As tireless as the rest of the Cannon Beach citizens, Amy had been involved in nearly every aspect of the center's work. Jenny burst through the door with Helen right on her heels and jogged to the small room where she stored the vet supplies she brought to every site. She never knew what type of animal she'd need to treat. Here, she mostly took care of shorebirds, but she'd also treated sea animals and the occasional house pet that had ingested oil.

Amy was leaning over a folding table, her arms wrapped around a medium-sized yellow Lab. Her little boy, Sam, was beside her, crying and holding a corner of the blanket that covered the dog. Jenny had seen the child here a few times, playing with Tia while his mother worked with the birds.

"Hi, Sam. Can you tell me your dog's name?"

"Buddy. Can you save him?"

"I'll do my best. How old is Buddy?"

Jenny moved to the table while she asked a series of questions, more to get Sam talking and relaxed than to get information. She'd learn what she needed from Buddy himself. She nodded at Helen, and as if they were communicating mentally, Helen stepped into Amy's place and put her hands gently on the still form of the dog.

Amy backed away and leaned against the far wall with Sam in her arms.

Jenny murmured instructions to Helen as she examined the dog. Outwardly, her voice sounded calm and her hands were steady as she checked the Lab's limbs, cleaned and sutured a large gash on his hip, and took X-rays with her portable machine. Inside, on the contrary, she was panic-stricken. What if he didn't make it? What if there was something she couldn't fix? When she was on the job, she had hundreds, sometimes thousands, of patients. Some made it, some didn't. She cared about every single one of them, but Buddy was different.

Jenny shaved the hair around another deep cut. This animal belonged to people she knew. She had always considered small-scale vet work to be less significant than what she did, but she'd been wrong. She glanced back at Amy and Sam, both with tear-drenched cheeks. The stakes seemed higher because she herself was connected to this circle of animal and owner, like when she had helped Danny with Piper.

Jenny finished the last stitch and snipped the end of the suture. Buddy had been nonresponsive to his surroundings at first, but he was beginning to look around again. Jenny motioned for Amy and Sam to come over to the table, and Buddy's tail weakly fanned the air when they came close.

"He has a slight concussion and two deep cuts. No broken bones. I gave him antibiotics, but I'd suggest getting him to your regular vet to make certain there's no internal bleeding or other serious problem. I can only do so much here, but he's stable and should be fine to move."

"I can drive you to Seaside," Helen offered.

Jenny got Danny and her parents to help move Buddy to Helen's car on a makeshift stretcher. Helen shut the door behind them, leaving her alone in the room with Jenny. "You were awesome," she said, walking over and hugging Jenny tightly.

Jenny's hands shook where they rested on Helen's back. She nuzzled into the warmth of Helen's skin and inhaled a scent of vanilla and spice. "Thank you for helping." The words were inadequate, but Jenny knew they both had experienced the same depth of emotion. Concern for one of their own, fear, a sagging relief. They didn't need to put words to the feelings to make them more real than they already were.

Helen pulled back and rested her hand on Jenny's cheek. "I'm sorry I left this morning. It was just...It's all too much...I love spending time with you and learning about you, but I want more."

Jenny put her palm over Helen's hand and pressed it close. "I do, too. I just don't have more to offer. My time is limited here, but maybe we can talk on the phone and write. Then the next time I'm near here, we can arrange to meet."

Helen shook her head. "I don't want a pen pal, Jenny. I want this." She put her arms around Jenny's neck and kissed her.

Jenny thought she had uncovered every side of loneliness in her lifetime, but until she felt its lack, when it suddenly and explosively vanished at the touch of Helen's lips on hers, Jenny realized she'd never truly understood what she had been missing. Jenny explored Helen's mouth gently with her tongue. The sweet, sweet taste of her. The passion between them stayed soft, hovering near the edge of the kiss, and Jenny felt its energy. Waiting to be unleashed, if only there weren't people waiting outside for Helen. If only Jenny didn't have to leave.

If only...

Helen pulled back as if she felt the good-bye in Jenny's kiss. "This is what I want, every day and every night. Not once a year when you happen to be passing near the West Coast on your way to someplace else."

She turned and walked out the door. Jenny dropped into the closest chair and rested her elbows on her knees. She wasn't sure what to think anymore. Her values hadn't changed since she'd come here, but the way she wanted to express them had. She stood up and started to put her instruments away. Her world was upside down here, and she wasn't sure how to handle the resulting vertigo. She'd have to fall back on her old standby. Hard work. She flipped off the light and went out to greet her next hundred patients.

❖

Helen dropped Amy, Sam, and Buddy at their house and drove slowly back to the center. Before she got to the street leading to the auditorium, she turned left instead and parked at the end of a beach access road. Yellow tape and warning signs marked the beach as closed, but she got out and climbed a concrete retaining wall that separated the parking lot from the shore. The sun was warm on the back of her neck and the sand in front of her was relatively clean already. A soft breeze lifted her hair.

A perfect day. The town should be filled to the gills with tourists. She should be sweating from the heat of overworked ovens in the bakery's kitchen, turning out tray after tray of baked goods for hungry beachgoers. A run to the bank in the late afternoon with a hefty deposit, and then back to work prepping for the next morning's baking.

Helen drew her knees up and clasped her arms around them. She had uprooted her life yet again to come to Cannon Beach, fooling herself with a deep certainty that she was finally coming home. She'd had nearly three months of promising sales before the spill changed everything. Now she was witness to the devastation of her beautiful new home and its inhabitants—human, animal, and avian. She'd worked harder in the past weeks than ever before, even when she had juggled three jobs during culinary school. Backbreaking, monotonous, sad work. She'd watched helplessly as her savings and sales had dwindled to nothing. She'd realized how ideal this place was for her while she was watching it slip out of her grasp. The people here, the laid-back lifestyle, and the constant exposure to a gorgeous natural setting: this was everything she'd dreamed of having, all those nights when she was shivering in an abandoned warehouse or enduring her uncle's tirades or laboring up to her elbows in greasy dishwater. Soon, within the next few weeks, the dream would be over.

She should be devastated, bone-tired, and in despair. She pushed her hair back and wiped wind-caused tears from her eyes.

Oddly enough, she felt lighter than she ever had. Not exactly happy, but filled with purpose and a sense of rightness. Banding together with her community had been a new experience for her. She might have been reluctant to get involved at first, preferring to protect herself by remaining aloof, but once she started working side by side with Mel and the others, she'd come to value the community spirit they shared. Jenny had been right—Helen could have delayed her bankruptcy a bit if she had quit spending so much time at the center and had stopped baking for the volunteers. But she wouldn't trade the kinship she'd experienced for any business success she would have celebrated all alone.

Getting closer to Jenny had been special as well. Helen had never felt such a profound attraction to another person. Looks aside—although Jenny's were enough to turn Helen's head—Jenny had character and integrity. No matter whether she kept up her grueling travel schedule or settled in one place, Jenny would doubtless spend her life in service to animals and the people who cared about them. She inspired Helen to be better, to look beyond her own needs and help others. Helen had trusted Jenny with her story and with her fears, and Jenny had done the same with her. She had found someone who excited her and, at the same time, settled her restless heart.

Helen jumped off the low wall and got back in her car. The morning had been a crazy one. She had woken early, safely wrapped in Jenny's arms, and she had quietly extricated herself from the embrace. Not because she'd wanted to go, but because both she and Jenny had to go. Jenny, to her next destination. Helen, to…well, she wasn't sure. She'd have to find a new goal and start from step one to achieve it.

Helen had sat in Jenny's room for almost an hour, watching her sleep and examining what she really wanted in life. A month ago, she wouldn't have been able to see any option beyond the bakery. It had meant independence to her, and the freedom to burrow into a life and not be forced to leave it again. Now she saw other paths her life could take. Would any of them coincide with Jenny's? Helen had never wanted a roaming lifestyle and she had done whatever it took to avoid living that way. But maybe the constant sense of being unsettled and insecure would be okay if she wasn't facing it alone. And maybe more kisses like the one she and Jenny had shared would eventually erase from Helen's heart any concern about moving. She'd be grounded by Jenny's touch.

Now, as she drove back to the center, she felt a growing feeling of acceptance. She'd accept the failure of her business with as much dignity as she could muster. She'd accept yet another disruptive move and an uncertain future. She walked into the auditorium and looked at the rows and rows of pens. Many were empty now, but a few animals and birds were being found and brought in every day. Her problems seemed puny in comparison.

Jenny was standing by the curtain leading to the washing area, talking to her father, but she hurried over as soon as she saw Helen.

"Hey," she said, pulling Helen into a big hug. "Thanks for texting me updates about Buddy. He's really going to be all right?"

"He'll be fine. He was already looking less disoriented by the time we got him home." Helen hesitated before telling Jenny everything the vet had said. Jenny had made it abundantly clear she was ready to go elsewhere as soon as she was done here. "He agreed with your diagnoses and said your suturing technique is the best he's seen. He's wanted to open a practice here in Cannon Beach, but he'd need to staff it."

"Cannon Beach needs its own vet," Jenny agreed. "I've met plenty of pet owners here, and they shouldn't have to travel far for decent health care. It'd be even better if he could find someone who could work on wildlife as well since there are so many animals and birds in the area. I might be able to come up with some names for him from contacts I've made."

Helen shook her head. "He wants you, Jenny. He's heard about the work you've done here, and Amy was a little dramatic in her description of how you helped Buddy."

Helen didn't mention her own addition to the conversation. The vet must have been left with the impression of Jenny as the Mother Teresa of the animal kingdom.

"I'm flattered, of course, but you know I can't stay here." Jenny shook her head as if emphasizing her words. "It's a wonderful town, and the job sounds tempting. *You* tempt me to stay here, to have a chance to spend more time with you. But I'm accustomed to traveling, and I'm good at what I do. I don't know how to stay in one place, how to really integrate myself into a community beyond the temporary way I connect during an emergency. I understand temporary. Permanence scares me."

"I figured as much," Helen said. She took a deep breath. Jenny had called her a temptation. She sounded as interested in pursuing their relationship as Helen felt, and the knowledge gave Helen the courage to do what she could to give them a chance. "I wanted to talk to you about that, actually. You already know I'm going to lose my business. I've been considering where I'll go from here."

"Are you sure? There must be something you can try."

Helen shook her head. "I'd take on another job doing anything at all to pay the bills, but no one is hiring right now. I sell a few items to locals, but a tray of brownies a day isn't going to keep the bakery afloat. I don't see any other way to—"

"Helen," Mel called out, jogging toward them from across the room, "I've been looking all over for you."

Helen sighed. She wanted to broach the subject of possibly going with Jenny to her next assignment and she was nervous enough about asking without being interrupted. "I'll be right over to help clean," she said.

Mel waved her hand. "Don't worry. You did enough by helping with Buddy. I just wanted to give you this order form."

Helen looked at the invoice Mel had handed her. Sandwich rolls, pastries. By the dozen. "What's this for?"

"Pam and I are organizing a series of tours to the Oregon Coast galleries. Everyone is suffering from the lack of tourism, and this is something we can plan even if the area's beaches are closed. The tours will have sack lunches and dinner in local restaurants. They'll have planned stops at galleries and stores."

"Sharing the wealth," Jenny said with an appreciative nod.

"What little there is," Mel said with a laugh. "But it's a start. I was hoping you could make those yummy soft potato rolls for the sandwiches, Helen. And sand dollars for dessert, of course. Plus, we'll make your bakery one of the after-lunch stops, and I'll let you know the dates and times to expect the buses once we've finalized the schedule. Oh, there's Glen. I need to talk to him about working as a tour guide. Talk to you later."

Mel disappeared again, and Helen stared at the invoice in her hand. She had already made the decision to let go of the bakery, but she couldn't stop her mind from running the numbers against her stack of bills.

"Awesome," Jenny said, looking over Helen's shoulder. "See? You've helped the community, and now it's helping you. Does this mean you won't have to close?"

"No...I mean, it's a generous offer, but I can't..." Helen added the numbers in her head again. She could stay open at least a few extra weeks if these tours were a success. Her bakery wouldn't be safe even with the big order, but maybe she could find other ways to...No. Staying would mean giving up Jenny, and Helen wasn't prepared to do it until she had at least given them a chance. "I still wouldn't be in the black. I'll help for the first few tours, but once the rescue center closes, I'll be ready to shut the bakery and move."

Jenny put her hand on Helen's shoulder. "Why rush? If the money buys you some time, then take it. I've witnessed this too many times to count. When you're caught in the midst of a crisis, everything seems doomed, but things will return to normal."

"Maybe I don't want normal. Maybe I want—"

Tia burst into their conversation. "Helen! There you are. We're having a town meeting on Friday for all the business owners. We'll brainstorm ideas to help each other through this tourist drought. I need you to bring about five dozen pastries, your choice, although you absolutely must bring some of those cinnamon ones. I've had six already today. And I'll introduce you to Gary, the owner of Chez Mer. He just lost his pastry chef to a big Portland restaurant and I told him you make exquisite éclairs. Do you? Anyway, if you don't already, I'm sure you can learn by Friday. Seven o'clock at the town hall. Here's a check for the goodies. Did you see which way Mel went? Oh, there she is."

Jenny laughed. "She's a dynamo." She rubbed her hands along Helen's upper arms. "I'm so happy for you. With these opportunities and all the other ones I'm sure you can think up, I know in my heart you'll be successful here."

Helen shrugged Jenny's hands off her arms and then captured them in her own. "This is amazing, all these people helping each other, but I've already made my decision. I've been trying to tell you that I want *you*. Not my bakery, not to live here, but to be with you. If I come with you on your next job, I can help with the work and give us a chance to be together. To discover each other more than we can in the few moments we've had here."

Jenny shook her head and backed away, but Helen wouldn't let go. "You've been through too much to make this decision, Helen. You're exhausted from working so hard and stressed financially and emotionally. Wait before you decide to throw your life away for someone like me. Give yourself a chance to make it here because it's a good place."

"And you're a good person. You're worth taking a chance on, Jenny. *We* are worth a chance. I can sell the business and come with you. We work well together and we obviously have a connection. Why not see where it takes us?"

Jenny finally broke free. "No, Helen. Because I know where it will take us. From place to place, crisis to crisis. Our relationship wouldn't have a chance because the next disaster would always be my priority. You'll resent me for dragging you around the globe, and I'll hate myself for it. It'll be just like…"

"You and your parents," Helen finished for her. It would be different, though, because Helen would have made a choice to go, and it wouldn't have been made for her. But she suddenly saw the truth behind Jenny's resistance. Jenny herself wanted out of the lifestyle she followed. She was the one who was resentful and angry. Until she faced her own responses, she'd never be able to accept a different kind of life. Helen turned and walked away before she made a fool of herself and begged to go with Jenny. She held Mel's invoice and Tia's check crumpled tightly in her hand. She'd put her energy back where it belonged, into her business and her new home here. Maybe, with the help of other business owners like these two, she'd be able to get through this rough patch.

But this town would never be the same for her. Everywhere she went, everything she did, she'd remember Jenny and she'd wish she was here. Finding a home had meant the world to Helen, but her true home was practically packed and ready to leave her behind.

❖

Jenny stood at the end of the inn's garden, watching a few gulls circle the tide pools below Haystack Rock. The skies around here had been eerily silent and empty for a few days after the spill, but birds were beginning to return. Maybe some of these seagulls were among the ones Jenny and her crew had released back into the wild.

The return to normalcy was rewarding to witness, but it also heralded the end of Jenny's stay here. Soon, she'd be packing her small bag full of possessions—including Pam's miniature oil painting—and hopping on a plane bound for who knew where. She always felt some small tug whenever she left one of her rescue efforts, tempting her to stay a little longer, but she never failed to control the urge enough to leave.

She couldn't fool herself this time, though. Everything about this trip was different, but all the differences were concentrated in Helen. She'd spent the night awake, thinking about Helen's words, her touch, her kiss. In a normal situation, she'd be able to date her and see where the relationship would lead, but this wasn't routine for Jenny. If she really wanted to have a chance with Helen, she needed to stay here or invite Helen to travel with her. Either one meant a complete upheaval of Jenny's familiar lifestyle. Was Helen worth the effort of learning a whole new way to live? Everything in Jenny's body and soul shouted *yes*.

"It's a beautiful beach," Eve said, coming up behind her. "We're ready to go whenever you are, darling."

Jenny nodded without turning around. As expected, her parents had decided to fly to Los Angeles and do some quick research before traveling to the Sudanese village. Jenny was torn between wanting them to stay and relief at seeing them go. They were her parents, no matter how frustrating they could be, and part of her had never given up on the dream of them being close and settled as a family. Funny how they had the opposite but similar dream of the three of them practicing medicine together across the globe. Neither was ever going to come true.

"I love it here," Jenny said, without looking at her mom. "I love the sunsets and the people and the way life is returning to the tide pools."

"Yes, it is very nice, dear. Do you remember the village we lived in when you were…what was it, eight? Nine? The one on the coast of Senegal. Your father and I were sent there because of the meningitis outbreak. You loved the beach there."

Jenny turned around. "I couldn't go to that beach because you didn't want to risk me getting infected. I had to watch the ocean from the back porch of our hut. Mom, did you and Dad ever consider coming back to the States? Maybe not permanently, but long enough for me to make friends or go to a regular school?"

"And have you miss the opportunity to travel and see the world? What school could have given you the experiences we did? Besides, you couldn't possibly have expected your dad and me to give up our life's work. You saw firsthand what a huge need there is for doctors like us. We couldn't be as selfish as that, Jenny, and you know it."

"I suppose not," Jenny said. But maybe the selfish act was constantly dragging her from one village to the next when she needed the stability of a home and the company of other children. When she needed her own parents to notice her needs, not just the needs of everyone else in the world. She didn't speak the words out loud, though. Her parents had made their choice, and she didn't need to fling guilt and recriminations at them. What she had to do instead was move forward without the past dragging her down.

"I'm going to make some changes," she said as they started walking back to the inn. "I can't go on like I've been doing."

"Finally," Eve said with a relieved sounding sigh. "We've been waiting for you to come to your senses. The work you've done is marvelous, darling, and we're very proud of you. But once you have your degree and can—"

"No, Mom. I'm not going to give up being a vet. I'm going to stay here and open a practice in Cannon Beach."

Her mom laughed, and then seemed to realize she wasn't joking. "Do you really believe you can be happy as a small-town vet? When you could do so much more?"

Could she be happy here? Jenny's heart said *yes* without hesitation. She might be working on a smaller scale than before, but the job was no less significant. Ask Amy and Sam. Or Buddy. Or Pam, who'd had tears in her eyes when she saw the seagulls return.

Or Helen, who hopefully would accept Jenny's apology for pushing her away. She had a long road ahead of her as she struggled to keep her bakery. Being with her and supporting her would be Jenny's life's work if Helen would give her a chance.

❖

Jenny drove on the winding Highway 26, pushing Mel's compact to the max as she hurried back to Cannon Beach. She had driven her parents to Portland's airport and dropped them off at the terminal. They had naturally spent the entire hour and a half trip trying to talk her out of her decision to stay in Cannon Beach, but she had been strangely unmoved by their arguments. She had expected to feel defensive, maybe guilty, perhaps more determined than ever to do her own thing and stay. Instead, she had felt the calm peace of a choice well made. *Her* choice, free of any baggage.

Tomorrow, during a break from work at the center, she would drive to Seaside and talk to Amy's vet about the possibility of collaborating on a practice in Cannon Beach. She'd appreciate the contacts and equipment an established vet would bring to the venture because she had few of her own. She was excited about the idea of settling down, but the details were overwhelming. She'd never had to find a place to live or grocery shop or cook or to set up cable and utilities. She'd lived in dorms and had been offered varied types of housing by the communities she'd helped, but an apartment of her own would be a new experience. She felt like a twenty-year-old, moving out on her own for the first time.

She'd need a car, she decided as she careened around a gentle curve. Mel probably wasn't planning on lending hers to Jenny on a full-time basis.

Jenny drove to the center and scanned the parking lot, searching for Helen's car. She wasn't there, but a short drive through town brought Jenny to the bakery. Although a Closed sign hung in the doorway, Helen's SUV was parked outside and a light was on in the back room. Jenny pushed on the door and it swung open, making a chiming sound that echoed through the empty store.

"Sorry, we're closed, but..." Helen's voice trailed off when she came out of the kitchen and saw Jenny in the doorway. "What are you doing here?"

"I came to see you," Jenny said. She wanted to close the space between them in two strides and fling herself into Helen's arms, but she approached her slowly instead. "I drove my parents to the airport and just got back in town."

"Ah," Helen said. She turned and went back into her kitchen. "Soon you'll be going to the airport yourself, I suppose," she called over her shoulder.

Jenny followed her into the back room and leaned against the counter while Helen jabbed her fist into a bowl of dough. Flour misted over her apron and shirtsleeves. Jenny laughed.

"You can't seem to bake without getting ingredients all over you," she said. She moved closer and used her thumb to dust flour off the arc of Helen's cheekbone. "That's one of the many things I love about you. You dive in and do everything wholeheartedly."

She heard the catch in her voice when her hand made contact with Helen's warm skin.

"*Many* things?" Helen asked. "What else?"

Her voice sounded rough with what Jenny hoped was a matching desire for her. *Please.* "I love how you gave everything you had to help the town, but you were still surprised when people were willing to help you in return. You never expected anything for what you gave. I love how you felt in my arms the other night. I love how—"

Jenny forgot what she was about to say when Helen suddenly pressed her lips against Jenny's open mouth. Jenny tangled her hands in Helen's hair and kissed her back, exploring the taste of her with an eager tongue. Flour and cinnamon and vanilla. The scents and flavors of home.

Jenny reluctantly pulled back. She needed to explain herself first, make amends. "I'm sorry I said no when you wanted to come with me. I knew how hard you'd worked to find a place and settle down. I couldn't bear to have you give up your dreams for me, especially not when I understood exactly what it was like to grow up without the things other people take for granted. A house and friends and a family that is always there for you. I wanted you to have everything."

Helen shook her head. "You don't understand. You became my new dream. We're good together, Jenny. I've been searching for love my whole life, but I thought it would be in the shape of a house with a picket fence or in the form of freedom to live as I liked. But it looks different to me now. It looks like you."

Jenny cupped Helen's cheeks in her hands and kissed her again. The temptation to linger was strong, especially when Helen scooted onto the counter and settled Jenny's hips between her thighs. Jenny felt the ache of arousal and a wet heat at the point of contact with Helen. She had to keep talking before she forgot how to speak.

"I was looking for love, too. From my parents, as if they'd finally realize what I needed and care more about me than the next child in line at their clinic. From myself, because I never felt I was doing enough. But things changed for me here. You changed me, Helen. Watching you give of yourself to these people and this place made me want to do the same."

Helen frowned and tightened her thighs. Jenny moved her hands to Helen's waist and helped anchor them together.

"All you've ever done is take care of others, Jenny. I didn't teach you that. It's the other way around. I didn't even want to volunteer until you."

Jenny caressed Helen's lower back, sliding her hands under Helen's ass and reveling in the warmth discernable even through her jeans. She felt Helen shift restlessly as her fingers flexed and probed. "Maybe we make each other better," she said, nuzzling Helen's ear when she spoke. "We're a good team."

Helen moaned softly when Jenny rubbed her hips between Helen's legs. "Does this mean you've changed your mind? I can come with you?"

"No," Jenny said. Helen grew still but sighed and melted into Jenny with her next words. "It means I'm staying here with you."

FLOTSAM AND JETSAM

A riana Knight slid her hand along the polished wood banister as she followed Melinda Andrews up the stairs and to the rooms she'd be renting for the next month. The place was perfect for her. The Sea Glass Inn had all the charm and character of an old house, but everything was freshly painted and papered in bright, clean colors. The ocean was beautiful, and Ari had barely been able to keep her eyes on the road and off the rocky shoreline as she drove up Highway 101 from her home in the mountains of Northern California. She'd be able to write here. To pour out her pain and grief on the page and finally process the emotions inside enough to make them go away and stop hurting her.

"You have a bed and desk in each room, so you can use them however you like," Mel said as she put Ari's suitcase on a folding stand. Ari dropped her heavy backpack next to it and went over to the window. Seagulls careened around the monolithic Haystack Rock, and only a handful of people were out on the beach.

"The beaches are open to the public again, but a few areas are still roped off," Mel continued. "Every now and again, especially if we have an autumn storm, more oil will wash onshore, so we have a place to wash and store beach shoes by the back door to keep from tracking it in. Tourism normally drops during the fall and the numbers are even lower than normal this year. You'll have plenty of peace and quiet for your writing."

Mel was obviously trying to maintain the cheerful demeanor of an optimistic innkeeper, but Ari heard the strain in her voice.

She had read about the spill three months ago and the damage to Cannon Beach, and she had felt an odd kinship with this place. They each needed to heal. Ari hadn't been able to write at home, and she had decided a retreat at the beach was the answer. She'd bring some tourist dollars to the near-vacant town, and in return she'd get the inspiration she desperately needed. Something about crashing waves and screeching gulls seemed to speak to other authors she knew. Maybe they'd reach inside her, too, and release the emotions she felt bottled up inside.

"This is wonderful," she said. "I can already feel the ideas starting to flow."

She tried to justify the lie by telling herself she just wanted to reassure her host. Mel had been very honest from the start about the state of the beach and the town, but Ari was self-employed as a novelist and she understood the financial burden of unpredictable paychecks and dry spells. Mel's relief had been palpable even over the phone when Ari called to rent the suite of upstairs rooms for an entire month. She didn't want to admit she was already feeling as blocked here as she had been at home because Mel might worry she'd back out of her extended stay. Maybe the sea air just needed more time to penetrate her sorrow and transform it into words.

Mel paused by the window. "My partner Pam has a studio in the garden. She said you're welcome to use it anytime. It's set up for painting more than writing, but there are benches and tables, and it's a very bright space."

Ari looked across the yard and saw the low wood-frame building with huge picture windows. The back garden was blooming with asters and mums, and a chipped old boat made an interesting corner arrangement. Just beyond a row of shrubs was the rough-waved Pacific Ocean and some towering rock formations. "I think the view might be too distracting," Ari said with a smile. "How does Pam focus on her canvas when all that beauty is beckoning?"

Mel gave her a sad smile as she turned away from the window. "Once Pam starts a painting, everything else seems to fade away for her. She did all the mosaics for the inn and she's a gifted artist, but the oil spill and all the damage it caused, especially the sea life that was harmed, seemed to shut her down. She hasn't painted for months now. I hope…I *know* she'll find her way back to art again, but the spill caused more harm than one can see on the surface."

Ari understood what it was like to lose the outlet of writing when she was hurting or confused or angry. She couldn't face the emotions in their raw form and had to mold them into sentences and images before she could manage them. Even hearing about another blocked artist made her insides churn with anxiety. She put a hand on her stomach, wanting to write away the knots and tension she felt growing inside, and said, "I'm sure a dry spell is nothing to worry about, especially after facing such a horrible tragedy. She must want to paint the sorrow she's feeling, and I'll bet she gets back to work soon, now that the worst is over."

"She will," Mel said with a decisive nod. Ari had a feeling Mel was the type to make things happen. Once she set her mind on getting Pam to paint again, she'd probably not rest until she had her in the studio with brush in hand.

Ari had never had someone take such an interest in her writing as Mel did in Pam's painting. Mel seemed to understand Pam's need to create. Ari's editors and publishers were supportive and encouraging, but they didn't have a stake in her work and life beyond a financial and friendly concern. Ari's girlfriends, few and far between, had been drawn to her as an author at first, fascinated by her bohemian lifestyle and titillated by the fantasies she created. The reality of life with her never seemed to live up to their expectations, though. She'd get stressed over a missed deadline, or they'd get jealous over her consuming passion for writing, and they'd disappear, leaving her to type stories of loneliness and frustration until those residual feelings disappeared as well. Mel seemed as unsettled by Pam's block as Pam herself must be.

Mel walked to the doorway. "I'm glad you're here, Ariana. Mostly because I can't think of a better or more lovely place for a writer to stay than within sight of the ocean, but also because I know it will be good for Pam to have someone else creating art here. I'm sure the sight of you working will inspire her to paint again."

Ari forced her features into what she hoped was an encouraging smile and not a grimace of terror. She couldn't even motivate herself, let alone be Pam's muse. She'd come here to ease the pressure, not add more. She carefully wore a mask of competence and ease whenever she talked about her writing to others, and Mel had clearly mistaken it for the real thing. She wasn't asking Ari to do anything Ari herself hadn't claimed was natural to her. Just write diligently, and Pam would be inspired to follow suit. No one ever saw the turmoil Ari felt inside.

"I'm glad I'm here, too," she said. Was it true? Yes, it was a pretty place, and yes, every writer friend she had seemed to see the ocean as a place of inspiration and boundless creativity. But maybe this wasn't the right venue for her. Too late. She had to give it at least a month, and then she could go home again. Or maybe to an artist's colony in New Mexico? An igloo in the Arctic or a tree house in the rain forest? Flowing words and phrases must be waiting somewhere...

"I'll leave you to unpack now," Mel said. "I've left brochures and lists of attractions and restaurants on the table over there. I know you're here to write and not to sightsee, but if you need a break, there are some spectacular places where you can hike or drive. If you need anything at all, just ask."

Once Ari was alone, she explored her new rooms. The third-floor suite had spectacular views and good natural light. Mel had put her suitcase in the first and smallest room, with slate-gray walls and bright white trim. A large oil painting of a jellyfish hung on the wall behind the bed. Fascinated, Ari stood in front of the painting and watched a sunbeam dance across the mosaic of white and clear sea glass embedded in the oils. Somehow Pam had brought life and movement where others might expect only stagnant inertia. Ari wished she had the same ability.

She turned away and checked out her second room. This one was brighter in color and mood. Rosy walls and a teal quilt on the bed were offset by the antique mahogany furniture. Ari didn't have much of an eye for design—she'd hired decorators for every room in her house except for her office—but she recognized style and class when she saw it. Dominating the room was another of Pam's paintings, this one of a kite festival. The sky in the painting was filled with kites of different colors accented with primary-toned sea glass. The crowds of people were out of focus, but individualized and given depth with simple brushstrokes.

She couldn't help but see symbolism in the paintings. She should assign the gray room as her bedroom, where she'd sleep in the presence of the slow-moving, land-bound jellyfish. The other room, with kites soaring in the breeze like she hoped her words and stories would do, was perfect for her office. She sat on the teal bed for a moment and tried to picture writing in there. Anywhere. She couldn't. She got up and moved her suitcase from the gray room to the rose one. She unpacked her clothes and carefully arranged them in the dark wood dresser and the closet. She'd sleep with the kites and work with the jellyfish. She felt as if she was lumbering along anyway. She might as well keep company with the beautiful blob of goo.

Ari took her backpack into the gray room. She moved a few shells and other trinkets off a shelf and stacked her reference books in their place. A pile of legal pads and a box of her favorite fine-tipped black pens went on top of the desk. She put her laptop on the desk as well, parallel to the front edge. She sat down and stared out the window. Maybe she should scoot the desk to the other side of the room, where she wouldn't be distracted by the view. Or would it help to stare at the repeated pulse of the waves?

She got up and went into the bathroom instead where she unpacked her toiletry bag and laid everything neatly on the vanity. She'd be here a month, but she wasn't planning to do more than sit at her computer, and Mel had offered her the use of a washer and dryer. So she'd brought very little with her, and unpacking took a disappointingly small amount of time.

Ari picked up a notebook and pen, more to soothe her conscience than because she had anything to jot down, and a map of Cannon Beach from Mel's welcome packet. She went downstairs and out the back door to Pam's studio. It was unlocked and empty, crisscrossed with interesting shadows from the windowpanes. The October sunlight turned gold in here, spotlighting some partially finished landscapes and a rough-hewn table. Ari sat at one of the split-log benches and put her notebook on the table. There was depth in this place and the air was heavy with the burden of artistic work. Ari shook her head. Not today. Today she would settle in her temporary new home. Maybe pick up a few snacks at the grocery store or buy some souvenirs for the neighbors who were watching her house while she was gone. Saltwater taffy sounded good. She could get some of that in town, surely. She got up and left the studio.

She'd write tomorrow.

❖

Ari walked along the sidewalk with her shopping bags dangling from one hand and a soft, cream-filled pastry in the other. She took a big bite and wiped powdered sugar off her lips with the back of her hand. She'd browsed through the nearly empty shops until she found just the right vase for her neighbors. It had been hand-blown locally and had bands of oranges and reds and yellows. The colors of a sunset. She had also found a powder-blue trinket box covered with tiny seashells and a generous coat of glitter for their young daughter. A bag of assorted flavors of saltwater taffy—heavy on the black licorice ones—would keep her company in her room at night.

She wandered slowly past shops selling toys, sailor-inspired clothing, and just about anything on which someone could glue a seagull replica. The gulls were kitschy but cute, and she figured she'd be the proud owner of two or three before it was time to go home. She could justify any purchase, no matter how silly she felt making it, because the local businesses needed her support. She was glad to offer it, especially if it gave her an excuse not to write for the day.

She stopped in front of an art gallery called Tia's Closet and stared at a washed watercolor of a woman on the beach. Her hair was piled up in a messy gray-blond bun and her back was to the artist. Something about the tilt of her hips as she walked barefoot in the sand made Ari think of her mom. She would have loved it here, and she'd have been wading through the shallow wake of waves even though the water was freezing and the beach wasn't pristinely clean. She would have grabbed hold of this month at the ocean in a way Ari never could. Her mom had always tried to pull Ari out of her head and into the world. She made everything an adventure and lived each adventure fully, while Ari preferred to stand a bit distant and observe. Later, when Ari would write her thoughts down on paper, she'd feel more alive and present than she had when actually there. Ari turned away from the painting and wiped her eyes with the sleeve of her green shirt. Where would she be when her mom wasn't calling her out of her shell and into life? Would Ari retreat completely?

Of course not. She would live and feel again someday, once she put her grief on paper and could handle its intensity. She saw a bookstore and hastily popped the rest of her pastry in her mouth before going inside. She needed a reminder that she had a presence in this world, and what better place to find it?

The gentle tinkle of a bell over the door made the woman at the counter look toward her. Ari paused, captured by the woman's eyes like a rabbit staring at the lights of an oncoming car. Her auburn hair was held in a neat french braid, with no wisps allowed to escape, and her eyes were large and Mediterranean blue. She was wearing a pumpkin-colored button-down shirt and dark khaki cargo pants. There was something elegant and efficient about her clothes, as if she could go from boardroom to a fancy restaurant with just a flick of her collar. She looked ready to cope with anything, and her cargo pockets were probably full of useful items like Swiss army knives and string cheese and a first-aid kit. She was helping a customer, but Ari barely noticed the other woman.

"I'll be right with you," the woman behind the register called to Ari, flashing a stunning smile. Ari nodded and ducked out of sight behind a shelf. She usually felt disheveled and gangly around capable-looking women like this one. Not that Ari wasn't capable, but she *had* managed to arrive at Cannon Beach with about a hundred pairs of underwear and only two socks. And she'd forgotten toothpaste, but Mel had kindly provided a tube. She just would never match such a stylish and unwrinkled state of being, no matter how hard she tried.

She found herself standing in front of a shelf full of nature guides for Oregon. Not what she needed—she'd better be too busy writing to wander around identifying trees and lichen. She came out of the alcove, quickly moving past the register on her way toward the fiction section, and she overheard a brief exchange between the clerk and her elderly customer.

"What did you think of last month's bundle, Rosalie?"

"It was perfect, of course. I don't know what made you choose the book on old sailing ships, but I couldn't put it down. I never would have picked it for myself."

"I'm glad to hear it. You might be surprised by one or two of this month's books, but give them a chance first. You can always bring them back for an exchange or refund if you don't want to read them."

"I've learned not to second-guess you, dear. You have an uncanny knack for choosing books I love to read."

While the transaction was being completed, Ari leaned around the end of a shelf and tried to read the titles on the counter. She was intrigued by the conversation and wondered, first, what this mystery woman would choose for her to read. Second, she wondered if she had ever recommended Ari's own books to a hungry reader.

The two women chatted some more, changing topics from books to the customer's granddaughter, and Ari lost interest. She found fiction and skimmed to the Ks. Knight, Ariana. All eight of her novels were on the shelf, and one was even a face-out. Not her best seller, but her personal favorite about an agoraphobic woman and the collection of friends she made online. Ari straightened the books slightly, making them flush with the front of the shelf. When she heard the door ring again, she turned away from her books and faced the shelf opposite them, not wanting anyone to associate her with her books and identify her as the author. She picked up a mystery at random and turned it over to read the back cover. Mel knew who she was, of course, but Ari had begged her not to tell anyone else she was in town. She felt embarrassed enough about her inability to write, even more so now that she was apparently supposed to be a good influence on Pam, and she couldn't face the questions she was bound to hear. How do you get your ideas? *I don't know. I don't have any.* When is your next book coming out? *Probably never, since I missed my deadline eight weeks ago.*

"Welcome to Cannon Beach and the Beachcomber Bookstore. I'm Jocelyn Sherman."

Ari shook the proffered hand. Jocelyn. A perfect name for her—sort of lacy and strong at the same time. A bit unusual, but not too far out there like Planetia or Iguana. Ari usually agonized for hours over the names for her characters and she liked when real-life people matched their names so well. Ariana had always seemed a little too ethereal for her, but she still used it instead of a pen name. She realized she hadn't let go of Jocelyn's hand yet while her mind had wandered off on a tangent, and she reluctantly dropped the contact. Jocelyn's handshake had been firm, as Ari had expected, but somehow mobile at the same time. Her fingers skimmed across Ari's palm as they let go of each other, and she felt the impression of them even after the warmth of Jocelyn's skin dissipated.

"I'm Ari," she said, using her everyday, incognito name. "This is a great store. Are you the owner?"

"Owner, chief cook, and bottle washer, as they say," Jocelyn said with a laugh. "Can I help you find something, or would you prefer to chance upon something unexpected?"

Ari nodded at the phrasing. Jocelyn understood book people. Ari loved the serendipitous finds she'd unearthed in bookstores when she wasn't looking for anything in particular, but today she didn't trust fate or dumb luck to throw anything good her way.

"Your last customer seemed to think you have a talent for picking the right book for people. Why don't you give me a shot?"

"Ah, a challenge. I love a challenge." Jocelyn's brow furrowed as she looked Ari up and down. "I don't know anything about you, but I'll give it a try on one condition. You have to read what I choose and not dismiss it at first glance."

"Fair enough," Ari said. She didn't mind challenges herself.

She had liked the sensation of Jocelyn's gaze on her at first, but she'd started to fidget after a few seconds, as if Jocelyn was reaching too deep and pulling something out of her.

"I've got it," Jocelyn said as she walked to the back corner of the store and chose a book off the top shelf. She grabbed another tiny volume on her way back and handed them to Ari.

Ari held one book in each hand. A slender paperback and the little hardcover. "I thought you might come back with the most expensive coffee table books in the store and tell me the oracle whispered that I'd particularly enjoy them."

Jocelyn laughed. She sounded like music, just like when she spoke. Ari wasn't sure how she'd write that sound if she ever made Jocelyn a character in a book. It was a subtle intonation, too fleeting to pin down and identify. "I'll have to remember that trick next time a gullible tourist comes in," she said.

Ari silently read the covers and then looked at Jocelyn. "A memoir about a beekeeper and a book about a monastery? I'm afraid to ask what your voodoo intuition told you about me to make you choose these."

"Someday I might tell you why," Jocelyn said with a shrug. "But not now. Are you going to read them, or are you backing out of our deal?"

"I'll take them," Ari said. She needed something to fill the hours while her creative mind was blank. She followed Jocelyn to the counter and pulled out her wallet. The vase had eaten up most of her cash, so she pulled out a credit card. She handed it over and was noticing how slender and graceful Jocelyn's fingers were when she saw her name clearly imprinted on the card. *Shit.*

"No way," Jocelyn said, her gaze darting from the card to Ari's face. "Are you really *the* Ariana Knight?"

"I'm *this* Ariana Knight. I'm sure there are plenty of us in the world."

"Are you the author Ariana Knight?" Jocelyn asked again. When Ari hesitated, about to fib and say no, Jocelyn pulled a tablet across the counter. "If you won't tell me, I'll just do a quick search online. Photo, author, Ariana—"

"Fine, yes, I'm *that* one." Ari used her finger to push the tablet out of Jocelyn's reach. "I'm here for a retreat, sort of. Finishing my novel and in the throes of artistic passion. Can't be disturbed."

Jocelyn rang up her books and swiped the tattletale credit card. "I wouldn't dream of disturbing you while you're writing one of your wonderful books. I respect your need for privacy." She handed the bag to Ari and tapped the credit card on the counter. "But…"

"But…what?" Ari reached for her card and reclaimed it forcefully out of Jocelyn's hand.

Jocelyn laughed at their brief game of tug-of-war. "But it wouldn't take much of your time to do a quick book signing and reading here at the store. Very intimate and small. No pressure."

No pressure on *you*, maybe. "I appreciate the offer, but I really don't have the time. Maybe on my next trip to Cannon Beach." Which would be when? How about never?

"Just give it some thought," Jocelyn called as Ari was walking toward the door. "You'd be doing us both a favor. You get publicity and sell books, while I get more people in my store. And sell books."

Ari looked back at Jocelyn and shook her head. Something in Jocelyn's expression told her she hadn't heard the last of this scheme. Ari hurried back to the inn, desperate to be alone with her troublesome but familiar writer's block.

❖

Jocelyn wheeled a cart full of metal folding chairs out of her storeroom and began to unfold them and form a large circle near the biography section. Once she was finished, she lugged a card table across the store and set it up near an outlet. Coffee, creamer, tea, sugar…she mentally checked off each item as she put it in place. A second table joined the first, but this one was empty except for napkins and paper plates. Members of her book club always provided the snacks, and soon the table would be full of goodies. Helen would bring something scrumptious from her bakery, and Mel usually contributed some variation of her famous scones. Jocelyn loved those scones, but tonight she'd prefer if Mel only brought one thing with her—one particular guest from her inn.

Jocelyn stood back and surveyed the room, rechecking to make sure she hadn't forgotten anything. She doubted Ariana Knight would come to the meeting. She had seemed reluctant to do a reading at the bookstore, and based on what Jocelyn had read online, she rarely made appearances as an author. The last place she'd want to be would be a bookstore full of readers and avid fans.

One more trip to the back room, this time for a box of paperbacks, next month's selection. She glanced at her file cabinets and tugged on one of the handles to make sure it was locked. She stored her information about all her customers in these wooden cabinets, and she treated the data as carefully as if it was personal health information or the notes from a therapy session. This afternoon, as soon as Ariana had left, Jocelyn had created a new file for her and placed it in one of the drawers reserved for the tourists she got to know by name. In the file, she'd written notes about Ariana's career and what little biographical details she'd gleaned from the generic bios on Ariana's website and the back covers of her books. She'd also listed the two books she'd recommended. If Ariana gave her feedback on them, Jocelyn would make note of her comments and be better able to hone her next suggestions.

Jocelyn ran her hand across the smooth-grained drawer containing Ariana's file. She'd been drawn to her from the moment she walked in the store. Ariana'd had the hungry look of a real book person when she entered. She'd not so subtly tried to read the spines of the books Jocelyn had chosen for Rosalie. Jocelyn would have done the same thing in her place, because she'd have been curious about what someone else was reading and hopeful about getting a good new title to add to her long to-read list.

But Ariana had been captivating for reasons beyond her potential as a book buyer. She was stunning, but in a dreamy sort of way. Jocelyn tended to date people like herself—driven, put-together businesswomen. She'd never had any real luck with dating, but still, she had her type and Ariana hadn't fit it at all. She had worn soft, faded Levi's and a yellow waffle shirt with a hole in the sleeve. Her seal-brown hair fell to her shoulders in what would be better called a cut than a style. Straight as a blade and glossy as polished metal. Jocelyn had wanted her hands tangled in that hair, and she had required a surprising amount of willpower to refrain from touching it.

Crazy. Jocelyn needed to visualize Ariana as an asset to the bookstore, not as someone to pursue romantically. First, because she didn't date tourists. And second, she repeated to herself, because Ariana was definitely not her type.

Jocelyn gave in to one smidge of temptation and pulled the cabinet key out of her pocket and opened the drawer. She reread the reasons for recommending the books she had. The beekeeper memoir was basically about family and home, and Ariana had somehow seemed like she was far away from both right now. The book about the daily life in a monastery was introspective and beautiful. A perfect fit for Ariana, who, when she talked to Jocelyn, looked as if she was carrying on a second conversation in her mind. One parallel to but much deeper than the one in the outer world.

Would the two books resonate with Ariana? Jocelyn was pretty sure they would. She'd been recommending books for a long time now, and her instincts were often undeniably accurate. Some of the locals called her the Book Witch. In a completely flattering way. Probably.

The bells on the front door announced the first arrivals. Jocelyn returned the file and locked the cabinet. She had similar notes on acquaintances, and much more detailed ones on permanent Cannon Beach residents. She recorded every interest, hobby, and idiosyncrasy she could discover. If one of her customers was going through a career change, dealing with a two-year-old, or adopting a dog from the humane society, Jocelyn put it in her notes. Then she scoured other bookstores and catalogs from small presses. She read like a fiend, too, wanting to really know the books she was recommending to others. People had certain expectations about bookstore owners. They thought she'd be retiring and shy, someone who wouldn't mind an empty store because she'd rather sit alone and read. Yes, Jocelyn was at heart all those things, but she had to be as aggressive as a stock trader to keep her business going. With big online stores and their discounts, independent bookstores were a high-risk venture. And now, since the ripples of the oil spill had swept through town and sent the tourists packing, times were even harder than normal. Jocelyn was prepared to fight for her store. Whatever it took. She'd battled for her life before this, from as early as she could remember, and she wasn't about to back down now.

She picked up the box of paperbacks again and set it by the register before greeting Helen and Jenny. They were both fairly new to Cannon Beach, but they'd quickly established themselves as locals during the immediate aftermath of the spill. Jocelyn gave them each a hug and then peered in the pastry boxes Helen had brought.

"Cream puffs and applesauce doughnuts," Helen said. She helped Jocelyn arrange the treats on serving plates.

"You're an angel," Jocelyn said. She hadn't stopped to eat lunch today, and the smells were very tempting. She'd wait until everyone was here before eating, though. "How's the Reynolds horse, Jenny?"

"Fifty-six stitches," Jenny said with a shake of her head. She had come to Cannon Beach to help organize the rescue efforts and she had decided to stay and open a vet clinic in town. Well, she had stayed for Helen. For the town as a whole, the vet clinic was a happy by-product of her decision. "He's going to be fine, but I have a feeling the equines in this town are going to be paying my rent until next summer."

Jocelyn shook her head. "Poor horse. What happened?"

"They're renting a pasture for him and the fencing isn't the safest. He stretched his head over it to reach some grass, and when he pulled back, he cut the side of his neck on a loose wire end. This is the third accident involving SeaHorse animals, and I'm thinking of holding a series of seminars to educate these kids and their parents on basic horse care and safety."

"That's a great idea," Jocelyn said. After the oil spill, the stable that organized beach rides had leased out its horses for a cheap fee and shut its doors until the next summer. Jocelyn had ridden on and off since she was a teenager, and she had splurged on herself for once and had a scruffy Paint boarded a few minutes outside of town. She had the benefit of the more experienced stable owner's expertise, but a lot of the horses were being leased by people who had no idea how to take care of them. She made a mental note to stock up on horse books. Maybe she could start a book club for kids with an equine focus. They'd learn valuable information, and she'd possibly make some sales. Win-win.

"Can you recommend some good books I can have on hand?" Jocelyn grabbed a pen and some paper off the counter and handed them to her.

"Definitely," Jenny said.

Jocelyn saw Mel enter the store—with a plastic-wrap covered platter but no Ariana—and she excused herself to go say hello to her. Jenny, furiously writing on the piece of scrap paper, waved her off.

"I'm glad to see you here, Mel," Jocelyn said. She always was. Mel was one of her best customers. During her first year running the inn, Mel had been in her shop buying books on electrical wiring and small-appliance repair and decorating. She had practically supported the store on her own. The best part of her buying sprees was the amount of time she'd spent in the bookstore, though. Jocelyn had missed Mel's company once the inn was renovated and full of guests. One of the main reasons she'd started this book club was to have a chance to see Mel and her other friends who were often too busy to spend long afternoons browsing. She'd also started her book bundle program for the same reason, and she spent the time her customers couldn't afford choosing books they could.

"Jocelyn, it's great to be here." Mel put her platter of scones on the table and shrugged out of her coat. "Pam sends her regrets, but she's swamped with the gallery tours right now. There'll be another busload coming by your store on Thursday about ten, so be prepared."

"Always," Jocelyn said. She had charts from every tour that had come by her store over the past months, and she was beginning to see trends. She knew exactly what books she'd display and stock before Thursday. "So…I met one of your guests today," she said. She'd been waiting for the chance to bring up Ariana, but she felt oddly tongue-tied and awkward, like a teenager with a crush.

"Ah, you met Ari. She's my only guest at the moment. What'd you think of her?"

Mel asked the question casually, but her expression changed as she watched Jocelyn try to think of a way to answer. What did she think of Ariana? Ari? She thought she was sexy. She was in awe of her. She had read every book Ari had written. They were heartfelt and intimate explorations of pain and sorrow and happiness. They were emotions laid bare. Jocelyn had kept her mind on the financial opportunity of having a famous author in her store, but her body and heart had other ideas entirely. Jocelyn felt her cheeks grow warm, and Mel laughed.

"All right, I have a good idea what you thought of her."

Jocelyn tried to compose herself. "I'm a big fan. Of her *writing*," she added when Mel laughed harder. "I suggested she do a reading and signing here, but she didn't seem too receptive. Maybe you could put in a good word for the Beachcomber?"

"I can try, but I get the feeling she wants solitude. She seems… sad, I guess. When she made her reservation she said she wanted a quiet place to work, and I think she has a project she needs to finish. I won't intrude on her space, but if the opportunity comes up, I'll talk you up. Oh, I mean talk up your store, of course."

Jocelyn gave Mel a playful bump with her elbow. She wouldn't push the issue of Ari with Mel right now, but she was determined to have a signing here before Ari packed up and left. She had to keep fighting, keep putting every ounce of effort she had into her store. She had projects in place to keep revenue flowing, and she was always on the lookout for new ways to remain solvent. An appearance by Ari would fill her store with readers and fans. It would also seriously disturb her equilibrium, but that was a chance Jocelyn had to take in the name of survival.

❖

Ari leaned back in her desk chair and watched the clouds scuttling across a vibrant blue sky. After a week of staring out the window of her upstairs room while pretending to write, she had moved the desk to the wall next to the door. The only result was that now she had an ache in her neck from twisting around to see outside. The tiny cursor on her laptop screen continued to pulse like Poe's telltale heart.

In her mind, she visualized the opening scene. A woman, distraught with grief and guilt, stands alone on a bluff overlooking the sea. Wind blows her light brown hair and she wraps her cardigan tightly around herself to fend off the chill in her heart. Ari had written the first sentence over a thousand times already, deleting each failed attempt, and the image in her head seemed frightfully clichéd and stale now. She wasn't sure whether the scene was a good one and it felt old only because she had been spending too much time trying to capture it in words, or whether it really did suck. She would feel compassion for the character and her sorrow, but then a critical part of her mind would sneer at the derivative symbolism and ask if Heathcliff was about to come stomping across the moors toward the woman.

Ari righted herself before her chair tipped over backward. She might as well go outside and experience the actuality of a windy fall afternoon at the ocean instead of dwelling on the fictional one in her imagination. She'd been sitting at the desk for three hours now. She hadn't typed anything worth saving, but the time spent at the desk should count for something. She deserved a break after doing absolutely nothing. She sighed at the sarcastic tone of her own thoughts and closed her laptop with a firm snap. She left the room and went down the stairs, pulling a thick plaid shirt over her sweatshirt. She slid her feet into a pair of low rubber boots Mel had provided for her, as protection against oil stains on both Ari's own shoes and the inn's floors, and went outside. The wind felt invigorating and bracing, and the sun was warm whenever it broke free from sporadic cloud cover. The sensations were welcome, especially after her forced confinement in the gray room, but even her enjoyment of the weather made her feel a nudge of guilt. She had always been able to transport herself away from the world and into her stories. She'd felt sun and wind and snow along with her characters without needing the medium of her own skin. Now, though, the story wouldn't let her in. She had to come out here to feel anything at all.

Ari went past the studio and waved at Pam, who was sitting on a bench next to one of the large windows. She looked as if she was sorting paint tubes by color, and a blank canvas was set on the easel behind her. Pam waved back with a friendly smile, but the expression vanished as soon as she returned her attention to the paints. Ari wondered if Pam would be able to create today or if she'd give up and escape to the real world like Ari had.

She climbed down the wooden staircase leading to the beach, pushing aside overgrown grasses whose dry yellow fronds swished across her face and arms. She jumped the last three steps and landed with a satisfying thud on the soft sand. She walked a few yards along the retaining wall before scrambling onto a huge driftwood trunk, almost half her height, and leaping off it and over a narrow rivulet that flowed toward the ocean. The physical effort felt good. She trudged across the thick sand and headed toward the wet, packed area where walking would be easier.

The beach was nearly empty. She saw a couple far ahead of her, walking like one person with their arms wrapped around each other's waists. A man stood near Haystack Rock, taking pictures with his cell phone. A woman on a small spotted horse was cantering along the packed sand, and Ari stood still to let them pass before she crossed to the water's edge. She frowned as the centaur pair got closer. Something about the rider was familiar to her…

"What a surprise to see you here," Jocelyn said in a breathless voice as she pulled her horse to a halt near Ari.

"I'm sure it is a surprise," Ari said, gesturing over her shoulder at the Sea Glass Inn. "Who'd have thought I'd be right outside the place where I'm staying?"

Jocelyn grinned, seemingly undeterred by Ari's sarcasm. "Right? Mariner and I just got to the beach and started our ride, and there you were."

Ari couldn't keep from smiling in return. Jocelyn's cheeks were red from the wind and her fast ride, and she spoke with a tone of shocked innocence. She looked stunning on horseback, connected to the beach and the creature she rode. She was full of shit, obviously, but stunning. Jocelyn seemed like someone who wouldn't relent until she got her way, and Ari needed to stay strong and resist. She made herself look away from Jocelyn and pointed again, this time at the masses of hoofprints in the sand wet from the ebbing tide.

"Looks like a whole herd of horses has been through here," she said. "Or maybe just one, back and forth a whole bunch of times."

"Hmm, I do seem to remember a van full of horses leaving the parking lot just as we drove in. Must have been them out here."

"Oh, okay. So…I'm new around here. Maybe you can tell me where I go to get a restraining order against a stalker?"

Jocelyn laughed out loud. "We take care of our own around here. No one will issue one against a poor business owner who is simply trying to make a living by offering to host a reading for a visiting author who will benefit from the evening and sell a bunch of books."

Ari shook her head at the breathlessly delivered rambling sentence. Every time Jocelyn mentioned the idea, she managed to make it sound as if she was doing Ari a favor. She couldn't help but admire Jocelyn's persistence—how the hell long had she been riding out here?—but admiration and attraction weren't going to be enough to make Ari relent. She got anxious enough at publicity events. It'd be even worse when she wasn't writing and felt like a fraud dressed up in author's clothes.

She started to walk along the beach, searching for a way to distract Jocelyn from her mission. The horse fell into step beside her and Ari reached out to stroke his neck. He was already getting his thick winter coat, and his mane sprouted every which way like a too-long mohawk. Ari used him as a diversion.

"He's cute. Have you had him long?"

"Only since the beginning of summer," Jocelyn said, giving the horse a pat. "There's a livery stable called the SeaHorse Ranch that offers beach rides for tourists. After the spill, the beach was shut down indefinitely, so they leased out as many horses as they could.

I couldn't resist a chance to ride again, and I knew I'd be helping the ranch owners by feeding and boarding him for a year, so here we are."

"Out a-stalking on horseback," Ari said. "Poor horse, unwittingly leased into a life of crime."

"We're not stalking you. We were just out for a nice ride on the beach and we happened to bump into you and I happened to mention an amazing marketing opportunity."

Jocelyn was definitely tenacious about this favor. Luckily, Ari could be equally persistent in her determination to change the subject. "What do you mean about getting to ride again? You look natural up there, like you spend a lot of time in the saddle." Ari made a concerted effort not to look where parts of Jocelyn met the saddle. She didn't need to go there—her willpower might not be strong enough to resist.

Jocelyn looked straight ahead, suddenly appearing as uncomfortable as Ari had been when the book signing was mentioned. "I rode a few times when I was a kid. At camps and stuff."

"Were you a Girl Scout?"

"Um, no."

Ari couldn't help herself. Whenever she wrote a character that was as evasive as Jocelyn was acting, there was some hidden reason behind her caginess. Ari tried to convince herself she was merely gleaning information she'd use in a future book—she loved collecting snippets of scenes or character motivation—but she was too aware of her growing interest in Jocelyn as a person. She was an enigma. At once vulnerable and hard as nails, gentle and pushy.

"What kind of camp?"

Jocelyn shrugged, as if answering the question was no big deal to her. "A camp for kids with cancer. I got a wish granted, and I had such a wonderful time with the horses that my parents sent me back each summer."

Ari stopped walking. "Cancer? I had no idea. I'm so sorry."

"I'm fine now," Jocelyn said. She pulled Mariner to a halt.

"I had AML. Acute myelogenous leukemia. I'm better now," she repeated.

Ari nodded, not sure what to say given Jocelyn's defensive tone. She rejected all the platitudes that came to mind and went with the first honest question that popped into her mind. "How much of your childhood was spent in hospitals?"

Jocelyn paused as if considering the question. "Between ages three and six, I'd say I was in hospitals and clinics far more than out of them. I had surgery and chemo, and once the cancer was in remission I had more intense chemo, and then a stem cell transplant from Maggie, my sister. She's my fraternal twin. After age six, I went back for regular screenings for over five years. I didn't go to a regular school until I was ten, but the doctors hadn't been convinced I'd even make it to that age, so I can't complain about having more nurses and doctors as friends than kids my age, or about watching other kids play from the sidelines."

Ari was silent. She'd learned a lot in a few sentences. She felt she understood the force of Jocelyn's determination a little better now. She probably saw challenges as life-or-death situations after facing such a huge one at a young age. And a twin? Ari was curious and wanted to ask more, but she sensed Jocelyn had shared enough for the moment. She had been hesitant to tell her story at first, and then had spit out the words as if trying to get their bitterness out of her mouth in a hurry. Ari started walking again, and Jocelyn and Mariner continued, too.

"You said you're working on a project while you're here," Jocelyn said. "What are you writing now?"

She didn't seem to have any doubt Ari would answer, and Ari couldn't find a good enough reason not to repay Jocelyn's confidences with at least one of her own. Trapped by reciprocity. Damn.

"It's a book about a woman who loses her mother," she said, pretending she was actually writing the novel and not merely staring at a computer screen and thinking about it. "They were estranged, and the main character is remembering their relationship and coming to terms with her residual anger and the guilt she feels because she's angry."

"I knew it," Jocelyn said with a triumphant grin.

"You knew what I was writing?" Ari asked, confused by Jocelyn's response. Did she know about Ari's own mother somehow? Had she searched hard enough online to learn about Ari's personal life? The thought made her feel exposed and she wrapped her arms around her middle, suddenly cold in the growing breeze.

"No. I recommended the book about beekeepers because it's really about family and home. Somehow I guessed you were wrestling with those issues, but I didn't realize it wasn't really you. It was your character."

"Do you moonlight as a psychic? Or do you use tarot cards to pick books for your customers?" Ari heard the challenge in her voice. Jocelyn had shared something deeply personal, but she still didn't have the right to delve into Ari's mind and emotions.

"Some locals call me the Book Witch," Jocelyn said, as if proud of the title. "I pay attention to hunches, is all. But your premise sounds interesting. You handle painful emotions very well when you write, and I'll bet this will be another best seller. What you need to do—"

"No." Ari hated sentences starting with the words *What you need to do* or *You should*. "I'm here on a working retreat, and can't let my attention be split between writing and making appearances."

"One appearance. Not even an appearance, just a small afternoon gathering where you read a few passages, sign some books, and answer questions. Nothing to it."

"It's not nothing. It would be too much of a distraction," Ari said, even though she had spent her entire visit to Cannon Beach searching for distractions to avoid writing. She halted again and faced Jocelyn. "I need to be left alone to write."

"Why?"

Jocelyn clearly didn't understand. Ari wasn't sure she did entirely, either. She'd always been nervous when speaking to readers, but she'd loved it at the same time. She couldn't stand up in front of people and claim to be a writer when she wasn't writing.

Her pain and grief were too close to the surface right now—what if the audience could see the real things she was facing, without the veil of her characters between them?

"Because," Ari said. The meaningless answer would have to be good enough for Jocelyn.

It wasn't. "I'd think a reading would be inspirational for you. It would be good publicity, plus you'll be adored by your fans, your ego will be boosted, and you'll sell books. That's the whole point, isn't it?"

"You mean *you'll* sell books." Ari had to laugh when Jocelyn shrugged and grinned at her without even a hint of shame.

"Tomato, tom-ah-to. You'll get royalties and I'll generate a little income to help my business survive." She leaned forward and balanced her arm on Mariner's neck. "We'll actually be helping each other."

Ari shook her head and started to back away. "As much as I'd love to help, this trip isn't about making money. It's about communing with nature. Synchronizing my spirit with the timeless rhythm of the waves." Ari spread her arms wide and shouted into the wind. "Becoming one with Mother Earth."

"Baloney." Jocelyn laughed. "I'll ask again."

Ari moved faster, glancing over her shoulder to make sure she was aiming toward the inn and wasn't about to trip over some driftwood. "And I'll say no again."

Jocelyn raised her voice as Ari got farther away. "Then I'll keep asking until you finally say yes."

Ari waved her off and turned around. She crossed the deep, loose sand and got to the steps leading to the inn before she heard Mariner's hooves slapping through the waves as Jocelyn cantered away. She climbed the steep wooden staircase, using the rough banister for support. Jocelyn was exasperating. She was so adorably and irritatingly confident that she'd eventually wear Ari down and rope her into the signing, that Ari was beginning to doubt her own ability to avoid it.

❖

Ari sat on the wooden step at the top of the bluff with her jacket pulled over her head to protect her from the misty fog. The day was gray and wet. The ocean rolled and heaved, only discernible from the sky in movement, not in color. Something, either very low clouds or a heavy fog, Ari wasn't certain, hid the fir-covered hills surrounding Cannon Beach from view. She hadn't been all the way down to the beach since her encounter with Jocelyn three days before. She kept watch for the horse and rider pair, but even though she hadn't even seen a hoofprint in the sand, she didn't consider herself safe from Jocelyn's relentless petitioning for a book signing. Ari tried to remain firm, but Jocelyn was a fighter. Ari had a feeling she was regrouping and planning her next attack. She stirred too many emotions within Ari—how long would she be able to withstand the turmoil of arousal and defiance she felt whenever Jocelyn was around? Soon she'd agree to anything Jocelyn asked, just to get some peace.

Unless, of course, she could avoid seeing Jocelyn entirely until she was scheduled to leave. The easiest way to accomplish the feat would be to spend every waking hour besides mealtimes in her room, diligently working on her new book. Or, to be more precise, starting her new book. Getting a sentence down on paper. She still struggled with the opening line, and she had used different tricks to get past her block. She'd tried starting a later chapter, writing some of the dialogue she heard playing in her mind, and doing every character-building exercise she had ever heard of. Nothing seemed to work, and after pacing in her room and staring out the window for several hours, she absolutely had to get outside.

And run the risk of seeing Jocelyn. She'd either gotten in her car and driven out of town or kept to the inn's garden path over the past few days, places where she was sure to be left alone by anyone other than Pam, Mel, and the other guests who'd arrived two days earlier. Those two, a pair of honeymooners from Eugene, Oregon, were far too wrapped up in each other to care about Ari at all. Just the way she liked it.

Ari understood why Jocelyn was as tenacious as she was,

especially given the circumstances of her childhood, but she still didn't have the right to bulldoze over other people to get her way.

"Are you okay out here?"

Ari startled at the voice and she turned to find Pam standing behind her. "I'm good." She pushed her makeshift hood back until she could look up and see Pam's face. "Not the greatest weather for being outside, but it's beautiful out here. Very powerful and ominous."

Pam laughed and sat on the step next to Ari. She didn't bother covering her head, and fine drops of mist settled on her short hair. "The ocean has many moods," she said. "This is one of my favorites, when it churns and everything is monochromatic. The atmosphere is more interesting than on a calm, sunny day."

The weather suited Ari's own mood better today than it did when it was milder. She should feel inspired by her environment and the hints of an incoming storm. Maybe she needed a full-blown autumn tempest to really get her creative juices flowing. She needed the waves pounding against the bluff itself and the wind blowing debris across the inn's garden before she could squeeze the depth of the moment out of her fingers, through the keyboard, and onto the page.

"Do you paint better when there's a storm than when it's quiet?" she asked.

Pam tilted her head to one side and considered the question before answering. "I don't think so. Right now, I'm not doing much at all, whether it's sunny or pouring rain. I came to tell you I'm done in the studio for the day, if you'd like to use it for a writing space. This doesn't really qualify as rain around here, but if you stay out in the drizzle long enough, you'll still get soaked."

Ari believed her. Already, she was getting chilled sitting out here. She dreaded the thought of going back inside or into the studio to face her laptop, so she kept the conversation going. "How did your painting go today?" Ari had seen Pam in her studio every day, and she'd also seen the range and beauty of the paintings she'd done for the inn. Surely such talent couldn't remain submerged for long.

"I have to admit my painting not only hasn't gone well lately, but it's been nonexistent. Today I organized my brushes and canvases by size," Pam said. "And I did get a nice pale ivory wash on one canvas, so tomorrow it'll be ready to sit on my easel and stare at me mockingly. How's your writing?"

Great. Never better. I'm churning out a hundred pages of brilliant prose a day. "I haven't written as much as I'd hoped by this time," she said. She hadn't written at all, but she wasn't ready to admit the whole truth. "I usually can process my emotions by putting the feelings into my stories and characters, but I haven't been able to lately. I guess I'm sort of lost, with no outlet for all the stuff inside. I'd rather live through my characters than have to face the pain and hurt directly."

"Wow," Pam said.

"Wow? Do I sound crazy?" Ari had been desperate to confess her inability to work on her novel to someone, and Pam had seemed the obvious choice. She was an artist and she seemed to be doing just about anything besides practicing her art these days. Ari had thought Pam would understand how terrible it was to be unable to create, but maybe she'd been wrong.

"Not crazy at all. I meant wow, because I've felt the same way before. I could paint feelings onto a canvas, and only then did I really seem to get what they meant. Then, when I went through the most terrible time in my life, I couldn't paint at all. All I could do was sit and stare at the pain. Until Mel came along."

"What did she do?" Ari had some idea about how Mel had taken care of Pam. She seemed to truly honor and support Pam's need to create. But it sounded like there was more to their story.

Pam laughed. "She somehow talked me into making the mosaics for this place. I didn't believe I could even get one of the six she commissioned finished, and I was defensive every time she asked about them, but she wouldn't let her vision for the rooms here go. She carried me along with her until I got all six done. Since then, well, I haven't stopped. Over the past year, I didn't need any special circumstances to create. I didn't need to feel pain or joy, or to have the temperature, lighting, and environment within certain parameters. I would see something and feel an emotion attached to it, and then I'd paint it." She sighed, a wistful sound. "I'd never felt anything like it, as if my connection to the world was healthy and... unhindered, I guess. It flowed."

"What happened?" Ari asked. Pam would understand what she meant. Why had the connection ended? Maybe Pam knew the secret most artists sought to comprehend—how creativity could be controlled. How one could stop it from leaving a person alone, groping in the dark.

But Pam didn't seem to know the answer. "I have no idea." She shrugged. "The oil spill happened, I guess. I saw the horror of it all around me, what it did to the wonderful birds and animals that live here. What *we* did to them. And now, with Mel worried about the inn, and more businesses going under every day...How could I paint everything I was feeling? And then I couldn't paint anything."

"Does it scare you? Do you worry you won't ever be able to paint again?" Ari's own fear bubbled to the surface of her mind as she talked to Pam. She bent her knees and hugged them with one arm, the other holding her jacket in place over her head so she didn't get wetter than she already was.

Pam put a hand on Ari's shoulder and gave it a pat, as if she knew Ari's questions were as much about her own work as Pam's. "I was terrified. I thought I was going through the same thing I did before, when I went for years barely picking up a brush. I still get frightened sometimes, but I'm slowly finding faith in my need to paint. I feel more confident about finding my way back to art when I'm ready for it. I'm just not ready yet."

"I wish I had your faith and confidence," Ari said. She let the jacket droop over her eyes and wrapped both arms tightly around her legs. "I've got all these emotions, and I need to write them out before I can get past them. I just can't get them organized and structured into sentences. Not even basic ones. Maybe it won't ever come back."

"I've read your books, you know. Jocelyn had us read one for her book club, and since then Mel and I have bought everything you've written. You're a storyteller, Ariana. You have a gift for it, and it's part of who you are. Mel and I talked about painting the other day. I think it hurts her as much as it does me when I can't create. She saw what it did to me when I stopped before, and she doesn't want me to go through it again. But she, always the practical one, said something that made me see what's going on in a different light. Both the catalyst for the last dry spell and the oil spill were profoundly serious for me. Maybe I had to actually experience them before I could paint them as subjects. It happened before." Pam paused and looked toward the sea.

Ari sensed Pam was looking into the past and not at the ocean. She was torn between wanting to give Pam privacy, and her innate need to understand other people. She gave in to her writer's curiosity. "What made you stop painting the last time?"

Pam was silent for so long that Ari thought she wasn't going to answer her at all, but she finally spoke. "I collapsed in on myself when my ex-girlfriend yanked her son out of my life. I felt like I'd lost my own child. Eventually I was able to finish his portrait and continue painting, but first I had to really mourn his loss. I can only believe I'll do the same thing after I get through grieving the oil spill, the dead creatures and ruined lives. Maybe one day I'll feel ready to paint the rescue center or the volunteers or the destruction and rebirth of the beach."

Ari was happy for Pam and her optimism, but she didn't feel the same hope for her future. Maybe Pam was better at facing emotions head-on than Ari was. And for a fact, Ari didn't have anyone remotely like Mel in her life to spur her on. Jocelyn was the closest thing she had to a muse right now. Her most persistent fan.

After Pam patted her on the shoulder again and went back to the inn, Ari continued to sit in the increasingly heavy rain. She gave Pam's suggestion a try and tentatively rummaged through the hidden cache of pain she held inside. Sadness, anger, and guilt performed their endless cycle until Ari felt queasy from the ride. She shivered and hunched her shoulders when the raindrops got big enough to drip through her jacket and run down her neck. She got up and ran past the studio and back to the inn. She couldn't face this alone, not without the help of her fictional characters. And she couldn't use them to help until she could get them out of her mind and into the manuscript.

She needed to find a way to *be* a writer again, without waiting for the readiness Pam was convinced would return. Maybe Jocelyn wasn't as wrong as Ari had originally thought. Would reading old passages and answering the usual questions about her writing and inspiration break something loose inside her? Would it remind her of what it was like to create and allow her to recapture the inspiration she so frantically sought?

Maybe, just maybe, if Jocelyn approached her again, she'd be willing to give this new plan a chance. She imagined Jocelyn's face when Ari would tell her she'd given in and would make an appearance in the bookstore. She'd probably wear a maddeningly triumphant expression, as if she'd known all along Ari would do her bidding. Maybe the whole damned thing was worth doing just to see Jocelyn's reaction.

Ari left the muddy, damp boots outside the back door and ran up two flights of stairs in her stockinged feet. She bypassed the room with her laptop and notepads, going instead into the kite room and flopping on the bed. She didn't feel like attempting to write anymore this evening. She watched television for a while, and then went downstairs to work on the jigsaw puzzle Mel had spread out on a card table. Ari picked up her phone and ordered delivery pizza for her dinner—why go out and make it easier for Jocelyn to find her?

When she had run out of ways to procrastinate, she got out the two books she'd bought from Jocelyn's bookstore and read them far into the night. She wanted to go back and ask for more recommendations since Jocelyn truly had pegged her as someone who understood solitude and who was wrestling with family questions. Maybe the next book Jocelyn suggested would be a guide to recovering a lost muse.

Jocelyn was on her mind all night. Had she given up on Ari, or would she launch another attack? This time, Ari wouldn't say no.

❖

In the end, Ari had gone in search of Jocelyn, not the other way around. And now she was standing in the empty bookstore, organizing her notes for the reading at the podium Jocelyn had set in the corner of her store.

At first she'd resisted the urge to go back to the store and face Jocelyn. But then she got bored enough to Google herself. She had thought reading some positive reviews of her books might give her a boost in confidence. Unfortunately, the first one she found was for her most recent work.

Award-winning novelist Ariana Knight disappoints with latest novel.

She should have stopped reading after the headline, but she didn't. She shouldn't have gotten in her car and driven directly to the Beachcomber Bookstore and told a delighted Jocelyn she'd do this stupid signing, but she had. And now here she was. Ready to disappoint again.

Jocelyn came over and broke Ari out of her self-pity mode.

"Do you need a glass of water up here while you read? Will you be comfortable standing behind the podium, or does it feel too formal?"

Jocelyn had been nothing but helpful and appreciative since Ari had arrived, and Ari had to admit that Jocelyn had thrown together an elegant, yet intimate setting on short notice. Ari wasn't sure exactly how short the notice had been. Maybe Jocelyn had been planning this night since the moment they met, confident she'd eventually wear Ari down.

"I like the podium because I can put my notes down instead of holding them," Ari said. No matter how she had ended up in this predicament, she'd do her best to make it a success for Jocelyn and her store. Ari was dealing with her own demons these days, but she could set them aside for one night. She had come here to help Cannon Beach as much as herself, and this was a way to support the town. Along the way, perhaps she'd remember why she loved writing in the first place. "And water would be nice."

Jocelyn gave her a wide grin and went to get Ari's drink. Ari watched her walk away with her long, patterned navy skirt swaying around her bare ankles and the sleeveless white top showing off her toned arms. Ari had come to this town with a heavy weight on her mind, and from the start, Jocelyn had taken up residence in her head. She preferred to focus on the ways Jocelyn irritated her. If she stopped being annoyed by Jocelyn, she'd have to face the even more disturbing fact of her attraction to her. To Jocelyn's body, her smile, and her wide blue eyes that seemed to look right into her customers' souls. To her persistence and ability to survive—so different from Ari's desire to escape and hibernate. And to her grace, whether she was riding her horse on the beach or walking across the store with a glass of water.

Jocelyn set the glass on the flat rim of the podium. "Are you okay?" she asked. "I have wine for the reception, but I can get you a glass now if you'd like."

Ari smiled but shook her head. A drunk reading—that'd be an interesting first for her. Who knew what she'd break down and say in front of the people who came. "I'd better say no, but thank you. I always feel a little anxious before events like this, but I'll be all right once it starts."

"I'm sure you'll do great," Jocelyn said.

She put her hand on Ari's arm, probably meaning it as a casual gesture of comfort, but her expression changed as the contact was prolonged. All at once, Ari couldn't read what Jocelyn was thinking, but the point of contact between her silk-covered arm and Jocelyn's bare hand grew warm and drew all Ari's attention, as if it was the only part of her body that was fully alive. Blood rushing through capillaries, skin shifting and tingling at the friction between fabric and Jocelyn's palm.

Ari, fascinated by her response to Jocelyn's touch, lifted her hand and cupped Jocelyn's cheek. She usually stayed in her head when she was in moments like these, with girlfriends or lovers. She'd overthink her actions and distance herself from the moment. Now, however, she went with her instincts. Caressing Jocelyn's high cheekbone with her thumb because it made her tingle deep inside her belly, not because it was what one of her characters might do. She wasn't remembering old love scenes she had written or planning future ones. She was present with Jocelyn, right beside her in the world the two of them created.

She stepped closer, bridging the distance between them, and her body twitched in surprise when she felt their lips connect. The time between wanting to kiss Jocelyn and actually doing it was near instantaneous. She hadn't wondered whether her advances would be welcomed or considered what repercussions might follow. She just kissed her. All her answers came when Jocelyn kissed her back.

She had imagined kissing her before this, too many times for her own comfort, and she had expected Jocelyn to be as ferocious in romance as she was in business. There was no battle of tongues or shoving Ari against the bookshelves, though. There was only a soft molding of the two of them to each other. Jocelyn's mouth was pliant against hers, welcoming and accepting her deeper inside until Ari thought she might be swallowed whole by the feelings coursing through her. Ari had initiated the kiss, but Jocelyn moved and brought her body in contact with Ari's. The touch of Jocelyn's hand against Ari's arm had been intense, but feeling the sensation in her entire body was overwhelming.

The chime of the bell over Jocelyn's door broke the spell as quickly as it had flared to life.

"Ouch!" Jocelyn bumped into the bookshelf behind her when she jumped out of Ari's arms. She hastily straightened the books and smoothed her hands over her hair and her face.

Ari leapt in the opposite direction and knocked into the podium, barely catching the glass in time to keep all the water from spilling.

"People are here," Jocelyn said with a wince. "I mean, obviously they're here, since the door opened. But I should get out there and greet them. You'll be okay? We're okay?"

"Of course," Ari said, although her insides were anything but okay. She picked up her scattered notes while Jocelyn went to the front of the store to greet whoever had so rudely interrupted them. Or maybe they were lucky to have been interrupted. Who knew how far the kiss would have taken them if they'd been left alone. Ari had never felt her body and its desires take such complete control over her. She hurried into the bathroom and stared at herself in the mirror.

She was slightly flushed, but not much more than she usually was when doing a publicity event. She'd expected to see a disheveled and stunned version of herself, but she looked unchanged and perfectly normal. On the outside.

Ari returned to the sales floor and let Jocelyn introduce her to the locals as they arrived. She stood at the front of the store and chatted on autopilot. *Thanks for coming. Yes, I've found Cannon Beach to be a perfect place for a writer's retreat. Yes, I'm inspired by the beauty around me here.* Say what they want to hear, don't whine about the writer's block and for God's sake don't admit to not having written a single word so far.

Ari turned around and jumped about a foot when she came face-to-face with a larger-than-life cardboard cutout of herself. She nearly apologized for bumping into the smiling and confident-looking version of herself. She hated being upstaged by a grinning piece of paper, so she moved away and over to the table filled with food. She stood next to Pam, who was watching her with an amused expression, and put some cookies and crackers on a plate.

"Mel sometimes gets me to do exhibits or painting demonstrations," Pam said, chewing on a carrot stick. "I resist, but I know they're good for me. I can get too wrapped up in my own little bubble of art, and I need to get out in the world to get fresh ideas and a break from introspection. I appreciate how she helps me out of my shell, but what I *really* appreciate is that she's never made me stand next to an enormous picture of myself."

"Yeah, thanks for sharing," Ari said before she took a huge bite out of a sand dollar–shaped pastry with a lemony filling. She wiped at the powdered sugar on her shirt and groaned. "And now the damned cutout is better dressed than I am. Maybe Jocelyn can put her by the podium and I'll stand behind a curtain and read, like the Wizard of Oz."

"I like the jaunty way you have your hand on your hip," Pam said, mimicking Flat Ari's pose. "You can put her at the book-signing table and reach through that space under her arm to sign your name."

Ari was about to make a retort when Jocelyn bustled up to

the table. "I think everyone's here," she said. "We can get started whenever you're...What's on your shirt? Hang on, and I'll get something to clean it."

She was gone again before Ari could say anything.

"Jocelyn is something special," Pam said. She put a large piece of the carrot cake Mel had brought onto her plate. "Everyone in town loves her, and she's given back more than we could ever repay. One positive outcome of that awful oil spill was the way it brought everyone together and really showed the true spirit of the people who live here. Jocelyn worked at the rescue center every day, cleaning birds and taking care of them. She couldn't keep normal business hours and do the volunteer work, so she'd take orders and deliver books in the evenings. I'm not supposed to tell anyone, but even though she was as hard off as all of us without the usual influx of tourists, she helped a couple other business owners stay afloat. She's gorgeous, too, but I'm sure you've noticed that already." Pam took a bite of carrot cake and licked the frosting off her fork. "She's single, too, although I can't imagine why."

"I'm not in the market for a girlfriend, so you can stop the not-so-subtle matchmaking." Ari could see Jocelyn's beauty and she sensed her kindness, so Pam could save her breath. Ari didn't need to be pushed toward Jocelyn—she was already there. What she needed to do was focus on her writing, not on anyone or anything else. Jocelyn appeared again, a damp cloth in hand, and Ari kept repeating her determination to remain detached in her mind while Jocelyn rubbed her front from collarbone to belly button. She felt heat explode under her skin, not helped at all by Pam's choking laughter. By the time Jocelyn was finished, after what seemed like hours of intimate contact, Ari felt ragged.

First the kiss, and now the extended contact. She knew Jocelyn had only been trying to make her presentable for the evening, but she'd taken her damned time doing it. Ari stood off to one side while Jocelyn gathered the guests and herded them into seats near the podium. She had drummed up more attendees than Ari had expected, but still the pile of books she was standing near seemed overly ambitious. She leaned one hand on the table to support herself. It was all too much to handle and she shouldn't have agreed to come. Writing, Jocelyn, her mother. Everything hit at once and Ari felt sucker-punched as she struggled for breath. Anxiety before speaking was one thing, but this was something new entirely. Something awful. She heard Jocelyn finishing her introduction and the applause from the audience as if they were muffled by the ocean's roar.

Ari pasted on a smile to rival Flat Ari's and somehow made it to the front of the room.

❖

Jocelyn stood next to Ari and handed her books to sign, introducing her to locals and telling her how to spell names. She had been worried sick about the evening, despite her calm assurances to Ari, and she had questioned her wisdom in pushing so hard for the signing. She wasn't accustomed to doubting herself, and the feeling wasn't a comfortable one. Ari had been polite but distant when she'd first arrived, and then their kiss had completely thrown Jocelyn out of orbit. By the time she had stood in front of the crowd and introduced Ari, she had become a sweaty-palmed, weak-kneed mess. Certainly not the Jocelyn she was accustomed to being.

She handed Ari a copy of her second book, Jocelyn's personal favorite. "This is Helen, Ariana. She's the one who made the lemon sand dollars."

"Oh, I remember those," Ari said, opening the book to the title page and writing an inscription. "I was covered with powdered sugar by the time I finished eating one and Jocelyn had to sponge me down before I got up to read, but it was totally worth it. Absolutely delicious."

Ari gave Jocelyn a quick wink and chatted a bit more with Helen before finishing her signature with a flourish. Jocelyn didn't hear a word Ari said after *delicious*. What was totally worth getting covered with sugar? Getting to eat the pastry or experiencing Jocelyn's cleanup effort?

She sighed and took the next ticket in line, giving Ari the appropriate book and name to inscribe. Ari had her in such a spin she wasn't sure what to do. She didn't date women like her, let alone kiss them in her store right before a big event. And she usually didn't make such a thorough and long-lasting job of wiping a few specks of powdered sugar off someone's blouse. She'd been aroused by Ari's unexpected kiss and annoyed when they'd been interrupted. She should have felt relieved, but instead she had sought out another way to make contact with Ari and to determine whether her reaction to the kiss had been a fluke or not. It hadn't been. The moment she touched Ari, even with a shirt and a cloth separating their skin, she had known she was in deep trouble.

No matter how personally disconcerting the night had been, the reading and signing had gone better than she could have hoped. Ari read a moving passage from her most recent book and a funny one from her third novel. She had an endearing shyness in front of the crowd and had answered questions as long as the audience wanted to ask them. Jocelyn watched her closely, too damned interested in her for comfort, and thought she could distinguish when someone asked something Ari had answered a million times before from when a question caught her by surprise with its freshness and thoughtfulness, requiring her to think fast and give a heartfelt and less rote answer. Jocelyn was happy with the number of sales she'd made, and she hoped to plan more events like this in the future. Most of all, though, she felt proud of Ari. She'd seemed detached and troubled when they had first talked at the store and on the beach, and Jocelyn had been wondering if the new book was going badly. Tonight, though, Ari had seemed more present during her reading and even more so during their kiss. Jocelyn hoped she had given Ari a break from the stress of her writing, because she seemed more at ease now. She loved the idea of helping Ari with her project, even for a very short time.

Once the last book was signed and the wine bottles and food trays were empty, Jocelyn felt the same push and pull she experienced so often with Ari. She wanted to be alone with her again, this time with no one to interrupt and no time limit imposed. But her common sense, usually her best and most trusted asset, told her to make sure Ari left along with the lingering guests. Jocelyn would be better off going home alone tonight.

"Do you want to take a walk on the beach?" she asked when the store was empty and Ari helped her carry the card tables to the back room. "The moon is nearly full and the tide is out. It's a beautiful night."

So much for common sense. Or any kind of sense at all.

"Um..." Ari looked as conflicted as Jocelyn felt by the offer. She bit her lip, drawing Jocelyn's attention to her mouth and making her momentarily forget to breathe. "Why not? It'll do me good to get outside after being around so many people tonight."

"You seemed at ease the whole time," Jocelyn said as they bundled into jackets by the front door. She turned out the store lights and locked the shop behind them. "I guess you've done enough of these events to be comfortable with them by now. And this was probably small compared to what you're used to."

"I was surprised by the turnout, actually," Ari said. She walked close by Jocelyn's shoulder, without touching, as they crossed the street and headed up the beach access road. "I've been to a few with more people, but this was a great group. They were engaged and interested, and I liked the questions they asked. Like they'd spent time thinking about writing and my books and really wanted to understand more."

"I told you the people around here are big fans. What a shame it would have been if you'd refused to do a signing for them while you were here."

Ari bumped into her and Jocelyn staggered a few steps, laughing. "You sound very smug," Ari said. "I'm sure everyone would have survived the trauma of not meeting me."

She sighed and grew quiet soon after, and Jocelyn tried to keep up with the sudden shift in mood as they walked along the beach. Moonlit ocean waves curled and foamed along the shore, and Jocelyn felt sand fleas bumping into her ankles as they jumped around in the sand. Maybe Ari was tired after being in the public spotlight—she didn't seem to seek it out as much as Jocelyn would have expected.

"We'll have to have you make a return trip once your new novel is published and on the best seller list," she said. She felt a stillness from Ari, as if she'd stopped breathing.

"Hardly worth the trip here from California," Ari said.

Jocelyn stopped and faced Ari. She felt a frown crease her forehead, and the resulting tension threatened to give her a headache. She had put a lot of effort into making the night perfect for Ari. Despite the distraction of the kiss, she had tried to be an ideal host, keeping both Ari and her guests happy and relaxed. She had mingled, starting conversations when there were lulls, and had served food and wine to anyone who had an empty plate or glass. What the hell more did Ari want?

"What's your problem tonight?" she asked, her voice louder than usual to be heard over the waves. "What more do you want? To be adored and complimented more? To make more money on sales? You seemed fine a few minutes ago, and now you're back to sulking."

Ari listened to her little speech with raised eyebrows. "I meant the book won't be worth a trip here because it probably won't get written. I didn't mean your event wasn't worthwhile. I couldn't have expected any more from you," she said. "I appreciate what you did for this event, and I managed to forget myself while I was there. Especially when we kissed. But it's over now. I have to go back to work, and I can't make it happen. I've written some version of the same damned sentence over and over for three weeks, and I've deleted it every time."

"Oh," Jocelyn said. Ari's books flowed with prose that seemed effortless and natural, so Jocelyn would never have guessed the process of writing would be anything but easy for someone with her talent. Jocelyn was the person in charge in her career—of course, she couldn't stop tragedies like the oil spill from ruining the tourist season, but she could rebuild her business with hard work and smart choices. Ari lived in a different world. Creativity couldn't be forced or scheduled, and Jocelyn could imagine the frustration of being out of control and unable to perform tasks. Being sick was the closest she'd ever come to feeling the way Ari sounded when she talked about her inability to write. Then no amount of wishing or organizing made any difference. She suddenly felt guilty for forcing Ari to do this signing when she was obviously having a difficult time with her writing, but a small part of her wondered if the event had been good for Ari. A chance to be around people, to focus on something besides her struggling project and maybe get unstuck. At least Ari was talking about her problem now, and not hiding the real reason for her reluctance from Jocelyn and everyone else around her. Jocelyn started walking again, hoping to keep Ari talking. "Do you know why you're having trouble writing?"

She felt Ari's shrug once they were walking side by side again. "I might be too close to the subject. I never felt this before, though, and I've always been able to use writing as a way to understand and cope when I'm sad or hurt or confused."

Jocelyn remembered what Ari had said about the premise for her book. She pulled her hand out of her pocket and curled her fingers gently around Ari's arm. "You lost your mom?"

"Yes," Ari said so quietly Jocelyn barely heard her answer. "Almost a year ago. I've been stuck since then, I can't write anything. I thought if I faced it head-on in a book, I could finally get to a point where I'm still sad, but I'm writing, too."

Ari took Jocelyn's hand in her own. Jocelyn held tight to her, feeling the fragility of Ari's emotions. She'd gotten to know a few artists, like Pam, here at Cannon Beach, and she saw the same changeability of mood and sensitivity in Ari. Nothing at all like the no-nonsense women Jocelyn dated and understood as well as she understood herself.

"Were you close with your mom?"

"Sort of," Ari said. "At times yes, other times not so much. I guess it's true with any family. She never thought writing was a suitable profession, and she would never even discuss my sexuality. I loved her, but I was angry because she didn't seem to accept who I am since I didn't make the same choices she did. We grew apart over the past five years and we didn't get to resolve any of our issues. I miss her and hate to have lost her, but sometimes the old anger comes back. Then I feel guilty for holding on to those negative memories. I want to write it. To face all the pain in a way I can handle and control instead of the messy and chaotic way it feels inside me right now."

Jocelyn realized she had been holding her breath while Ari talked, and she exhaled softly. She had shared the story of her childhood with Ari, and she knew this was as big a revelation as hers had been. Tonight at the reading, Ari had carefully avoided talking about her personal life and her current work—referring to it only vaguely when asked directly about it. Jocelyn knew she didn't give this information to just anyone. She wanted to put her hands over her ears, to avoid hearing the words because she was being drawn in to a life she couldn't comprehend. One that didn't match hers at all.

"Why can't you write something else for now? Something less loaded emotionally and less hurtful. Something less close to you. Then, when you've worked through the mourning process, you can go back to this story you want to tell."

"You mean figure it out first, and write it later?" Ari asked. When Jocelyn nodded her head, Ari shook hers vehemently. "That's not the way I work. I can't figure it out on my own. I need to see it happen through my characters before I can sort it out in my own mind."

"Maybe your relationship with your mom deserves more than that. Maybe it was important enough to deserve having you explore and examine it directly instead of assigning it to a character. I'm sure your way of handling emotions is fine for some situations, but this is huge. It shaped who you are and probably made her a different person as well. You should look at the two of you, your lives and your interactions, not at two fictional people who are shadows of your mom and you."

"It's not as easy as you make it sound—"

"Of course it isn't," Jocelyn said. She stopped and pulled her hand out of Ari's grasp. "Life never is. Don't you think I would have preferred to write a book about a kid with leukemia instead of having to sit in a hospital bed in real life, getting jabbed with needles and told I probably wouldn't see age ten? But I couldn't assign my life to some made-up person. I had to fight to survive, no matter how much I wanted to bury my head in the sand and pretend it wasn't happening to me."

Ari shoved her hands in her pockets again. "I'm sorry about what happened to you. No child should have to go through that, and no family should have to experience it. But we're different people in two very different situations. This is how my mind works."

"Well, this time it isn't working for you." Jocelyn wasn't certain why she was this angry with Ari, but she couldn't control it anymore. The night had fluctuated too much, too fast. Why had she caught Jocelyn in her swing from sexy to charming to maudlin? "So you should change how you work through emotions. Handle the pain of life, and tell stories. They don't always need to be intertwined."

"Don't tell me what to do," Ari said, her voice cold and flat.

"I'm not. I just…" Actually she had told Ari what to do. She wasn't a stranger to this conversation since she'd had some variation of it with girlfriends in the past. She tried to fix things. To bring everyone into her fight-to-survive-at-all-costs camp. Make a decision and do it. Make the change necessary and follow through. Ari was a different breed altogether. She'd never be like Jocelyn. Emotions would catch her like a leaf in the breeze, tossing her this way and that until she figured out how to right herself again.

"Good night," Ari said. "Thanks again for everything you did to plan the reading. I'll walk from here and pick up my car in the morning."

She started walking toward Haystack Rock and the Sea Glass Inn. Jocelyn wanted to call out an apology and ask Ari not to go. To hold her and let her cry about her mom and her past until she was emptied of the sorrow. To tell her she was fine the way she was. Whatever her creative method was, it had worked for her in the past.

Jocelyn could have run after Ari and said all those things, but she stayed still. Ari would figure out her own life and manage it how she wanted. Her choices were none of Jocelyn's business, and she was better off not being emotionally involved.

She stood on the empty beach for another hour, until sand flea bites and an increasingly cold wind forced her to go home.

❖

Jocelyn walked along the boardwalk in Seaside, window shopping as she slowly made her way to the café where she was meeting her twin sister. Maggie was never on time. She was one of the most compassionate and capable people Jocelyn knew, but she couldn't seem to grasp the concept of time unless it was related to her work in some way. At the hospital, she was punctual and precise. In life outside her job as an oncologist, she was a flake. But she was Jocelyn's flake.

The lack of tourists was more noticeable in Seaside than in Cannon Beach, even though the former was a much larger town. Cannon Beach still retained the feeling of a sleepy, tight-knit community, but Seaside was a tourist town, pure and simple. Both had been hit hard by the oil spill, and Jocelyn saw a few *For Rent* signs in empty storefronts. For the most part, though, Seaside was still healthy. These were business owners who really understood the fluctuations of their trade. This year would be one of the lean ones, but those were anticipated and accepted risks of doing business here.

Jocelyn passed two kite stores, a shop selling humorous souvenir T-shirts, and a general store with everything a tourist would need, from flip-flops to beach towels, in its windows. None of them had more than three customers inside, but they were all open and fully stocked. Jocelyn was beginning to see hope for the future of these beach communities. The summer had been hard, and no one had been able to look much beyond the present day. Now, even though the number of visitors was much lower than the average, she felt a shift in the atmosphere. They were through the worst and ready to hunker down for winter. Next year would be a fresh start.

"Joss, over here."

Maggie's voice cut through Jocelyn's introspection. She had been so wrapped up in her thoughts she had taken longer than expected to get to the restaurant, and Maggie had actually beaten her there. She wove through a cluster of empty wrought-iron tables to where her sister was sitting. "Hey, Mags."

Maggie stood to give her a hug. They were fraternal twins, but alike enough to be easily recognized as siblings. Maggie's hair leaned more toward red than Jocelyn's deep auburn, and she was an inch taller—something she had lorded over Jocelyn ever since she had sprung ahead in height during high school.

"Do you mind sitting outside? We can go in if it's too cold for you," Maggie said, hovering next to her chair. "Or I can go to my car and get you a jacket."

Jocelyn sat and pushed Maggie's chair out with her foot. "Sit down, Mags. I won't die of hypothermia while we're eating."

Maggie winced at the phrasing, and Jocelyn reminded herself to watch what she said during their lunch. She forgot and joked about things Maggie would never find funny. She still treated Jocelyn like the fragile and sick child she had been years ago, and Jocelyn wasn't convinced Maggie truly believed she was healthy now. If Mags had her way, Jocelyn would be in the hospital for monthly scans and diagnostic tests, just to be certain. Jocelyn put up with Maggie's caretaking and worrying because Maggie had saved her life.

"Your book signing was awesome, sis," Maggie said after they ordered sandwiches. "Although I'm wounded because you didn't tell me you and Ariana Knight are an item."

"An item? We're friendly, but nothing more. Besides, who calls couples an *item* anymore?"

"I do," Maggie said, taking a sip of her lemonade. "And don't change the subject. I saw how the two of you were ogling each other. If I'd had any doubts, they disappeared when you were feeling her up at the food table."

Jocelyn swallowed her soda the wrong way and started coughing. "I did not!" she said when she could speak again. "She had powdered sugar on her shirt and I was wiping it off."

Maggie snorted. "Oh, please. I thought I might need to turn the hose on you. At least she didn't seem to mind."

Jocelyn stayed silent. She wanted to protest and deny any feelings she might have for Ari, but the more she denied it, the guiltier she would look. Besides, Mags knew her better than anyone. She'd spot Jocelyn in a lie from a mile away. She'd obviously seen the attraction Jocelyn had been feeling for Ari—exacerbated by their kiss—but hopefully no one else at the party could read her well enough to suspect any involvement between the two of them. Well, Pam had been laughing during the powdered sugar incident, as if she'd noticed something. Just Maggie and Pam, then. Of course, Pam would most likely tell Mel. So only three people knew…

Jocelyn's head was beginning to hurt. She nearly overlooked Maggie's last comment, but the words sank in eventually. "You really think she liked it when I…well, the whole shirt thing?"

"Are you kidding? What woman wouldn't? Besides, she didn't swat your hands away, so I think you've got a shot."

"We kissed before the party," Jocelyn admitted after their lunch was served. She picked up a potato chip and waved it for emphasis. "Nothing serious. Just a casual kiss."

"Liar," Maggie said. "Okay, you kissed before the party and rubbed her chest during it. Spill. What happened after?"

Jocelyn took her time chewing and swallowing some of her sandwich before she answered. She didn't like this part. She chose her words carefully, not willing to share Ari's confessions with anyone, not even her twin. "We kind of argued. She's having issues with her new book, and I guess I sort of gave her unwanted advice."

"No," Maggie said in a fake-shocked voice. "You? You got bossy with a girlfriend and pushed her away once you started to get close? I don't believe it."

"I'm not bossy."

"You're a control freak and you know it. You have intimacy issues. Big deal, welcome to the club."

Jocelyn frowned and put her sandwich back on the plate. Maggie never prevaricated with her. She spoke her mind, no matter what. Jocelyn was the same with her, and she wished she could find the same level of trust and honesty with a romantic partner. She sensed Maggie did, too. Neither had found it yet.

"She was stuck in an emotional wallow. I was trying to help."

Maggie shook her head. "You had a choice in that moment. What was your other option?"

Jocelyn thought back to the conversation on the beach. She had been faced with a choice, just like Maggie said. She could have supported Ari. Listened to her and let Ari use her as a sounding board. She was opening up about a sensitive emotional topic, and Jocelyn had shut her down. She could have been Ari's muse, but instead she pushed her deeper inside herself.

"You've read her books, Joss. They're powerful. She captures something profoundly human and universal in her stories. Do you think someone could write like that, yet not be more emotionally sensitive than your average person? Of course not." Maggie answered her own question. "Remember our book club meeting when we read her book? Her words spoke to everyone there. We each saw something of ourselves in her stories, and we understood ourselves a little better after reading them. I think that kind of gift is worth a wallow now and again."

Jocelyn thought back to the comments made during that night's book club. Maggie was right, again. Ari's process for understanding emotions and writing them out might not be efficient or sensible or painless, but it was *her* process. Because of what she wrote, readers were able to work through their emotions in turn. A cycle of expressing and ruminating, moving closer to clarity with every turn.

"You're right. I shouldn't have tried to fix her."

"You can't help yourself. It might not be who you were born to be, but it's who you are. You see everything as a challenge and you're always determined to win because winning means life. But relationships aren't cancer or a business challenge or a marathon. You can't conquer them."

Jocelyn wanted to argue, but she couldn't. Maggie knew her too well, plus she spent most of her days with patients like Jocelyn herself had been. She understood how the struggle to survive could become a way of life. Jocelyn did have one final card to play, though.

"Everything you're saying makes sense, but it doesn't change the fact that Ari and I are too different. Even if I stopped trying to change her, we'd never be a good fit. She withdraws to deal with the world in private, and I rush out and try to tackle it."

"Sounds familiar," Maggie said quietly, reading the dessert menu and not looking at Jocelyn.

Jocelyn waited until they ordered sundaes before she spoke again. "What sounds familiar?"

Maggie shrugged. "How alike are we? We have some similar values and interests. We have the same nose and forehead shape. But aren't we as different as you claim you and Ariana are?"

"Yes, I guess so." Since the topic of cancer had come up already, it brought one example to Jocelyn's mind immediately. Their different but related experiences with leukemia had led Maggie to a career helping others with the disease. She had also grown up to be more fearful—although Mags called it *careful*—than Jocelyn. Jocelyn had become fearless.

"Maybe we should stop seeing each other, then. Give up our weekly lunches and stop talking on the phone all the time. Since we're so different, you know."

Jocelyn scraped the whipped cream off the top of her sundae and licked it off the spoon. She pushed the tempting and unexpected image of Ari covered in cream aside and answered Maggie's foolish question. "We're sisters. We're allowed to be different. Besides, we balance each other in a lot of ways. I'd be half the person I am if I didn't have you."

Maggie merely looked at her without speaking.

Jocelyn sighed. "Yes, I get your point. But I think there's a difference between two people who are balanced with each other and two people who are opposite extremes."

"Fine. Give up your chance to have a famous, talented, sensitive girlfriend. Keep looking for another one like Horrible Heidi."

Jocelyn laughed and would have flung a spoonful of ice cream at Maggie's head if they hadn't been in public. Heidi really had been horrid. Clicking around in her heels and power suits, running casual lunches like high-stakes boardroom meetings. Jocelyn had taken her attraction to competent and successful women a little too far that time.

"Do you really want to start criticizing ex-girlfriends? Because I'd be happy to talk about Crazy Kat and her fetish for—"

"Fine," Maggie said, covering her ears. "I'll stop if you will."

"Deal."

Jocelyn and Maggie kept to safer topics during the rest of lunch. They laughed and chatted while they finished their desserts, but Ari hovered in the back of Jocelyn's mind the whole time. She had been drawn to her from the start—even before they met, she had been captivated by Ari's voice in her books. Was Maggie right about finding balance? Jocelyn had spent years searching for mirror images of herself. Women who had the same outlook on life and problem solving. But those similarities had never been able to keep relationships alive, or even to help them through rocky patches. Was Ari a good match for her? Would they mesh or would they clash?

Jocelyn had felt connected to Ari during their talks on the beach and in the bookstore. They had argued a little, but they'd also opened up to each other in ways Jocelyn rarely did, and she suspected the same was true for Ari. And that kiss…There was no question of their connection in the physical aspect of a relationship.

Still, Ari would be going back to California soon. They hadn't even spoken of a relationship, and when Ari walked away from her the other night on the beach, she had done so with a sense of finality. Even if Jocelyn wanted to pursue something with Ari, Ari most likely didn't feel the same way. Ari needed someone special in her life, someone who would help take care of her talent and her emotions. Someone who recognized her strengths. Could Jocelyn be the person Ari needed? She wasn't sure.

But that kiss…

Definitely worth a shot.

❖

Ari looked up from her laptop and checked the clock on the wall. She had been writing for an hour—twice as long as yesterday. Not her personal best by any means, but much better than three hours of typing and deleting a single sentence. She saved her document and closed the screen. She was happy and relieved to be back to work, even on a small scale, and she didn't want to push it and scare her newfound ideas away.

She grabbed her notebook and a heavy wool sweater and jogged down the steps with a renewed sense of energy. When she crossed the backyard and passed the studio, she saw Pam inside. She was sitting at the wooden table with a pile of multicolored sea glass in front of her. They waved at each other, and Pam went back to sorting while Ari walked to the staircase and down to the beach. She hoped Pam would be creating again soon, and not just looking for menial tasks to do in the studio. Although she had talked to Pam about her rediscovery of her ability to write, Ari had carefully refrained from offering any advice or cheery encouragement. She and Pam both understood how difficult stagnation was. Ari was crawling out of the hole she had dug for herself, but Pam was still inside hers. She'd find her way out sooner or later, with Mel's support and her own drive to paint.

Ari climbed on the tall driftwood trunk and sat with her legs dangling over the side. She gently kicked her heels against the wood while she opened her notebook and started to write. Not a story, but a journal. She started with details, like what time she had gotten out of bed and how her new novel was progressing, and then she jotted down some of the memories from her teenage years she had recalled this morning. She was still using words to explore the turmoil of emotions she felt, and not working them out internally, but at least she was writing as herself and not filtering her feelings through a fictional character. Someday she would create a novel using these notes, her image of the woman on the bluff, and the premise of loss and guilt. Just not now.

Ari stared at the waves. They were calm and gray-green today. She closed the notebook and sat still, matching her breath with the steady thrum of the vast ocean. She wasn't about to offer unsolicited advice to Pam, but she had been willing to take the words Jocelyn had thrown at her and act on them. After her anger had ebbed, Ari had considered Jocelyn's suggestions. They *had* been pushy and intrusive, but slowly Ari had recognized the sense behind them. The night of the book signing, she had made notes until two in the morning for an idea she had thought of during her stay at the inn. She had ignored the unfolding story at first because she was determined to write the novel about mothers and daughters, but it had remained buried in the back of her mind. Once she turned her attention to it, the words and sentences began to flow.

Pam had told her about her ex-girlfriend's child, Kevin, and how he was slowly becoming part of her life again. Ari had been intrigued when she heard how Mel's son Danny and Kevin were bonding like brothers even though no actual blood or legal relationship existed between them. Ari had changed most of the details in her story, including turning the brothers into sisters, but she'd kept the basic theme of people who were creating a unique family for themselves. Some of the concepts overlapped the book she eventually wanted to write about her mom, but most of it was unrelated. She had been determined to hold on to a project that wasn't working, and she had nearly overlooked this new one. Her fingers stalled sometimes, hovering over the keyboard and trembling with doubt, but she always managed to write the next word, and then the next sentence and paragraph and page.

Ari spotted a horse and rider in the distance, cantering toward her end of the beach. She jumped off the log and was going to meet them when she realized it wasn't Jocelyn and Mariner. She stood still while the young girl and her chestnut horse passed by.

Once they were nearly out of sight, she turned and went back up the stairs and circled around the inn to get to her car. She was stronger now, and ready to face Jocelyn.

She drove the short distance into town and parked in front of the bookstore. She sat in her car for a few moments and watched Jocelyn through the window. She moved along a shelf, running her index finger across the spines of books. Every once in a while she pulled out a book and added it to the pile she held in her arms. Probably acting her part of Book Witch and choosing a bundle for one of her devoted customers. Ari loved the way Jocelyn paid attention to her readers. She connected with the people who came in her store, bringing them together with books and with other locals through her recommendations and book clubs.

Jocelyn might have cited money as a main reason for having the book signing, but Ari didn't believe it after watching her during the event. She united her neighbors with each other and against the threat of business failures and closures. She talked like someone who only saw goals to meet and challenges to overcome, but there was something more inspirational and relatable inside her. Ari had benefitted from Jocelyn's attention and observation once she had gotten past the bossy language it'd been housed in.

Ari got out of her car and went into the shop. Jocelyn came out of the stacks with a smile that grew wider when she saw Ari.

"Hi, Jocelyn," Ari said.

"Hi."

This was going well. Ari wasn't sure how to proceed. She had made quite a few decisions since the last time they spoke, and she wanted Jocelyn to hear every one of them.

"My month at the inn is almost over," she said. The smile faded from Jocelyn's face and she put the pile of books on her desk.

"I guess you'll be going back home, then? I hope you enjoyed your stay at Cannon Beach."

Jocelyn's tone had grown stiff. Ari shook her head. "No, I mean, yes, I'm glad I came. But no, I'm not going home yet."

Jocelyn had been fidgeting with the books. She stopped and looked at Ari. "Not going...Are you planning to stay at the inn longer?"

"That'd be too pricey long-term. I rented a room in town, just a block from the beach."

"Long-term?" Jocelyn laughed. "I keep repeating what you say. I'm just surprised. I didn't expect you to want to stay."

Ari closed the distance between them and stood next to Jocelyn without touching her. She wasn't sure how Jocelyn would react to what she was going to say, and she didn't want to push her. "I guess I found my inspiration here, but not where I expected. I thought I'd be inspired by the waves or the smell of salt in the air or the cry of gulls. But I found it in you."

Jocelyn shook her head and bridged the gap between them, resting her palms on Ari's hips. "I didn't inspire you to do anything. I should have let you find your own way. Better yet, I should have helped you through this block by being a sounding board and just letting you vent. Instead, I pushed you into a book signing and told you how to handle your own pain and creativity."

"I needed a push. I was stuck in a spiral of sadness and guilt, and the more time I spent not writing, the worse it got. You showed me a different direction to take." Ari paused, overcome by the emotions of the moment and tempted to run away from the intensity. The realization that Jocelyn cared enough to want to support Ari's writing spread a beautiful warmth through her, but doubt followed quickly with an icier chill. Would she be able to reciprocate? What could Ari give Jocelyn in return? Only the steady anchor of Jocelyn's hands on her kept Ari from bolting to either her keyboard or the highway home. "I'm writing again, Jocelyn, and I have you to thank for it."

"You've started the book about you and your mom?" Jocelyn raised one hand and caressed Ari's cheek. Ari saw a mixture of pride and pleasure in her expression.

"No. Something else." She kept her answer vague, but Jocelyn would be the first to read her new book. Ari had never felt the urge to share her work—her life—so intimately with someone else. "I'll return to the one I envisioned someday, but I need to take a step back and spend more time with my memories and emotions before I transform them into fiction."

"But I was the one who was wrong," Jocelyn said. "Your books, the way you write, they're important to people. Your characters resonate with readers because their emotions are genuine. And they're genuine because they're things you've actually felt and experienced. Don't let something I said take that away from the work you do."

She put her hand on Ari's shoulder and Ari covered it with her own, letting their fingers intertwine. "You didn't take anything away from me. I'll always write about the things I feel, but some emotions have to be mine for a while longer before I can give them away." Like the one she was feeling right now. Someday she'd write about this wave of love flooding through her, but for now it belonged only to her and Jocelyn.

She leaned her forehead against Jocelyn's and sighed. She had come to Cannon Beach a broken and blocked writer, but also one too focused on herself to see past her own needs. She had wanted healing, not for herself but for her ability to distance herself from the pain she felt. Jocelyn had healed her heart, instead. What could she offer in return?

Jocelyn wrapped her free hand around the back of Ari's neck and held her close with a firm but gentle pressure. "So you'll be staying here a little longer?"

"Indefinitely," Ari said. She brushed her nose against Jocelyn's and kissed her cheek. "No one is waiting for me at home except a few houseplants." She paused and finally put her concerns into words. "You were here for me when I needed someone honest and strong, but I don't want you to think I'll always take and never give. I want to support you. To discover you. Hopefully, I can be what you need, too."

"What I need? Hmm…I don't suppose you'd be interested in doing another reading and signing while you're here? I'm thinking over the holidays would be good because we should have a tourist surge during those times."

"Mercenary," Ari said with a laugh. She captured Jocelyn's mouth in a hungry kiss and nibbled on her lower lip. "I'll do anything you ask."

Jocelyn's hand tightened on Ari's nape. "Forget the signing, then. I can come up with some much better ideas for you."

"I can't wait." Ari's arm went around Jocelyn's lower back and pinned them hip to hip. Jocelyn braced her hands against Ari's shoulders and her smile faded.

"Can I be honest again? I was attracted to you from the moment you walked into my store and tried to spy on the books I'd recommended to Rosalie. Before I even knew your name. But I was too caught up in what I thought I needed, and I tried to control the way my feelings were growing. With a little help, I've realized how exactly perfect you are just because you are you. Not a version of me." She relaxed the pressure on her hands and let Ari pull her close again. "We balance each other. I'm glad you're staying."

Ari felt the steadiness of balance already, with Jocelyn in her arms. She was sure they'd clash at times, but they'd also bring peace and clarity to each other. She kissed Jocelyn again, her tongue exploring and promising. Jocelyn's breasts were pressed against hers, and she felt when her breath came faster. She pulled away from the kiss and whispered, with her lips just grazing Jocelyn's ear, "I'm not leaving here until I know how my new story ends."

UNDERTOW

Heather Grant honked and flashed her high beams before pulling into the oncoming lane and sailing by a slow-moving camper. Fucking two-lane roads. Passing lanes were few and far between out here on the highway from Portland to Cannon Beach. Once she was back in her own lane, she stepped on the gas pedal and accelerated to her comfortable cruising speed of ten miles an hour over the limit. Until she crested the next hill and found herself stalled behind a semi.

She tapped restlessly on the steering wheel as she slowed to match the truck's pace. The road wound through national forests and the Coast Range foothills, and the dense trees and vegetation occasionally opened up into wide swaths of clear-cut emptiness. Heather was focused on the road and not paying much attention to the area's flora, but she noticed the lack of beauty when she drove past the acres of felled trees and torn-up shrubs. She didn't have time to stop and mourn the forest or its inhabitants, though, since she was already hours behind her schedule. Her unaccustomed tardiness didn't bode well for her enforced vacation.

As soon as the road widened enough for her to pass, she was zooming along again with her lights illuminating the empty road ahead. She'd wanted to get this drive over during the light of day, but she'd stopped by the bank on the way out of town. She just needed to check on one loan for one customer, but then she had moved on to one other and one other. Three hours had elapsed before she turned her voice mail on and her computer off and locked the door to her office. Now she was traveling on unfamiliar, unlit roads as the early dark of winter enveloped the wilderness. She leaned forward, peering over the steering wheel, as if the extra inches would give her yards of visibility. She saw a shadow at the edge of her headlights' range. A flash of movement.

Heather braked hard. She felt the back end of her Volvo push the car into a skid, and she heard the click of antilock brakes and the squeal of tires searching for traction. She had been sitting too close to the steering wheel in her attempt to see the road ahead, and her head smacked into something sharp.

One stretched moment of confusion, screeching, and hurt. And then silence. Heather gasped to catch her breath after the adrenaline dump. She sat in the silent, stopped car on the shoulder of the road with the smell of burning rubber in the air, blood dripping from her forehead and her broken thumbnail. A fat and shimmery raccoon stared at her car before ambling across her path and disappearing into the woods.

"Damn." Heather rummaged in her glove box and found a pile of fast food napkins. She wet them with bottled water and blotted her forehead. She was going to have one whopper of a headache in the morning. She winced as she gingerly peeled off the broken piece of thumbnail—her head and hand must have collided when she'd snapped forward. Once the semi roared past, rattling her car in its wake, she got out and checked the road to make certain she hadn't hit anything. She'd seen the raccoon walk away unharmed, but what if it had been traveling with another one? She didn't see any sign of animals either under her car or along the shoulder, so she got in and carefully pulled onto the road again.

She drove much slower now, her eyes glancing left and right instead of staring straight ahead toward her destination. Her hands trembled on the wheel as her initial shock wore off. Her head and thumb throbbed, and she slammed on the brakes every time she saw the glint of light reflected on the side of the road. She saw several deer and an opossum, but none of them ran in front of her car. She sighed with relief when she saw the turnoff for Cannon Beach. Lights from the small town and an increase in traffic gave her a sense of being back in civilization after too long away, and she slowly let the tension release from her shoulders and neck.

Her GPS guided her along the quiet main street. A teeny grocery store and a post office that looked more like a gnome house than an actual building for humans weren't a promising welcome to this town. A few elegant restaurants and a dozen or so art galleries were more suited to her taste, but how long would they keep her entertained? She was supposed to stay here two weeks, but she doubted she'd last more than one. Her doctor wanted her to take a vacation and see the sights. If she made an effort, she could get through his annoying prescription in half the time he'd suggested.

She pulled into a parking place next to a huge and ancient house, and her headlights flashed on a sign for the Sea Glass Inn. What looked like glass tiles in a hundred colors glimmered like a rainbow, and Heather sat in her car staring at it for several minutes. She finally turned off the engine and got her suitcase out of the trunk. She was late enough as it was without wasting more time.

Heather went through the front door and heard a chime echo through the house. She waited in the foyer until a tall woman wearing jeans and a yellow sweater came out to greet her.

"You must be Heather. I'm Mel. I was beginning to think you might be lost since we expected you...Oh, goodness! What happened to you? Do you need a doctor?"

Heather put her fingers to her forehead and felt a crusty blood trail curving over her eyebrow and down her right temple. "I'm fine, really. I'm late because I had to get some work finished before coming here, and I hit my head when I stopped to let a raccoon cross the road. Really, it's nothing."

Mel looked skeptical, but she didn't argue. "There's a first-aid kit in every room. Just, please, let me know if you need anything else."

"I will. I just need to clean up and I'm sure it'll hardly be noticeable."

She signed the register and followed Mel upstairs. The place was old. Freshly painted and decorated, yes, but Heather would have preferred something more upscale. A five-star high-rise complete with day spa and a thrumming, flashing nightclub. Sights and sounds and sensations that would occupy her mind and distract her. Her work usually did, and her vacations should, too. What would she do here? Think all day? She was supposed to be resting for her health, but the thought of a week or two of boredom made her blood pressure spike.

Mel led her into a spacious room. The walls were painted a soft pale green, and a painting of a beach after a storm dominated the space over the bed. Heather looked at it long enough to recognize the talent of the artist and the beauty of embedded sea glass, but the subject was too much. She was used to surrounding herself with bland, nonprovocative landscapes and meaningless color-blocked pieces, like the art hanging in her bank. Or like the cheap oil painting hanging over her desk, depicting a generic old barn in the middle of a field. She turned away and set her suitcase on a folding luggage rack. A window behind it looked out over the backyard and the ocean. Heather couldn't hear the rhythm of the ocean waves through the glass, but she felt it inside when she saw the hint of foam-tipped waves in the darkness. A small building sat sheltered in the garden. Large-paned windows were lit from inside, and Heather saw people moving around.

"That's Pam's studio," Mel said, coming to stand next to her. "I told you about the retreat she's holding this week when we spoke on the phone. Four of the people attending are staying in the inn, and three others live nearby and are commuting. They'll be spending most of their time in the studio and shouldn't get in your way much at all."

"I don't mind a full house," Heather said. She knew Mel and the other business owners at Cannon Beach had lost an entire tourist season after the oil spill, and now they were offering a variety of activities and special events to draw tourists in during the traditionally lean winter months. She had gotten a good deal on this room because she'd come during the retreat week and Mel had offered her the participant rate, so she certainly wouldn't complain about the extra guests. Besides, if she were here on her own, she wouldn't be able to escape the attention of her hosts. This way, she'd be one of a crowd—a very small crowd of five, but still...

"We normally serve breakfast and no other meals, but since the artists sometimes work so long they forget to eat, I've been keeping the fridge stocked with sandwiches and fruit and other healthy snacks. You're welcome to share as well. Just help yourself."

"I might take you up on that," Heather said with a relieved sigh. She had originally planned to get to town and do some sightseeing right away before going out for dinner and a glass of wine. The idea of going out right now was unappealing. "I wouldn't mind a walk and a quick bite to eat before going to bed early."

Heather surprised herself with the admission. She wasn't usually the quiet evening in and early-to-bed type. Quite the opposite. Maybe the long drive coupled with her raccoon scare had worn her out. A good night's rest, and she'd be back to her old unfazed and active self.

"Sounds like a nice plan," Mel said. She got the first-aid kit and a clean towel out of a cupboard in the bathroom and set them on the counter. Heather picked up a binder with information about Cannon Beach and nearby towns. Mel had included a list of tourist destinations and things to do in the packet.

"Can I keep this list?" she asked when Mel came back.

"Of course," Mel said. "I have plenty of copies, so take what you like as a souvenir of your time here."

Heather ripped the pages out of the packet. Souvenir? No way. She was planning to check off all the activities on the list and send it to her doctor. Then he wouldn't be able to lecture her about not taking enough time off.

Once Mel left, Heather took off the dusky blue suit she had worn to the office. She cleaned the blood off her face and squeezed some ointment on the small cut on her forehead. Once she had finished, the damage looked minimal, and except for a small headache and partially missing thumbnail, she was unscathed. She pulled a bulky fisherman's sweater over her head and put on a pair of black sweatpants. Not an attractive outfit, but who was going to see her out here?

She found her way to the brightly lit and welcoming kitchen with its blue cabinets and cozy breakfast nook. Mel had said breakfast was served in the dining room, but Heather thought this looked like the perfect place to sit with a cup of coffee and a newspaper. Maybe Mel would let her bypass the group meal and sit here by herself instead.

She snagged a ham and cheese sandwich and an apple out of the fridge and started eating as soon as she was out the back door. She followed a flagstone path as it curved around the garden and past the studio. She hesitated in the shadows and looked inside. Eight people—the artists and Pam, Heather figured—were seated around a large wood table on benches that looked like halved tree trunks. Different types of art projects in various stages of completion were set up near the windows where they must get wonderful light during the day. Four paintings, two clay sculptures of figures, a twisted heap of metal, and something that looked like a pile of coat hangers. Heather's gaze skimmed past them to a life-sized sculpture of a human figure. As she walked by the studio, the path brought her closer to the window and she could see some of the details of the sculpture. The figure's chest was molded with the texture of a tree trunk and its feet were entwined with roots. Some type of plant had been roughly drawn on the sculpture's neck and into its hair. The expression on the face was one of almost terror as the human tried to escape the elements of nature. Heather thought of the clear-cut areas she'd traversed today on her drive. Some humans seemed to have turned their backs on the environment more easily than this carved person was able to do. The piece had been shaped and molded with a subtle touch, and even in this early stage, the skill of the artist was evident.

Heather chuckled to herself at the idea of buying the piece and putting it in her office at the bank. Once finished, it was sure to be powerful, a statement about people and the world they inhabited and destroyed. She was supposed to remain neutral about such topics at work, not display her personal beliefs in such a public and symbolic way. Heather shrugged and kept walking. What did she know about the piece, anyway? Maybe the sculptor had something completely different in mind, like a statement about fashion or a protest against Arbor Day.

Several of the people in the studio looked up when she passed. They were a diverse group, as different from each other as their works were. One was even wearing an honest-to-God beret. Heather paused when the beret-wearer turned toward her. Pale skin and wide eyes, with short, untidy white-blond hair. Young. A bit too bohemian-artist for her tastes. Still, she found it difficult to look away. Was this the woman whose sculpture had captured Heather's attention? Somehow, she was sure of it.

She finally got herself together enough to walk past the studio and down to the end of the garden. She stood there for a few moments, chewing her apple and listening to the waves crash below. A huge basalt formation rose out of the sea like the kraken, a deeper shadow in a world full of them.

Heather sighed and turned away, heading back to the inn. She was too cold and tired to stay outside any longer. Besides, she had accomplished her goal.

Look at Haystack Rock.
Check.

❖

Aspen Carter spread another handful of clay on her sculpture's torso. It felt cool and tacky to her touch as she smoothed it into an even layer. She wanted to make the waist thicker to keep the androgynous look of the figure, but she didn't want to lose its slender grace. She was having trouble finding the right balance and had already added and taken away what felt to her aching arms like eighty pounds of clay.

Once she thought the shape looked right, she used her fingers to gouge the furrows that would eventually be the rough bark of the tree-trunk-encased upper body. Too deep. Damn. She filled in the divots and smoothed the clay again before making another try at the subtle forms.

This sculpture had given her more grief than any of the others she'd done. The transition from an image in her mind to a physical manifestation of it had been challenging and frustrating. Almost every step along the way had required repeated attempts before she was satisfied with her work, and even now she was second-guessing—or was it twentieth-guessing?—the curve of the sculpture's thighs. She'd had moments when she'd wanted to throw the figure over her shoulder, carry it down to the beach, and dump it in the ocean.

She'd never been happier in her life.

She sighed and stepped back to survey her progress. She'd been at the inn for three days now, and the amount of improvement she'd made was obvious to her. Pam's keen eye had helped her through her usual trouble spots. The transition points of knees and wrists and neck had always been tough for her to get right. She usually erred on the side of making these areas too slender because she wanted to show grace and delicacy in her figures. Pam had suggested she add more size and fullness to them instead. She had been skeptical, but she was here to learn, so she had ignored her accustomed tendency and had slapped on more clay. After only one knee, she had been able to see what Pam meant. Suddenly, the proportions of the entire leg were more balanced and elegant, not bulkier as she had expected.

Aspen slowly circled her sculpture. She had never had the type of feedback she was getting from Pam and the other artists. She'd taken art classes in high school and college, but she'd mostly been self-taught and self-critiquing since then. When she'd heard about the retreat and the discount on a room at the inn, she had nearly emptied her savings account to come here. Already, only days into the two-week seminar, she had more than gotten her money's worth.

Her stomach rumbled, but she ignored her hunger and decided to keep working through breakfast. She wanted to finish the torso today, and the texture of the bark still didn't look right to her. She needed to make sure it was recognizable as a tree but keep it subtle enough so it looked like part of the person and not something wrapped around it. She was about to wipe away—yet again—the lines she'd made, when she saw the same woman who'd been outside the studio last night walking along the garden path.

Aspen peered around her sculpture. Like the night before, the woman was wearing old sweats and a thick sweater. Her hair was tangled and had what looked like twigs caught in it, reminding Aspen of her own sculpture where nature and human met and clashed. The real human in front of her seemed less troubled by the connection to the natural world, though. Her cheeks were red, probably from the wind and cold of the winter morning. She walked with purpose, just as she had last night after turning away from the art and the studio's windows.

Aspen wasn't sure what captivated her about this unknown person, but she felt helpless to ignore her interest and curiosity. She quickly covered her clay form with moist towels and plastic sheeting. Maybe she wouldn't skip breakfast after all.

By the time she came out of the studio, the woman had already disappeared, presumably through the inn's back door. Aspen followed, stopping briefly to wash the chalky film of dried clay off her hands in the downstairs bathroom before joining the others in the dining room. The three other artists who were staying at the inn were there, and Pam and Mel were bringing dishes of food out to the table. Aspen had hoped to sit next to the woman, maybe talk to her and find out her story, but the two empty seats weren't next to each other. Aspen sat down in one of them, and moments later the woman came into the room and sat across from her. Even better. Aspen was finally able to see her without distance and plate-glass windows between them.

Mel called her Heather, and Aspen met her eyes and smiled when they were introduced. Heather must have raced up to her room and back because her hair was neatly combed and de-twigged, and makeup hid the windburn on her cheeks. Except for a Band-Aid on her forehead and some gauze wrapped around her thumb, she was as impeccably groomed as someone about to have luncheon with society friends. She'd even changed into a pair of dark brown slacks and a pale lilac sweater, quite a contrast to Aspen's mustard-yellow sweater and gray cords—both thrift store finds. Still, if Aspen could learn Heather's secret to getting dressed and ready in such a short time, she'd never be late to work again.

Aspen scooped some eggs onto her plate and added a cherry scone and some hash browns. She ate without paying much attention to the conversations around her and stared at Heather while trying not to be too obvious about it. Aspen estimated her age somewhere in her midthirties, probably ten years or more beyond Aspen's age of twenty-four. Young looking for her age, but something in her expression seemed older and weary. Aspen's hands tingled with a longing to mold clay into the delicate triangular shape of Heather's face and the slope of her neck into her collarbones. She'd felt the same urge many times before, whenever something beautiful or meaningful caught her attention and begged to be sculpted, but she had never experienced the desire to follow the contours and curves of a woman's body like she did Heather's.

"I saw you leave early this morning, Heather," Pam said. Aspen had been focused on the strange yearning she felt to explore Heather more thoroughly, and she gladly abandoned that troubling line of thought when Pam and Heather started talking. Aspen was curious about her, as if understanding Heather would help her understand and control her own reaction to someone who was nearly a stranger to her. "We were surprised to see you up before dawn since you got in late last night. Did you go for a drive along the coast?"

"I did," Heather said. She flashed what seemed like a self-satisfied smile before it faded again, leaving her as expressionless as she'd been before. "I walked to a bluff in Ecola State Park and watched the sunrise, or what little you can see of it with the mountains in the east. I drove to a lookout and saw the lighthouse, and I even spotted a herd of elk."

Heather ticked off the items with the fingers of her left hand, as if crossing them off some sort of list.

"I didn't expect the elk," she continued, "but they're on the list of things to see around here, so they count. Local wildlife. There were about six of them in a grassy meadow next to the highway, all shrouded in fog. Stunning."

Most of Heather's words had been precise and clearly enunciated, but the last two sentences were mellower and spoken with a real smile. Aspen couldn't figure her out. She seemed aloof and businesslike part of the time, with her fast walk and quick, careful speech and elegant appearance. But at other moments, like when she had looked at Aspen's sculpture through the studio window last night or when she talked about the elk, she softened around the edges and made Aspen's breath catch in her throat.

Mel sat and cradled a cup of coffee in her hands. "What a busy morning! I hope you find some time to relax while you're here. You shouldn't have to work harder at your vacation than you do in the office."

Heather nibbled on a piece of toast with some of Mel's homemade strawberry-rhubarb jam on it. She'd barely eaten half of it, but she'd already had three cups of coffee. Aspen, on the other hand, had worked her way through something out of every bowl on the table, and she was on her second scone.

"I want to make sure I take full advantage of everything Cannon Beach has to offer," Heather continued. "I'm signed up for a yoga class on the beach this afternoon, and I'm sure that will be relaxing. I need to call and sign up for one of those cooking classes at the culinary school in town, and I'll go to Tillamook tomorrow."

"Tillamook? Where they make cheese?" Aspen asked. She had been content to listen and try to puzzle out Heather's shifting personality. She was vacationing with a vengeance, and Aspen's curiosity was growing more ravenous every moment. She surprised herself by interjecting into the conversation, but she'd spoken without thinking.

Pam nodded. "They have some interactive exhibits and a shop where you can buy ice cream. Marionberry Pie is my favorite flavor."

"I want to go," Aspen said. She looked at Heather. "I don't suppose you'd mind some company?"

"Oh, I...well..." Heather looked as disconcerted by Aspen's request as she had felt suggesting it. "Aren't you going to be busy with your retreat?" Heather asked in a relieved-sounding voice, as if she was happy to have come up with an excuse to go alone.

Pam spoke up before Aspen could answer. "Tomorrow's retreat activities are scheduled early in the morning and after dinner at night. The artists work at their own pace during the day, and there's plenty of time for a fun sightseeing trip."

"Besides," Aspen added, "I'm sure *take a sculpting student to get ice cream* is on a list somewhere of the top things to do while in Cannon Beach. After tomorrow, you'll be able to cross it off as accomplished."

Heather gave her an inscrutable look, but then her expression collapsed into softness again. She smiled. "Okay. But only because I don't want to skip any of the Cannon Beach highlights, and I'm sure this sculptor–ice cream thing is one of them."

"Then it's a date," Pam said before Aspen could respond. "You two will have a great time tomorrow. Be sure to go to the Air Museum, too."

"And there are a couple of wineries along the way," Mel added. "They're on the page from your welcome packet, Heather. I'll mark all these places on a map for you."

The two of them launched into a tourism board advertisement for Tillamook, Oregon. If she and Heather went to even half the places mentioned, they'd need more than an afternoon. Heather listened to their suggestions with an unreadable mask on her face again, and Aspen ignored most of what they were saying and tried to justify crashing Heather's plans. She'd been working hard on her sculpture since she'd arrived, and a break would do her good. Plus, she might get some inspiration for future works in a new setting.

Besides, she wasn't a commercial artist anyway. She would take full advantage of Pam's lessons and learn as much as she could while she was here, but her art wasn't her livelihood like it was for the other participants. She was a barista in Seattle who sculpted when she had the chance and the cash for materials. She was playing a part here, but it wasn't one she'd take on full-time. While she was at it, she'd play along with her body's reaction to Heather and give in to its enthusiasm about spending some time with her tomorrow. These two weeks were a game, and she'd win if she left here with some new skills to apply to her art. That's all.

Aspen excused herself and left the table without another glance at Heather, but her image was visually imprinted on Aspen's mind. Time to get back to the studio and back to her creation.

❖

Heather sat in the living room at the inn and waited for Aspen to finish her morning sculpting. She wasn't thrilled about spending too much time with any of the other guests, especially since she had a mission to accomplish, and she hoped Aspen would be ready for the speed-dating version of sightseeing. She would have been more annoyed with her for inviting herself along if Aspen hadn't looked as surprised to be suggesting she come as Heather was to be asked. Still, Heather would make the most of her unexpected company. Aspen was lovely and interesting, and Heather thought an afternoon talking about her sculpting would be a nice change of pace. Heather and her coworkers never had in-depth conversations about art or culture, tending instead to stick with mundane talk about the weather and the bank. Aspen didn't strike Heather as the small-talk sort. Besides, Heather could use a witness to vouch for her if her doctor didn't believe she had really done everything on her vacation list.

She sat down at a table with a large puzzle depicting a colorful picture of a seaside amusement park and idly put several pieces together. Before she knew it, she was searching in earnest through the jumble of pieces in the box for the remaining edge ones. She hadn't done a jigsaw since grade school, and she had forgotten how addictive they were. She could spend the entire day in this chair, putting together sections of boardwalks and roller coasters. Instead, she was about to embark on another round of intensive tourism. She realized her insistence on completing the long list of Cannon Beach attractions was a passive-aggressive way to send her doctor a message to butt out, but she couldn't stop now that she'd started. She didn't want to be told what to do, and she didn't want to have the unseen and scary medical issues that had prompted his insistence on this holiday. Most of all, she seemed incapable of standing still long enough to really think about the underlying causes of those issues. Over the past couple of years, her growing tension and dissatisfaction had become too uncomfortable—and now threatening—to fully ignore. She had to push herself even harder than before to keep from acknowledging them.

Heather completed the upper edge of blue sky pieces and started to work on the left side. Her doctor should be pleased with her hour-long bout of yoga yesterday. She'd disliked every minute of it. The wind had blown grit in her eyes and had flipped the corner of her yoga mat into her face every time she did the downward dog pose. The shifting sand under her feet made balancing poses—something she sucked at even in a normal studio—impossible to perform. Not to mention, it had been fucking freezing out there. Whose brilliant idea had it been to do yoga on a beach in December? Every business in town seemed determined to find unique ways to make money. That was definitely not one of the more successful ventures.

Of course, everyone out there except Heather had seemed to find a version of nirvana during the class. She had a feeling they were all as miserable as she'd been. They just hid it better.

"Hi," Aspen said.

Heather looked up from the puzzle. Aspen stood in the doorway to the living room wearing a sweatshirt that looked like it doubled as a painter's drop cloth and a pair of clay-smeared cargo pants. She was a mess, but an irresistibly adorable one. She had a glow about her, and Heather took a guess as to what caused it.

"Did your sculpting go well this morning?"

"It was amazing," Aspen said. She came over to the table and picked out a puzzle piece Heather had just spent ten minutes trying to locate. Aspen snapped it in place while she talked. "I've been struggling with the tree-trunk torso and I couldn't get it to look like it was organically part of the figure. Pam and I talked about ways to make it look less symmetrical, and I ended up extending the bark pattern partway down one of the thighs. It looks awesome, but I never would have come up with the idea on my own. I'm lucky to have someone as immensely talented as Pam helping me."

Heather watched Aspen talk, the puzzle completely forgotten.

Aspen was sparkling with passion, a joy in learning new aspects of her craft and the thrill of accomplishment. Had Heather ever felt the same way? She couldn't remember.

"I'll clean up and be right back," Aspen said. "I'm already a little late and I'm sure you're ready to get going."

She left the room before Heather could answer. If she had been going to Tillamook alone, as she'd planned, she would have left long before now. She'd been forced to wait for Aspen, but she'd had more fun sitting there doing the puzzle than she had doing all the other things on her tourism list. She wasn't about to admit that to her doctor, though.

By the time Aspen came downstairs again, Heather was in the foyer with her keys in hand. Once they were in her car and driving south on Highway 101, Heather reopened their last conversation. The subject matter—passion for work—wasn't a comfortable one for her, but she couldn't seem to shake her curiosity about what it must feel like to be so in love with a hobby or career.

"The retreat sounds like it's been worthwhile for you, especially with the advice you're getting from Pam. I thought most artists had mentors, though. Teachers or agents or whatever." Heather had sought mentors from the first moment she had chosen her career in banking. College profs, industry leaders—she had carefully researched their accomplishments and had done her best to emulate them. She'd been proud of each positive step she had taken, but she knew without a doubt she'd never had her face light up with pure joy in her work like Aspen's had today. "Who sells your sculptures?"

Aspen visibly shuddered. "No one. I don't sell them. I've donated some to parks in Seattle, but usually I give them to family or friends."

Heather frowned. "You're not serious, are you? You could make a fortune with your work."

"Ugh. Sculpt for money? I'd end up a sellout, trading my artistic vision for cash."

"Or you could create the art you love, and people who appreciate it would buy it," Heather said. "I've never heard of someone *not* wanting to make money."

"I earn enough to support myself," Aspen said. "Being rich isn't everything."

"No, but it's a damned good start. What do you do for a living, anyway?"

"I dream and sculpt and experience the world for my *living*. I work in a coffee shop to pay my rent and buy food."

Heather couldn't stop herself from rolling her eyes. Aspen sounded idealistic and naive. "Eventually it'll need to be the other way around. You'll need to make a living from your work and have art and experiencing the world as your hobbies. You should be saving and investing in your future, and you're fortunate to have enough talent to make your passion pay for that future."

"You'd want me to sacrifice the integrity of my art and my soul just to have more money and buy more things?"

"Yeesh, no," Heather said with distaste, even though she wondered if she herself had sacrificed something important along the way. She was envious of Aspen—she had the talent to attain the best of both worlds. Make a lot of money doing what she obviously loved to do. Working in a coffee shop probably meant long hours and minimum wage, a little extra if tips were good that day. "How much time do you have to sculpt, anyway?"

Aspen shrugged and looked out the window. During the rest of her argument for the nonmaterialistic lifestyle, she had challenged Heather with a direct glare. Heather realized she'd struck a nerve.

"Art supplies are expensive, especially if I'm casting in bronze," Aspen said. "Sculpting makes me feel good and energizes me, but I don't like to bring too much negativity with me to the studio. So if I have a full shift or cranky customers, I don't always feel up to creating. But I have the freedom to make those choices."

"So you have the freedom to sculpt when and what you want, but not always the money or appropriate energy to do it. Sounds like you're a slave to your work just like a lot of other people. Haven't you heard of making your avocation your vocation?"

"Are you speaking from experience? What do you do?"

Heather hesitated. Aspen sure as hell wasn't going to be

impressed by Heather's job title. Why did Heather even care what she thought? Still, she answered the second question and ignored the first as she pulled off the main road and into the parking lot next to the huge hangar housing the Air Museum. An avocation? She'd have a hard time even defining one, let alone giving up her secure lifestyle to pursue it. Maybe she was trying to protect Aspen from making the same choices she had. Maybe she was angry with her for having other choices available.

"I'm a senior loan officer in a bank."

"A very successful one, judging by your car and your clothes," Aspen said. "Are you happy there?"

"What does happiness have to do with it?" Heather asked. "For most people jobs are for making money. Not everyone has the chance you do." She got out of the car and slammed the door shut. If she really believed what she was saying, and what she had told herself throughout her entire career, then why did she feel so upset?

She and Aspen bought their tickets at the snack bar counter and went into the museum in silence. Heather looked around at all the planes on static display and sighed. She was only interested in aircraft if she was sitting in a first class seat inside one, but she dutifully walked around and read some placards. She'd started this obstinate quest to conquer Cannon Beach in all its touristy glory, and she couldn't seem to stop herself. She watched Aspen as she followed a parallel path to hers, but one row over. Aspen seemed to feel an uncontrollable urge to touch everything she saw. Any part of a plane that was close enough to the velvet ropes for her to reach, the etched lettering on display signs, and the displays of World War II flight suits and equipment. Heather was less a tactile person than a verbal one. She lived inside her head, while Aspen sought to reach out to the world around her. Heather definitely saw the advantage in Aspen's way of connecting with the world. She'd be an amazing lover. Heather stopped walking and pressed her hands to her cheeks, feeling the thrum of her pulse and the heat of arousal. Perhaps she should add *Have torrid affair with an artist* to her vacation to-do list...

A tempting thought, but one Heather would keep in her imagination. Still, she'd been pushy with Aspen for reasons Aspen wasn't aware of and hadn't intentionally created. Heather didn't like having anyone tell her what to do or how to live her life. She'd followed enough of other people's rules along the way and had gotten stuck in their visions of her life, and she was certain Aspen didn't want to be bossed around, either.

"I liked my job well enough at first," she said, catching up to Aspen near an open-cockpit triplane and continuing their conversation as if it hadn't been interrupted. "I love learning new things, just about anything, and I feel a lot of satisfaction when I set and meet goals. It's just…"

"It's just…what?" Aspen put a hand on Heather's sleeve, and Heather wasn't sure whether she was offering sympathy or just obeying an urge to touch the nubbly texture of Heather's sweater. Either way, the simple gesture was uncomfortable because it felt too good. Heather was on this trek to Tillamook and the other tourist highlights because she needed to distract herself from thoughts of work and happiness—not because she wanted to explore them. She couldn't seem to stop talking once she started, though.

"I met my goals. I chose the bank I wanted to work for and I moved through the ranks ahead of even my overambitious schedule. Last year, I got a big promotion, and now I'm where I always wanted to be. My salary, my home, and my possessions are exactly what I wanted. I guess I'm feeling adrift because I've achieved my dreams and I don't know where to go from here. Maybe a different bank, maybe a higher-paying job. I don't know. I'm in limbo, and I don't like it. I'm sorry I took it out on you. Sculpt or don't sculpt. Be a professional artist or a weekend hobbyist. It's your life."

Aspen opened her mouth as if she was about to say something, but she closed it again and walked to the next plane. Heather followed and read the sign, memorizing a few random facts about the Spitfire in case her doctor asked questions about what she had seen here.

"Did getting everything you wanted feel as good as you thought it would?" Aspen asked after a few moments without speaking. Heather wondered if this was what Aspen had been about to ask, or if she'd been thinking of something else entirely. She wished Aspen had asked anything but this.

"Of course," she lied. "I have the security of investments and a great health care plan. I get a lot of pleasure from my car and apartment. I'm just the kind of person who needs to have another goal in sight. I'm in between right now, but I'll decide where I want to go next and get myself there."

"Seems like if you were made truly happy by any of your possessions or job titles, you wouldn't be so desperate to move on to something new."

Heather had been able to push the same paradigm-changing seed of thought deep inside her heart, where she rarely ventured. Aspen's words brought it out where Heather couldn't help but acknowledge and recognize it.

"I'm an ambitious person and have been all my life," Heather said. Had she really? She'd certainly been that way since the time she figured out how to please her parents and make them proud of her. She'd never looked back or slowed down after those first words of praise—if she had, they'd have stopped immediately. "I'm not going to change, and I don't want to. I just need to figure out my next big step. And today's next big goal? The Tillamook cheese factory."

"Sounds like a worthy one," Aspen said. "I'm sure it's the key to a successful life."

"Then what are we waiting for? Let's go."

❖

The drive from the museum to the huge cheese manufacturing plant was a short one, but Aspen wished it had lasted longer. As much as she despised obvious signs of luxury and materialism, she had to admit Heather's car was an understated and damned comfortable ride. The seat warmer barely had a chance to take some of the chill from the enormous open-doored hangar out of her bones before she had to get out again, though. She didn't think Heather would be willing to skip the factory and go for a long, warm ride along the coast, so she didn't suggest anything to take them off course.

The parking lot was nearly empty. Tuesday afternoons in the dead of winter, only months after an oil spill, didn't seem to be high traffic times in this coastal area. Aspen didn't mind crowds because she was always looking for unusual body types and interesting facial features to incorporate into her sculptures, but she figured Heather preferred the quiet. Not because she was contemplative, but because then she could speed walk through the exhibits and barely bother to look at them. She had hardly looked at the planes in the air museum, seeming to prefer instead to read the informational signs about them as if she was studying for a test. Aspen really didn't care about the planes or the cheese, either. She was here because she had been drawn to Heather for some reason, and she wanted to listen to her intuition. Maybe she'd get some inspiration from being around her, such as an idea for a sculpture of a woman drowning in cash and flailing for help, or one of a woman sitting on a briefcase wearing a fitted, expensive business suit and an expression of loneliness and emptiness.

Try as she might, though, she couldn't see Heather as merely someone caught in the meaningless rat race. There was more to her, more even than Aspen had been privileged to see yet—she was sure of it. Heather was sexy and Aspen's fingers wanted to smooth the lines of evasion and tension off her face, and then work their way over the rest of her body. She was also bossy, talking to Aspen like a smug old guidance counselor lecturing an unmotivated teenager. She was nothing like the go-with-the-flow women Aspen usually met and dated—of course, rarely did she find herself in contact with smart businesswomen, unless she was serving them expensive and high-maintenance lattes. Heather was intense and challenging and irritating.

And correct. Aspen reluctantly got out of the car and jogged to catch up to Heather as she walked across the lot. Aspen's ideals kept her from becoming a tainted professional artist. Her need to eat and find shelter meant she had to work. Her job and the people she had to serve drained her to the point of exhaustion every night, and she barely had time to get out her clay and tools, let alone spend hours perfecting the lines of a sculpture.

Why was she squandering this one chance to spend two weeks learning from Pam by spending the day with Heather and not in the studio? Just the day, she promised herself. She had worked intently this morning and had needed a break by the time she came back up for air. She'd continue tonight until long after dark with a fresh mind and perspective. This short rest would be good for her as an artist.

Besides, the chance to spend time with someone like Heather wasn't something she had every day, either. Even though Heather's questions made her uncomfortable, she needed to pay attention to them—maybe *because* they made her uncomfortable and resistant. Even though Aspen had nearly perfected the art of acting placid and serene even when her insides were in turmoil, as they often were when she wasn't molding clay and carving wood on a regular basis, Heather made her emotions roil to the surface.

Aspen loved a challenge, and Heather certainly provided her with one.

"I hope we'll slow down long enough to get ice cream on the way out," Aspen said as Heather rushed past her toward the gift shop and food counter. "I'll bet eating a scoop of chocolate peanut butter would give you extra credit points in your tourism class."

Heather paused on the stairs leading to the self-guided tour area. "Tourism class?" she asked with a tilt of her head.

"We're all making bets on why you're so gung-ho about seeing sights you don't seem to care about seeing."

"What are some of the guesses?"

Aspen grinned in response to Heather's barely suppressed smile and she leaned her elbow next to Heather's on the handrail. "A blogger, an aspiring tour guide, a spy for a rival bed-and-breakfast— that's mine—or the inventor of a new extreme sport. Marathon sightseeing." Aspen rattled off some of the options they'd come up with when they were supposed to be having a brainstorming session last night. Most of the discussion had been devoted to Heather's puzzling interest in everything *Cannon Beach*. "I've been appointed as a mole to uncover your real reason for taking the town by storm."

"Is that why you offered to come with me today?" Heather asked, looking at Aspen with eyes so blue they almost appeared violet. Aspen tried to imagine her in a bank, staring at loan applications and credit reports all day. She couldn't place Heather in her work setting, though, and instead pictured her staring out at the ocean with the sunset reflecting a rainbow of color in her beautiful eyes.

"No," Aspen said. She swallowed and licked her lips, her mouth unaccountably dry as she saw Heather's gaze flick from her eyes to her lips and back. "I don't know why I did that. But I'm glad I did."

Heather leaned closer, as if about to tell Aspen a secret. "So am I."

An occasional visitor walked past them on the staircase, but Aspen only noticed them as shadows passing by. All she saw, smelled, and heard was Heather. Her low-pitched voice and the aroma of an exotic, floral-spicy, and most likely expensive perfume. Aspen's body felt numb except for the alive and agitated patch of skin where their arms touched.

"Are you going to tell me the real reason you're working instead of relaxing on your vacation?"

Heather shrugged, and the movement rippled through Aspen's body. "I have some health problems. From years of living on coffee and danishes and working overtime, I guess. My doctor insisted I take time off, and someone from work recommended Mel's inn. So here I am."

Aspen rested her palm in the center of Heather's chest, wishing she could heal whatever frightening things were happening inside Heather's body. She had a feeling the issues were more mental and emotional than purely physical. She'd seen and heard hints of Heather's dissatisfaction and aimlessness today. "Did your doctor tell you to work harder on the trip than you do in the office? Seems counterproductive to me."

Heather sighed audibly, and Aspen felt the echo reverberate

through her palm and into her own body. "I'm being stubborn, I suppose. I didn't have much choice in the matter, and I thought I'd cross off everything on the list and throw it on his desk when I get back. It started as a silly idea in my head, and has turned into..."

"Your new goal?" Aspen offered when Heather paused.

She nodded. "It keeps me busy." She stepped back, moving up a step, and Aspen's hand dropped back to her side. "So, are you going to tell everyone what I'm doing here?"

Aspen shook her head. "I'll go with my story. You're scouting the place for another hotel in town and you're trying to put together the perfect list of tourist attractions for it. You're stealing Mel's ideas."

Heather laughed and started walking up the stairs again. "She'll kick me out, and how will I accomplish my goal without her morning scones as fuel?"

"Get some protein bars," Aspen suggested. She liked the banter between them. She had a feeling Heather hadn't told many people—if any at all—about her health concerns. She seemed the type to hold them inside, probably what got her into this mess in the first place. Aspen liked having Heather confide in her, but she felt helpless to stop her from self-destructing either here or at home and in her job.

Aspen was ready to follow Heather on a whirlwind tour of the cheese factory, whatever Heather needed to do to make herself feel in control again, but Heather surprised her by spending most of their visit standing in front of a huge picture window and watching blocks of cheese move about on conveyor belts. Aspen stayed close to her. She had to admit the repetitive movements of the process were mesmerizing, especially with the workers who moved around as if they'd been choreographed, wearing masks and thick hairnets.

Heather tapped lightly on the glass with her index finger. "You know, if you really want to continue sculpting without making any money, you should switch media. You probably could make something cool out of these blocks of cheese."

Aspen nodded. "I could sculpt the moon. Or carve holes in it and make a Swiss cheese out of cheddar. How ironic would that be?"

"And you won't have to worry about the masses buying your sculptures and diminishing your vision somehow, because they'd reek something awful after a few days."

"Hey, you're right," Aspen said, paying more attention to a smiling and relaxed Heather than to the view through the window. "The pieces would eventually just mold away to nothing. I'd be making a statement about the nature of art."

Heather turned toward her, laughing, and her shoulder rubbed against Aspen's. "And if you get hungry while you're working, you can eat the scraps."

"Another bonus. Plus, it'd be cheaper than buying clay and carving tools. All I'd need would be a cheese knife and a cutting board."

"Throw in a baguette and a bottle of wine, and you can have a cocktail party while you're sculpting."

They leaned against the glass while they laughed and kept trying to outdo each other with cheese jokes. When their hilarity died down, Heather gave a sad-sounding sigh and looked around them at all the interactive exhibits.

"Want to read more about the process of cheesemaking?" Aspen asked. She'd liked having Heather present with her. Teasing and wiping away tears of laughter. Connected to her and the moment, instead of rushing through it. She felt as if Heather was about to slip away again, and she saw the mask of determination settle over her expression, but then Heather shook her head and the façade disappeared.

"Not even a tiny bit," she said, pushing away from the glass and grabbing Aspen's hand. Aspen felt her palm and fingers mold to the shape of Heather's. She'd never felt such a sense of coming home, except when she held a wire modeling tool and carved something of her own out of a blank lump of clay.

Heather pulled her back toward the stairs. "Let's skip the lesson and go directly to those extra-credit ice cream cones."

❖

Heather spent the next day alone, wandering through the downtown shops and galleries. Mel had included a list of local businesses in her welcome packet, and Heather was determined to buy something from each one of them. She'd get all her Christmas shopping done in one afternoon, or maybe she'd send one present to her doctor every day for a month.

What had started as an obstinate way to symbolically blow a raspberry at her doctor had somehow turned into an amusing game. Heather was actually having fun. She couldn't remember the last time she'd felt this playful. She went out with coworkers regularly, celebrating birthdays and Fridays and promotions. She favored loud bars on those nights when her restless thoughts that there had to be something more to life kept her awake. She'd sit alone for hours, nursing a weak whiskey sour and reading over paperwork at the bar while the strobe lights and booming music keep her thoughts at bay. She even dated once in a while, when she could stir up enough interest in someone to sit in a restaurant and make small talk for an hour or two. But those conversations were usually work related since she tended to meet and socialize with other businesswomen.

Yesterday had been a turning point for her. She had been sightseeing with a vengeance since she had arrived, and she expected to do the same with Aspen in tow. She had started their afternoon together by taking on the role of older sister or mentor and encouraging Aspen to make different career choices, but soon she had given up her attempts to create distance by lecturing and advising. She had started to recognize her own jealousy over Aspen's passion and her irritation that Aspen was giving away the chance Heather could only dream of. To work with passion and joy. Aspen's probing questions had kept Heather from backing away from the self-discovery. She would normally have sought to numb the realizations with more work and with crowded places, but yesterday she had allowed them to surface in her mind. The acknowledgment of her feelings didn't change them or solve her life issues, but somehow she felt lighter.

Light enough to play. To joke and tease with Aspen. They had sat in the small café and swapped tastes of ice cream and toppings.

Then they had wandered through the gift shop, touching lightly and laughing with an ease Heather hadn't experienced in ages, with another person or with herself. When it had been time to drive back to the inn for Aspen's evening art class, Heather had returned to her room and crossed off another two tourist activities with a flourish. Then she had gone downstairs and helped Mel finish the jigsaw puzzle.

Her good mood had lasted through today, as well. She had hoped to see Aspen last night, to rekindle the laughter and maybe light another spark between them, but Aspen and the others had stayed in the studio until Heather got tired of watching for her and had gone to bed. Miraculously, she had been able to remain lighthearted on her own. After a brief chat with Aspen at breakfast—little more than their plans for the day—Aspen had gone back to sculpting and Heather had hit the town.

She leaned back on a bench by the sidewalk and pulled her navy pea coat tightly around herself. A few rays of sunlight made it through the thick cloud cover, but they weren't enough to warm her. At least she wasn't on the beach stretched out on a yoga mat while goose bumps peppered her skin. She opened a pale pink bakery box and took out a puffy creation called a sand dollar, apparently good enough to rate an asterisk on Mel's list of musts. Must do, must see, must eat. Heather was still planning to do them all, but now it felt like a lark. She wished Aspen were with her, because she would appreciate Heather's temporarily changed outlook. Heather would be the same person she had been once she was back at work in Portland, but she could allow herself to be someone else here.

She bit into the layers of flaky pastry and reached the dark chocolate cream inside. Mel hadn't steered her wrong. This deserved at least four asterisks. She licked her fingers and leaned forward so the powdered sugar coating sprinkled the ground at her feet and not her dark wool coat. She finished in four bites, resisting the urge to dive back into the pastry box and eat another. Later. Now she had more shopping to do.

Heather got up and wrapped the handles of her packages around her wrists. She'd been to nearly every place on Mel's list, including the Beachcomber Bookstore. The owner, a gorgeous but too-perceptive woman, had watched her with a disconcerting intensity. Heather knew what she was seeing. Exactly what Heather had seen this morning when she'd looked in the mirror, as if by acknowledging her mental unrest she had suddenly shifted her perception. She had been denying the doctor's concerns and her test results, refusing to admit she had moments of low energy and sadness, but this morning the signs had stared back at her from the mirror, and she had seen some of what had worried him. Dark circles under her eyes, too little weight in her face and on her body, and a resigned but defiant frown. The bookstore owner had seemed to absorb Heather's mood and expression with clarity, too, and then she had brought her three books to buy.

Heather shifted the heavy bag. One of the books was an autobiography of a dancer, the second was a guide to operas and their stories, and the third was about Gothic architecture. Heather wasn't sure why they had been chosen since she wasn't an architect, a ballerina, or an operagoer. Each one seemed to remind her of old interests, however, and she had willingly bought all of them. She had taken an opera class in college because she had to add a few fine arts credits to her economics ones in order to graduate, and she had enjoyed every moment, especially when they attended performances. She had never designed a house or building, but she had been drawn to interesting structural shapes and forms and would sometimes wander the city streets for hours at night, searching for new ones to admire. She was a stiff and nonrhythmic dancer, but she loved music.

Heather would have time to read later. Now she had to finish her shopping spree. She pushed through the door of the Seascape Art Gallery and was surprised to see Pam standing behind the counter, shuffling through a stack of invoices.

"Heather, what a surprise! I'm glad you caught me here since my hours have been inconsistent lately."

"Hi, Pam. I didn't know you owned a gallery," Heather said, walking over to the counter. "How do you find time to do this and paint and teach?"

"I usually have help in here, but after my student hire went back to school, I didn't hire another clerk. I sort of…well, after the spill, I couldn't paint for a long time. I'm slowly starting again, but now I don't have help here, so I'm juggling running the gallery and the seminar with my own painting. I'm not doing a very good job of it right now, but I'll get there. At least the seminar is inspiring to me. Working around other artists is giving me the push I needed to pick up a brush again."

"It must be hard not to be creating," Heather said, thinking of Aspen and her willingness to sculpt less because she scorned being a professional. Heather wondered if her reluctance had more to do with fear than concern over losing her artistic integrity.

"It's a horrible feeling," Pam said. "And I think it was almost as hard on Mel as on me because she understands how much I need to paint to really comprehend the world around me."

Heather understood a little of what Mel must have felt during Pam's dry spell. She had seen the rapture on Aspen's face after her morning sculpting. If she had to witness the light being snuffed out, she'd do anything in her power to help Aspen find her passion again. "Are any of your paintings here?" Heather asked. She'd been gradually deepening her appreciation of the storm painting in her room. It had disturbed her at first, maybe because the destruction on the beach reminded her of the turmoil in her mind, but now she was able to glance obliquely at her unfulfilling job and her fear that she had made a bad decision too long ago to rectify. Could the tempest-tossed debris in her mind be cleaned away? Or would she need to return to her old habits of ignoring and anesthetizing? Maybe a souvenir painting of Pam's would help her remember how she had felt here, as long as the memories weren't too painful. She'd prefer a memento created by Aspen, though. Something to remind her of yesterday and her revelations and their laughter, like the hazy memory of reality during a lucid dream.

"I have a couple full-sized ones near the window," Pam pointed across the gallery. "And in the display case on the back wall there are some miniature oils I've done because a lot of our guests want something similar to the mosaics in the rooms. Why don't you put your bags behind the counter while you look around? I see you've been shopping and apparently singlehandedly keeping Cannon Beach merchants safe from bankruptcy."

"I'm doing my best," Heather said, putting her bags down with a sigh of relief. "I've been to almost every shop Mel had on the map in my welcome packet."

"You do realize those lists are meant to be helpful suggestions for our guests and not mandatory assignments, don't you?"

Heather laughed. "Yes, I do. I started working through them as a way to make a statement to someone who isn't even here, but now it's turned into a game. I'm having a good vacation in my own goal-oriented, obsessive way."

"As long as you're having fun, we're happy," Pam said.

"Best vacation I've had in a long time," Heather said. It was a completely true statement, especially since she couldn't remember the last vacation she had taken. She'd been barely old enough to legally drink.

"Good." Pam smiled and went back to her invoices while Heather wandered through the gallery. She looked at Pam's paintings first, admiring one with gulls circling Haystack Rock and another of a calm sea with a pod of gray whales in the far distance, along the horizon. She admired Pam's subtle touch with oils and glass, and her subjects that seemed to have meaning beyond their actual beings. When she looked through the display of smaller oils, however, she found the one she wanted to own. It was a smaller section of her storm painting, zeroing in on a segment of the beach with windblown grasses and scattered driftwood. Maybe it would remind her of the moments of doubt and clarity she had found here, even when she returned to her mind-numbing life.

Heather held the little oil painting as she examined the rest of the gallery's offerings. A few pieces caught her eye immediately: a blown glass wall hanging that looked like a waterfall in blues and teals, a portrait of a sea captain at the helm of his ship, and a turned wooden sculpture of an abstract figure. She wanted to run her hands over the piece, feeling the grain of the wood and the smoothness of its finish.

"You remind me of Mel when she first came in here," Pam said. Heather turned abruptly and found Pam watching her. "She made a beeline for the highest-quality pieces in here, just like you did."

"I just picked my favorites," Heather said with a feeling of heat in her cheeks. Why was she blushing and trying to avoid the compliment?

"They're mine, too. If I didn't need the gallery to make money, I'd have nothing but works like those three."

"I agree," Heather said. "But I can see what you're offering with the other types of artwork. They'll keep you in business and satisfy the customers who want to buy a memory." She gestured toward a few pretty but unremarkable paintings of the ocean. Then she pointed at some more abstract works with vibrant colors and pleasing shapes, but little depth beyond them. "Or the ones who want to buy art because it'll make them feel good to have something attractive in their house or office even though they don't know much about what they're looking at."

Pam nodded slowly, watching Heather with an unreadable expression. "You have a good eye," she said eventually.

Heather was about to protest again, but she let herself receive the compliment with a quiet thank you. She paid for Pam's painting and gathered her bags again.

"See you back at the inn?" Pam asked.

"Not until later tonight," Heather answered, using her elbow to open the gallery door. "Next on the list is a cooking class at the culinary school. I think we're making salmon."

Heather was halfway back to her car before a memory resurfaced that had been nagging at the edge of her mind while she'd been in Pam's gallery. She'd been maybe ten or eleven and had brought home some papers from her classes. Her parents had been pleased with the A-plus on her science experiment and had chastised her for making spelling errors on a short language arts essay. They hadn't even mentioned the picture she had drawn for art class, and later that night Heather had found it crumpled in the trash. As if the one memory was a trigger for others, she recalled too many times when her mom or dad had steered her away from beauty and toward more practical pursuits. Music, art, and literature were fine as sideline activities, but not as the focus of her attention. She'd heard phrases like *waste of time* and *not a subject you'll need to master for your degree* too many times to count, and they had insinuated themselves in her mind, making her nervous when Pam praised her for something her parents would have dismissed.

Heather was under no illusion that she'd have possessed the talent of someone like Aspen or Pam, even if she'd been encouraged to explore her artistic side. Perhaps what she had been missing in her life wasn't an all-consuming passion and gift in one area, but an appreciation for art and beauty and music in general.

She wasn't certain what to do with these revelations she kept uncovering. They were making her nervous and not helping her make a decision about how to inject more life into her career. Instead, they managed to emphasize and magnify her feelings of discontent.

Heather stowed her bags in the trunk of her car and drove to the small culinary school and catering company. She had been in kitchens before and had no expectation of uncovering a latent talent to be a world-class chef, but she was looking forward to the evening anyway. She thought of Aspen back at the inn, working on her sculpture with the single-minded intensity of a true artist. She had something magnificent to offer the world. What did Heather have to offer? What would be her legacy when she was gone?

A thousand completed to-do lists.

❖

Aspen used a small sculpting tool and carved excess clay from a tendril of ivy until it was as thin and delicate as she envisioned. She glanced at her sketch pad to make sure she was following her original plan, and then she rolled another narrow snake of clay. She stepped back and checked her progress, consulting her drawing yet again, before she pressed the rolled clay into the figure's neck.

An intricate filigree of ivy and flower stems covered one side of the sculpture's neck and face. The plant life blended up into the figure's hair. The lower portion of the filigree transitioned to slender human veins on the shoulder and left breast. Aspen felt the movement of the tendrils, just as she'd hoped. The lower parts were embedded in the person, into its very veins. The upper reaches of vines and flowers were growing and stretching upward, pulling locks of hair with them.

She took a few steps back again, searching for balance points and a continuity of the natural elements as they infiltrated the human. She was completely immersed in her work, but she still was aware of the moment when Heather came along the path and stopped outside the window to watch her. Aspen didn't acknowledge her at first because she needed to remain focused on the task at hand. The ivy was the most subtle part of her sculpture, but it would be the main focal point. The viewer's eye would automatically be drawn to the face of the figure first of all, where the patterned stems and the hand clutching them were located. Pam had spent hours with her retreat class, looking at photos of sculptures and paintings as well as actual ones in the local galleries until they were able to spot the center of any work of art. Not the physical center, but the point where an observer would focus before branching out to the edges.

Aspen made some minor adjustments to the curve of stems, extending them a few inches farther around the figure's neck, like either a noose or a loving embrace. She had never been comfortable with an audience while she worked, but somehow Heather's presence was unobtrusive and supportive. Maybe she was becoming more used to having others around during her creative process. Since leaving school, where she'd sculpt and draw among other students, Aspen had worked alone. Friends and family saw the finished products but never the work in progress. This week, Pam and the other artists had been with her every step of the way, offering encouragement and suggestions. Some she had taken— especially the ones Pam gave her—and others she considered and rejected. Her ability, her *potential* was expanding because of the input, whether she acted on it or not. An unexpected and beneficial side effect of the retreat.

Was Heather somehow part of the retreat experience in her mind? Aspen enjoyed feeling Heather's gaze on her. She liked sharing this intimate and personal process of sculpting with her. She had a feeling her willingness to let Heather in this part of her life—even though she had been as pushy about Aspen's future as an artist as Pam and others had been—had more to do with her as a woman than as another aspect of the group setting here. Having Heather watch her create brought them closer together, connecting them in a way Aspen hadn't felt before with her girlfriends. Heather's presence helped her expand her awareness until she was no longer sculpting for herself but for the connection it created between Aspen and the world around her.

She turned abruptly, pleased with the texture and form of the filigree, and waved at Heather, beckoning her inside. Heather looked surprised to be noticed, as if she thought Aspen was too deep in her work to see anything else but she recovered quickly and came through the studio door.

"I hope I didn't interrupt you," she said, standing respectfully far from Aspen and the sculpture. "I was heading to the beach and saw you in here. Once I started watching, I couldn't stop."

Aspen grinned at the compliment. She liked having Heather enthralled by her, even if it was just by her work and not her as a person. She gestured at the sculpture. "What do you think? Honest opinion."

Heather moved closer when Aspen gave her permission, and Aspen appreciated the unwillingness to intrude on her process.

"I love how you've created tension here. The bark is solid, the roots on the lower legs are pulling the figure downward, and the ivy is reaching up. The figure is in the center, trying to break free. We have to look at this and ask questions. Should we try to break away from nature? Is it confining, or freeing to be part of the living Earth?"

Aspen wanted to kiss her. She seemed to understand exactly what Aspen had been attempting to say through her mute work.

Heather bit her lip and circled her hand around the neck area of the sculpture. "Are you going to do something more with these stems where they blend into the hair?"

"I have some sculptured flowers I'm going to place here and

KARIS WALSH

here." Aspen went over to a worktable and got a plastic bin. She showed Heather the small irises she had made two days ago, with their fragile beards and arcing petals. "Once I have them in place, I'll blend them in to the hair so they seem to be part of it."

Heather nodded. "I like them. They'll add visual interest up there, and they'll also make a more interesting profile. The area is beautifully sculpted but a little…"

"One dimensional?" Aspen offered when Heather's voice trailed off. Heather nodded. "I totally agree," Aspen continued, her words tumbling out as she found it exhilarating to talk to someone else, especially Heather, about her process and choices. "I was going to sculpt them in relief but the area looked too flat, more like a drawing than a sculpture. So I made them separately and I'll incorporate them when I've finished the ivy and stems. They'll protrude a little and represent how the figure is almost pulling them free from its body."

Heather leaned closer to the clay. "The hands are exquisite. I can see every muscle and bone where the human is clawing at the vines. Hands seem to be a difficult body part to get right but you've done it beautifully."

Aspen took Heather's hand loosely in her own and raised it until it was level with the sculpture's face. "Recognize them? They're yours."

Heather gave her what seemed to be a surprised but pleased look and examined the figure's hand more closely with hers right next to it. "How did you…? When?"

Aspen squeezed Heather's fingers, not wanting to let go. "When we went to Tillamook. I watched your hands on the steering wheel. Memorized them. I didn't even need to sketch them but I carved these to match the image in my mind."

Aspen didn't add how many times she had pictured Heather's hands touching her, caressing her body. Even the act of sculpting them had been an amazingly erotic experience. Aspen had never felt anything like it. She had been tempted to throw this sculpture in the trash and start a full-body one of Heather. If she could be that turned on by carving mere hands, what would molding and forming

• 154 •

Heather's entire nude body do to her? She was almost desperate to find out.

"You're a gifted artist, Aspen. I feel privileged to have a chance to see this work in progress, like the veil is being lifted for just a moment and I can share your vision. Do you have photos of some of your other sculptures?"

Aspen pulled her phone out of her back pocket. "I have more on my laptop, but here are some. Just swipe through."

She handed her phone to Heather. She was planning to let her see the pictures without any commentary but she gave in and leaned over Heather's shoulder, pointing and explaining when and why she had carved each one.

Heather finished looking through the photo gallery, and then she scrolled quickly through them again. "These two aren't as sophisticated as the others," she said. "The message is a little heavy-handed, like you were young when you carved them. This one as well, it looks rushed and maybe not the right scale, as if you were low on supplies and in a hurry to manifest your vision. I wish you'd revisit it sometime when you have time and supplies to make it a larger and more imposing piece. The others are gorgeous, though, and give a strong impression of your personal style. They're easily identifiable as yours but each is unique. If you were going to build a portfolio, you should leave the three out and just put in photos of the rest."

Aspen listened in disbelief as Heather suggested an order for the photos, moving from the simplest to the one with the most visual impact. Would she ever stop trying to make Aspen into the ambitious person she herself was?

Heather gestured at the nearly finished piece. "This one should be first. Hit them with your best work, and then let the rest follow an uphill progression."

"Well, thanks for the advice, but the most I'll do as an artist is give my work to someone or sign up for another retreat like this one. I don't need a portfolio to do either."

"It'd be a waste of talent, Aspen," Heather said. "You have a brilliant gift. You shouldn't keep it hidden away or squander your time and energy on a job that keeps you from expressing yourself fully."

"I'm not hiding my art," Aspen said. She felt cornered and heard the edginess in her voice. "I'm sharing it in my own way. It's my passion, not my livelihood, and that makes it more meaningful, not less."

"It could be both." Heather paused and looked intently at Aspen. "You get very defensive whenever the subject comes up. What are you scared of? Compromising your art or taking a chance on being a professional and running the risk of failing?"

"Art isn't my job," Aspen repeated more loudly, as if volume would make Heather accept the statement. She was angry, but even in her emotional state she had to recognize the truth behind Heather's accusations. Who wouldn't be afraid of turning out their best work, pouring their heart into creating something, and having it rejected by the public? No one criticized a free sculpture. But if they were paying thousands? They'd maybe expect more than she could deliver. She couldn't admit the truth to Heather, though, and she lashed out instead.

"Don't try to turn me into you and expect me to set goals of selling so many sculptures a year. Lists and ambition and possessions might be the rewards you chase, but they don't work for me."

"Fine," Heather said in a clipped voice. "Go back home and hide behind your coffee counter. But don't do it because you worry that being a professional artist would make you materialistic and shallow like you think I am. I found a generic career where I could make progress. I never had a talent to pursue and nurture like you do. You're actually being more like me when you stay in a job that saps your energy and erodes your soul."

She turned to leave but Aspen grabbed her arm and held tight. "I never called you materialistic or shallow. I don't see you like that at all. It's just—"

"Not everyone can float through life like you want to do, Aspen. Some of us need to have goals and work toward them. And most of us need to feel in control of uncertain futures by saving and investing money. If you want to be an unfettered free spirit, go ahead. But stop using your art as an excuse not to do the hard work your talent requires of you. Being an artist means a hell of a lot more than picking up a sculpting tool and shaping some clay. Just ask Pam. She runs her gallery, connecting people with art. Yes, some of it is commercial, but some is pretty spectacular. She holds these seminars and helps younger artists like you discover new skills and learn how to collaborate. And in between, she works on her own paintings."

Aspen was surprised to feel the ache of tears in her eyes. She let go of Heather's arm and took a step back, afraid she'd trip and fall. She admired Pam and had seen her in the studio at all hours of the day and night, whenever she could fit in a spare moment. She was turning blank canvases into pictures full of life and meaning. What had Aspen done? Added a few new swirls to her sculpture's neck.

"You should have been given this talent," she said in a whisper. The realization of how she'd squandered her gift and how Heather would have cherished it made her feel queasy. "Just think what you'd have done by now. How many sculptures you'd have sold or shown in exhibits. What a name you'd have made for yourself."

Heather shook her head and put her hands on Aspen's shoulders, anchoring her in place and supporting her. "You don't know that. You couldn't. I was never encouraged to develop any talents unless they'd help me be a success in some traditional, nine-to-five job. There's a good chance I'd never have even discovered the skill you so obviously treasure. I might have something like it inside but by now it's buried too deep to ever uncover. You've been freely sharing what you do with other people, and the only reason I keep pushing is because I can see how much more you could do. How many people you could reach with your message, how many questions and new ways of thinking you could inspire."

Aspen put her hands on Heather's waist and pulled her into a tight hug. She felt depleted after her flash of anger and her sadness over missed opportunities.

"I'll never be like you," Aspen said, her voice muffled against Heather's shoulder. "You and your lists and your goals. I don't believe they've made you happy but I can see how much you've accomplished. I know someday you'll find the passion you seem to be missing, and I have no doubt you'll push yourself hard enough to be a great success."

"Maybe, someday," Heather said. Her breath ruffled Aspen's hair when she spoke. "But I have a feeling we'll both stay the same. Change is hard. I'll probably go back to Portland and aim toward the next goal at my bank. Work my way up the ladder, step by step, until I'm branch manager or whatever. And you'll go back to working when you have to and sculpting when you can."

Aspen closed her eyes as the truth of Heather's statement burrowed into her. She wanted to deny it but even as she was recognizing the possibility of pursuing art full-time, she was aware of inertia holding her back. She'd need to keep working while she got herself set up as an artist and found her niche. She'd need to have a gallery showing or sell some pieces, and to do that she'd need money for supplies and time to sculpt. To do *that*, she'd need to work more hours at the coffee shop. The cycle wouldn't stop, and it would lead her further from her art at every turn.

And their journeys toward unwanted goals would lead them away from each other. Aspen had never really expected her relationship with Heather to be more than an interesting diversion while she was on her retreat. They'd had fun together, and she'd come to understand the depth of Heather's character in a way she hadn't anticipated when they first met. But unless they made drastic changes, they'd always want more for each other and never would fully understand why the other person was settling for an unfulfilling life.

Aspen leaned back and brushed her fingers through Heather's hair. The sensation was as whisper soft, as if she were sifting through downy feathers. "How can you feel so perfect for me sometimes, and completely the opposite of what I need at others?"

Heather laughed quietly and took hold of Aspen's hand. She kissed her palm and moved her lips along Aspen's wrist. The spot where Heather's mouth met Aspen's pulse point came alive with a jolt. Electricity seemed to travel from her lips into Aspen's bloodstream, shocking her entire body into a state of arousal.

"I know exactly what you mean," Heather said. "You should be with someone equally sensitive and passionate, and I should be with a woman with whom I can share my drive and ambition. We'd be much more comfortable. But, damn it, all I want is you."

Heather kissed her then, and Aspen felt as if an unseen shell of cast bronze had encased her heart and was now broken, releasing her. They had both admitted they were a poorly matched pair but they both were willing to turn away from logic and fear for one moment of togetherness.

❖

Heather hurried into the inn with Aspen close behind. She fumbled with the lock on her bedroom door and flung it open, grabbing Aspen by the hand and pulling her inside. Laughing, they fell against the door and it slammed shut with a bang. Heather wrapped her hands in Aspen's short blond hair and kissed her, meeting Aspen's tongue with her own and gasping for air when the kiss deepened.

Aspen's hands were everywhere on her, with the same tactile intensity she always showed. Cupping Heather's cheeks, kneading her shoulders like clay, rubbing her back. Heather felt every touch and she was amazed by the various responses Aspen was able to draw out of her. A light, almost ticklish brush of the fingers sent shivers up Heather's arms and made her hypersensitive to even the movement of the air or the brush of her sweater. Stronger pressure on her shoulders and lower back made her moan in pleasure as knots of tension released. They kissed with the gasping, reaching, groaning need of two people who knew they had only minutes to share before reality separated them again.

Heather gave herself no time for second thoughts. She had already gone through them time and again since meeting Aspen. She was too young, too unmotivated, and too talented for someone staid yet driven like Heather. Aspen would frolic through life never fully activating and managing her talent. The thought made Heather sad, but the choice was Aspen's to make. Heather had her own demons to slay, and she would do that by pushing herself to ever-evolving goals. Maybe someday one of them would fulfill her...

Right now, though, a temporary fulfillment was within her grasp, and Heather planned to take full advantage of it. Aspen wanted her, too—Heather could feel mutual desire connecting them as they kissed as if their survival depended on air the other could supply. Neither expected more than the immediate present offered them.

Aspen steered her over to the bed, and Heather fell backward onto the mattress with Aspen on top of her. Her hands curved around Aspen's hip bones, and all their fumbling and kissing and touching settled into a rhythm coming from somewhere inside. This was new territory for Heather. Every step of her life was accompanied by a list. Chores, loans, goals, and things to buy. Plan the work, then work the plan. Now all of Heather's being was condensed in this one driving, reaching need. She bent her knees and placed her feet on the bed, settling Aspen snugly between her legs. Aspen moved her hips in a thrusting, circular motion. She stretched out fully on Heather's body, her mouth biting and sucking on Heather's neck, just below her ear, and her hands curling under Heather's shoulders. Her fingers dug into Heather's flesh, and Heather responded by arching even closer.

Heather cried out as her orgasm caught her by surprise. *Everything* connected with Aspen surprised her. She closed her thighs tightly against Aspen's sides and felt her shudder once, twice, and then lie still.

Heather's hand weakly rubbed Aspen's back until Aspen raised herself on one elbow and gave her a slow, deep kiss.

"You startle me," Heather said. In a world full of sameness and predictability, this quality of Aspen's most scared and exhilarated her.

"You ground me," Aspen said, resting her cheek on Heather's breast.

After a few moments of rest, Aspen rolled to one side and lay next to Heather. She stroked her with one hand as if trying to memorize the feel of Heather with her hands.

"Have you always been this tactile?" Heather asked, playing with Aspen's hair. "Sculpting and molding things with your hands seems to be part of who you are."

"It always has been," Aspen said. "I was making sculptures from the time I could grab hold of any material to use. My food, Play-Doh, or even piles of fabrics and scrap metal. Any old junk, or real clay, I didn't care. I never really saw myself as different or unusual because of it until we made papier-mâché jack-o'-lanterns in school one time. I'd never worked with the stuff, and I loved feeling how malleable it was. The other kids made globs of sticky fabric or basic shapes like triangular eyes but mine was a pumpkin house with windows for facial features. It's like something clicked and I was a person who sculpted. I've tried about every medium I could find since then."

Heather couldn't stop her sigh but she tried to keep it from being too dramatic or wistful. "It must feel good to be special. To have a gift you feel compelled to use."

Aspen swatted her playfully. "You're special, too. You're talented and successful and obviously very good at what you do."

"It's not the same, but thank you. I'm not a gifted loan officer or someone who is completed by doing this work. I studied hard and followed carefully chosen examples to get where I am today. Anyone could follow the same career path if they had the desire and the willingness to do the work. Not everyone, no matter how hard they try or how much they practice, can replicate your abilities."

Aspen put her hand over Heather's rapidly beating heart. "Everyone has passions, though. What moves you? Or what moved you when you were still young enough to be open to the world?" She tapped her fingers on Heather's chest. "And I don't mean skill. I mean, what do you love even if you're not good at it?"

Heather had to travel a long way back in her mind to find unfettered passion. "I remember standing by the ocean for the first time when I was a child. We were living in Vancouver, Washington, and we went to Ocean Shores for the weekend. I'd never seen or felt anything like it. The waves and the spray of sea mist and the sun glinting off the water and making me see spots. It was one of those moments when you see something so beautiful you feel a stinging in your eyes, like you're going to cry just because you are looking at whatever it is in front of you." Heather paused, frustrated because she couldn't explain herself well and sad because she hadn't felt that press of tears in far too long.

"I used to seek that feeling. I'd find it sometimes but usually when I wasn't expecting it. I'd hear a piece of music or see a picture or find some out of the way view in nature, and suddenly I'd be moved by indefinable emotions. I guess, in a way, beauty was my passion. I didn't create it or bring it to life in any way. I just looked and saw it."

Aspen laid her head on Heather again and held her close, as if understanding the tears threatening Heather's vision. This had nothing to do with beauty and everything to do with sadness. What good did it do to recognize a passion when it wasn't anything worthwhile or meaningful? Was Heather going to quit her job and travel around looking at pretty objects and scenic overlooks? No way in hell. She was going to go back to doing what she had made herself good at doing. Maybe she could keep some of these memories intact and make more of an effort to see beauty on her weekends and—God forbid—vacations, but she had a feeling it would be easier and less despairing to keep her blinders on and see only work, her apartment, and her things.

"You create beautiful art, and I love to look at it," Heather said. "We approach both art and life in very different ways."

"I know," Aspen whispered. "And I'm not agreeing because I think the skills I have are better than yours. I'm agreeing because you make me feel shame, for not giving more of myself to my sculpting, and a desire to be a better artist at the same time. You confuse me."

"And you make me realize how little I've lived in alignment with my passions, and how little talent I have for following them. Two people in a relationship should make each other feel good and strong and uplifted, not even more aware of their own weaknesses."

Heather pushed herself to a standing position and held her hand out for Aspen. She pulled her off the bed and into a hug.

"This afternoon was wonderful," Heather said. She felt Aspen stiffen in her arms as if she realized she was hearing a good-bye speech. "Your body, your mind, and your talented hands amaze me. I love being with you, and having a chance to hold you close was more than I dreamed of, but I think we both know how this ends. You have to get back to the studio, and I have a few more items to cross off my list."

Aspen stepped away from her and cupped Heather's cheek in her hand. "You called me a coward earlier and said I was hiding behind the coffee counter. You were right, but you're just as afraid to live all the way, with passion and joy, as I am. You hide behind your lists and your anger and your self-pity because you don't have the skill of an artist. And now you're disguising your fear as logic and pushing me away."

Aspen gave her one last kiss and walked out the door, leaving Heather alone with only the painting of the storm for company.

❖

Aspen put her energy and emotion into her sculpture. She finished it in a rush of activity after her heartbreaking afternoon with Heather. She had to take short breaks when she'd remember their lovemaking and Heather's final speech—her hands would shake and she'd need to walk away from the clay figure until she was under control again. But now she was done with the sculpture. Every last detail had been carved and defined until she was satisfied with the piece as a whole and slightly awed by the largest and best work she had ever completed. She couldn't deny the fact that she was able to produce something special when she was able to devote herself to it full-time and not fit in only an hour or two a day on a small project if she was lucky.

Making the mold for the bronze was her favorite part of the process, partly because she felt as if she was wrapping a huge Christmas present that she herself would eventually get to open, and partly because this step required just the right amount of mental attention. She had to keep focused on the layers of latex, rubber, and plastic that encased the clay so they were even and filled every nook and cranny of her sculpture, but most of her mind was free to wander. She had expected this seminar to be a fun break from the coffee shop and a chance to fully engage with her work for a change. The reduced-cost two weeks at a gorgeous B&B on the coast was an added bonus. Aspen hadn't expected the seminar to be life-changing.

She washed her hands after the final clamp was applied. Now what? She and Pam were taking the mold to a foundry in Portland, but not until tomorrow. She wanted to search for Heather and find some way to break through to her, but she hadn't seen her since their afternoon together.

She knew what she needed to do. After hours of intense thought during the past few days, she had come to a decision. She wasn't going to hide behind the coffee counter anymore. She gave her mold a final pat and left the studio, getting in her car and driving back to Tillamook.

She drove past the cheese factory and was tempted to go in and stand where she and Heather had stood the other day, but she kept driving to the office supply store. She wasn't here to relive their first "date." She was here because she needed a one-hour photo shop and a big-box office store. The memories of Heather and their conversations kept her going, though, even when she was tempted to back out of her new plan before she got it started.

Aspen was new to the goal-setting business. Once she had finished school, she had fallen into her job and apartment, taking the first ones she found. She'd taken the easy way out every step of the way. She had justified her lack of drive by claiming she was protecting her art, but she was neglecting it instead. When she had talked to Heather about her childhood and her discovery of sculpting, she had felt sad about the way she had let herself create distance between herself and sculpting instead of creating art. She had always been touching and molding and shaping, from preschool onward. Did she still create every waking moment? No. Did she miss the physical connection between her and the objects and materials around her? Yes. With all her heart.

She drove back to the inn and sat in her car in the parking area while she hastily shoved photos of her work into plastic sleeves. She tried a few different combinations and orders of pictures. She was particularly fond of one of her earlier pieces—one Heather had suggested she leave out of a portfolio—and she hated to omit it from her collection. She'd been going through a tough breakup and a stressful time at work when she'd sculpted it, and she saw it as a personal triumph that she had created something beautiful and lasting out of her pain. When she looked through the pages now, with a more critical eye, she saw what Heather had seen. The piece was sentimental for her, but it didn't fit with the rest of her work in tone or subtlety. She put the photo aside, deciding instead to frame it and hang it in her apartment as a symbol of sculpting's ability to heal. She put the rest of the pictures, including a temporary one of her clay figure, in the order Heather had suggested and got out of the car.

She went through the back gate, hoping to find Pam in her studio. As she came around the house, she heard Heather and Pam talking on the patio. She hesitated, still hidden by shrubs and not wanting to intrude. She could have walked up to them, but she had a feeling Heather didn't want to see her anymore now that she was ready to go back home, to her lists and her promotions.

She shouldn't be eavesdropping, but she couldn't seem to move when she heard Heather's voice. She was going to miss the sound of it, and the way Heather gestured when she spoke, moving through space with a grace and refinement Aspen adored. In her moment of indecision, she heard the last part of their conversation.

"Just promise me you'll think about it," Pam was saying. "Give it a day or two."

"Okay, but I don't want to waste your time. I can say no right now, or I can wait until tomorrow and say it then."

"Humor me. Tell me tomorrow."

Heather's laugh carried over to Aspen's hiding place. She heard humor in it, but something else as well. A tension Aspen only heard when Heather talked about her career and her life in Portland.

"Fine. I'll wait. But I don't have any training or skill or—"

"Please, Heather. Make your decision based on what you want, not on what you think you have to offer. I wouldn't have asked if I didn't believe in you."

Aspen practically felt Heather's shrug in her next words.

"All right. I guess we'll talk again tomorrow. But it'll be a short, one-word conversation."

Pam laughed in response, and Aspen thought she sensed something confident in it. Pam always seemed sure of herself, though, a trait Aspen didn't share. It would be a helpful one if she followed her heart with her career as a sculptor, but she was going to have to try using blind hope and nagging doubt instead. Much less helpful traits.

Aspen heard the back door shut and she came out of the bushes cautiously, in case Pam had been the one to go inside. Heather must have, instead, because Aspen saw Pam walking along the path toward the studio. She wanted to follow Heather. Ask how she was, what the offer Pam had made was, and why Heather seemed so defensively opposed to it. Aspen sighed and headed after Pam. Heather didn't want her input or her presence.

Pam was setting out paints and an easel when Aspen entered the studio. She was humming to herself and had a hint of a smile on her face. Aspen recognized the signs of an artist about to create, and she hurried into a conversation, not wanting to disturb Pam more than necessary.

"I've been thinking about what you said, about trying to sell some of my sculptures and do this as a career, and I think I might want to at least give it a try. For a while. Maybe."

Pam turned toward her with a grin. "There were a lot of qualifiers in that little speech, but I believe in you. Give this a shot, and you'll start to believe in yourself as much as I do."

Aspen sighed. She wasn't positive that would ever happen, but she was dying a slow death without art on the center stage of her life. She had to make this change. "I didn't realize until this seminar how much I need to be sculpting all the time. Being here, without having my energy sapped by distractions, has been amazing. I'm working better, and I feel more at peace."

In her mind, not in her heart. Heather had broken that into pieces, but Aspen would use her pain and create with it. Even though the ending of their brief relationship was a sad one, Aspen had to acknowledge how Heather had changed her life.

"And meeting Heather made a difference, too. She talked to me about goals and having more respect for my gifts. She made me rethink how I had been living my life. I guess I've been too scared of failure to really follow my dream, and I masked my fear with sort of an artistic self-righteousness."

Pam laughed. "We've all been there. But we create because we want to connect people with places we've seen or ideas we've had. Art is made to be a collaboration with an audience, whether it's a single owner of one of our pieces or a crowd of people walking through a gallery. You've made a portfolio?"

Aspen clutched the slim vinyl folder to her chest. "Not a real professional one. I had some photos printed in Tillamook this morning and bought this at an office supply store. I just wanted to show you and get your feedback."

"Gladly," Pam said. She hesitated a moment before continuing. "You'll need to let me see it first, though."

Aspen reluctantly handed the portfolio to Pam. She paced nervously while Pam looked through the pages.

"I'm planning to replace the first pictures with ones of my bronze, once it's cast."

"Mm-hmm," Pam muttered. She came to the end of the photos and closed the book. "When you applied for this seminar, you emailed a gallery of your work, but a few are missing from your portfolio and the order is different."

"Yes, well…" Aspen berated herself for not adding her sentimental piece to the collection.

"They're good changes," Pam said quickly. "This is a cleaner presentation than the one you sent me. It shows growth but a strong sense of personal style and imagery. Very well done."

"Oh, whew." Aspen sighed with relief and an awkward sense of pride. She hadn't wanted to blame Heather when she thought Pam wasn't happy with the finished product, but now she was pleased to give her credit. "The changes were all Heather's ideas. She suggested the order and what sculptures to keep out of the portfolio."

Pam looked through the pages again with a thoughtful expression. "Yes, she has a good eye. She recognized your talent right away, you know."

"She seemed to like my sculpture." Aspen wasn't sure what else to say about Heather. Somehow, speaking about her in such a casual way helped her control the rampant emotions she had been feeling lately whenever Heather came to mind. In other words, all the time.

"It's an astounding piece," Pam said, handing Aspen the black folder. "I want you to feel proud of this. You made this entire seminar worthwhile. Just to see your growth in such a short time, as well as the quality of the finished piece…To be honest, Mel and I planned these retreats as a way to get guests back again after the spill. I never realized how much I'd enjoy teaching them, and how much my students would inspire me to paint again. You made a difference to me, too."

Aspen was speechless. She had spent enough time with Pam during critique sessions to know she wouldn't fling meaningless praise Aspen's way. Pam got a piece of scrap paper and wrote a few lines.

"Here are the names of some local galleries. Take your portfolio to them and ask for a showing. You don't have enough pieces for an entire show, but they often do events featuring two or three new artists. It'd be a good start for you. Other than that, keep creating, as much as you can. My studio will always be open to you, if you decide to stick around here."

The thought was tempting. Aspen could always find work in a coffee shop here, if sculpting didn't work out for her. But she'd have to live surrounded by memories of Heather… She waved the paper. "We already went to the galleries in town as a class. How will

I know these people are interested in me and not doing you a favor if they offer me a showing?"

Pam laughed. "I understand self-doubt. You'll probably never get rid of it completely, but you'll need to learn how to work in spite of it and using it. The names I wrote down are all in Manzanita. They know me there, but they won't associate you with me unless you tell them. That's your choice."

Aspen grinned and put the folded paper in the pocket of her cords. She wouldn't tell. She had to do this part on her own.

❖

Heather walked as close to Haystack Rock as the tide allowed. The sun behind her threw the rock in dark shadow, but the wheeling gulls streaked flashes of white across its craggy surface. Waves lapped and curled around its base, sending the occasional spray of foam and glistening drops of water into the air.

She remembered her first night here and rubbed the fading mark on her forehead from where she'd hit her head on the drive to Cannon Beach. So much had changed since she'd arrived. She'd come out to the beach to see the town's landmark basalt formation merely to check it off her list. Look, then done. On her way to it, she had first spotted Aspen—bohemian and beautiful—and her magnificent sculpture.

The nagging jealousy she'd felt because she didn't have the raw talent of an artist had been steadily and unexpectedly fading since Pam's surprising offer the day before. Heather had listened in disbelief while Pam told her about needing someone to help in the gallery—not a student clerk as she'd had before, but a real partner who would help ease Pam's responsibilities and free her up for more painting and retreats. She hadn't been offering Heather a job but had been giving her the opportunity to buy in as a partner.

Heather shook her head. What would her parents say? She had a good guess, but their imaginary voices were drowned out by her own shouted reasons why she should refuse. What did she know about art? Pam had called her a discerning viewer, and Heather had told Aspen about how she had sought visual moments of beauty when she was a child, but she'd had no formal training apart from an elective class or two in college. Pam would expect her to purchase pieces for the gallery—high-quality ones as well as commercial works with wide appeal. She'd help retreat students and other artists who came to Pam as a mentor with the logistics of being an artist in a world that favored those with more traditional jobs.

Heather snorted, and the sound of her humorless laughter was carried away by the wind. No salary. No ladder rungs to climb. This would be her job, and commission on sales not yet made would be her pay. There wasn't a secure base salary, just the dream of potential commission. Heather shuddered. She'd done everything in her power to avoid the unknown, unpredictable life Pam was now dangling in front of her. She'd been aggressive in her career, but always by following high-powered mentors who'd paved the way in a career that had easily discernible and quantifiable steps to success. She'd never taken a chance on herself, by herself, with the huge risk of failure she'd face here. Her savings would buy part of the business. Her intuition and artistic taste would have to step up and take care of the future.

She'd be insane to consider it. And she'd never have given it a second thought if it weren't for Aspen. Aspen, who asked questions and made Heather think about passion in a whole new way. Aspen, who had amazingly talented hands and imagination, but little business sense or concept of how to make a career out of her art. She'd told Heather she wasn't interested in pursuing sculpting as a full-time job, but others like her would want the chance and would need someone like Heather to help. Pam had talked about needing Mel to ground her, encourage her, and help her navigate the real-life aspects of life as an artist. Heather could be that person for artists young and old who wanted to recreate their lives. She'd also be the one to ease Pam's burdens at the gallery, freeing her to paint and mentor more.

Heather walked along the shore, not because she needed to cross it off her list—she already had marked off *walk on beach and collect sea shells* days ago—but because she felt more able to think and plan out here. There was something limitless in the waves and the tang of salt and the gray sky meeting gray water on the far horizon. Something hopeful, something nudging her toward a new life and a new chance to live with more passion than she'd dreamed.

By the time she turned back toward the inn, the sun was sinking low in the west, over the ocean. She saw a silhouette on the top of the inn's part of the bluff. Aspen, as if summoned by Heather's thoughts. She took a step back from the staircase, maybe retreating in case Heather saw her there, watching, but Heather waved and beckoned her down the stairs. She went slowly to meet Aspen. Too many things needed to be said, even after such a short time apart.

"Hey," Aspen said once she got close. She was wearing a ragged green and brown sweater that looked hand knit and had a blue scarf wrapped snugly around her neck. No beret this time, and her short blond hair was mussed by the breeze.

"Hey. I've missed you." Heather reached out and took Aspen's hands in hers, half expecting her to pull away. Aspen squeezed her tight, instead.

"Me, too. I wasn't meaning to invade your privacy, but I saw you out here and I couldn't…I just wanted to see you."

Heather's heart felt as buoyant as a gull soaring with a wind current. Decisions fell into place with startling ease as she stood here, face-to-face with the woman she loved.

"We need to talk." Heather saw Aspen's frown at the trite breakup phrase and she shook her head quickly. "Not bad talk. Just talk. I'm staying here at Cannon Beach. I'm going to be partners with Pam and help run the gallery."

Heather hadn't even told Pam her decision—hell, she hadn't made it for certain until seconds ago. Aspen deserved to be the first to know. Heather saw Aspen's confusion, but she kept talking. "I want you to stay, too. I know how different we are, in age and approach to life and goals. But the afternoon…that afternoon when we…anyway, we talked about how we each seem to make the other person more aware of weakness. Maybe that's not a bad thing. Maybe that's how growth occurs. I want to learn from you, Aspen, how to be freer and happier. I just want to be with you." Heather took a deep breath. Aspen needed to know she was accepted and loved, not worry she was Heather's project or first gallery acquisition. "Just stay here, as you are. Work in a coffee shop or the bakery or the bookstore if you want. Sculpt when and how *you* want. I'll support whatever you decide. I just want you to be with me."

Aspen shook her head, and Heather wasn't sure what she was answering in the negative. She held her breath until Aspen spoke.

"I want to be with you. I'd already been thinking of staying, and that's part of the reason I was looking for you. I made a portfolio, just like you suggested. Nothing fancy, just some pictures thrown together, but I got a show, Heather. A gallery in Manzanita is going to display my work with two other artists next month. I'm going to work in Pam's studio to get pieces done for it."

Heather grabbed her and pulled her close. Even if Aspen hadn't added the part about wanting her, she would have been as happy with the knowledge that Aspen was going to seriously pursue her art. Heather felt the same tight twinge of tears she'd always experienced in moments of beauty. Aspen would provide her with a lifetime of this kind of passionate response.

"What made you change your mind?" she asked, keeping her face buried in the curve of Aspen's neck. Their bodies molded together as if Aspen had sculpted them out of a single block of clay.

"You, mostly. I've always been alone with my sculptures, but in these past few days I've realized I'm not anymore. Pam's voice is there, giving me suggestions and challenging the way I look at my work. The other artists, too, are there with all their different ways of solving problems and expressing what they see and think. Mostly, though, it was you. You became part of me because you burrowed into my heart. Part of me as a person and me as a sculptor. I'd never felt such a connection with other people, and I never had a community of artists before. I'd never have grown much or had the same opportunities if I'd continued to steal moments of time and work by myself without feedback. And I'd never be able to bring the same depth to my work as I will with you in my life."

Heather sighed and pulled back enough to look in Aspen's

eyes. She kissed her, feeling the warmth from Aspen's lips seeping under her weather-chilled skin and making her feel alive and vital again. What they had was special, and no one else would ever get as much of her as she was offering to Aspen. But in smaller ways, she'd be able to help other artists find their community and their artistic freedom and voice. She might not ever pick up a paintbrush or sculpting tool, but she'd bring more art into the world in her own small way.

And Aspen would take the world by storm once she completely dedicated herself to her work. Heather was sure of it. She deepened their kiss and then broke away, leading Aspen up the stairs and past the studio. There was time for everything else tomorrow. They'd start making plans in earnest—Heather's specialty—and she'd be careful to offer support to Aspen without dumping all of her overwhelming drive and goal-setting skills on her at once. They'd make a life here, full of passion and beauty. Tomorrow.

Tonight, Heather had a different kind of passion in mind. She and Aspen held each other close as they hurried back to the inn. Tonight, Heather would be the sculptor, molding the desire she felt for Aspen into a living work of art.

SPINNAKER

Once Tamsyn Kalburg had sailed her sloop a short distance past Haystack Rock, she flaked the halyard in a loose figure eight to keep it from snagging and turned onto a steady downwind course. She intentionally made the turn wider and smoother than she would have if she had been alone, but even with her precautions, her passengers looked ready to puke.

Tam started gathering the blue and white spinnaker, stuffing the lightweight sail under the boom and down the hatch. She pointed at the beach. "Hey, Pam. The inn is over this way now."

Pam was leaning over the railing, staring at the open sea as if it might calm her stomach. She and Mel had driven down to Newport this morning to join Tam on a sail up the coast because Pam wanted to see the Sea Glass Inn from a new angle and make a whale's view painting of it. The two of them had seemed excited at first, but they'd grown quieter during the short sail to Cannon Beach.

"All she'll remember from this trip is dangling over the railing and being sick," Mel said. She was sitting on a red-cushioned bench with her knees hugged to her chest. "We'll be giving you paintings of the side of your boat for your next five birthdays."

"Maybe I'll make a portrait of you, Mel," Pam said in a weak voice. "That green tinge on your cheeks is a very flattering color."

"I'm not sick," Mel said in an indignant tone. Tam might have been more convinced if she hadn't noticed the same color Pam had. "It's a new makeup. All the rage now. The beautiful blush of seasickness."

Tam laughed. She had met Mel almost a year ago, when the oil spill hit Cannon Beach and Tam was called here from her Newport office of the Department of Fish and Wildlife. She and Pam had been acquaintances for ages since they had both spent part of their childhood here on the shore. Mel and Pam had been the first people to welcome Tam back to what she loosely considered *home*, and although her homecoming had been anything but pleasant, she had been grateful for their readily offered friendship. She liked hearing the playful banter between them, companionable and intimate even though they weren't feeling well. Tam, on the other hand, felt great. The rough seas and salt air nourished her more than food could ever do, and she relished the tactical thrill of sailing out here where skill and confidence could mean the difference between living and drowning.

She sat with a relaxed hand on the tiller while Pam eased herself away from the railing and onto the bench next to Mel. Her life vest rose up when she plopped down, bumping her in the chin, and she pulled it back into place.

"I should probably tell you now how happy we are that you've moved back here, Tam," she said, picking up her pad and squinting toward the shore. "Because I doubt I'll be speaking to you after the return trip."

"I'm starting the not-speaking-to-her thing right now," Mel said. "I don't know why I bothered to pack a nice lunch for us when I won't be able to hold any food down. Oh, Pam, look at the way the sunlight's hitting the studio. How lovely."

"I see it," Pam said, her charcoal pencil rapidly capturing the scene in front of her. Her voice grew steadier the more she worked. Even Mel seemed captivated enough by the view of her inn from the ocean to perk up somewhat.

Tam watched with interest as the beach and the large house unfolded on Pam's paper before her eyes. Pam shook her hand and continued working with short, brisk flicks of her pencil.

"Can you hold the boat still for a minute, Tam?"

"Yeah, sure. One of my special sailing skills is calming the seas." Tam shook her head with amusement. She brought people sailing with her on occasion, usually preferring to be on her own in the middle of water and waves, and most of them got the same queasy look she was seeing in Mel and Pam. She didn't think she had a particularly strong stomach or any immunity to being sick, but she always took more care to keep stunts to a minimum when she had guests on board. Most of her passengers were undone by what she'd consider an easy sail.

"This is the Pacific Ocean, not the lake at summer camp," she said. She gently adjusted their course to give Pam a change of angle. "Besides, I thought the two of you said you'd sailed before."

"We have," Mel said in an indignant voice, ending with a sheepish laugh. "On the lake at summer camp."

"Never again," Pam said, never taking her gaze off the scene before her. "I'm not even getting on one of those fake boats in Seaside's kiddie park, just in case they slip off the track and fall into the water."

Mel laughed, and then groaned and leaned back in her seat. Tam handed her a ginger ale from the cooler and Mel took it with a moan of thanks.

"I blame you for this, too, Pam," Mel said. "You've known her for years and you should have warned me about how she sails. Remind me not to let her drive us home."

"I'm a great driver," Tam said with pretend indignation. "I never get speeding tickets."

"Because no cop can catch her," Pam said, chewing on the end of her pencil and tilting her head as she examined the back of Haystack Rock. "Can you take us a little closer? And over thataway."

She waved toward the south side of the large basalt formation, and Tam shook her head with caution. She'd been much closer than this before, maneuvering delicately around the rock with one hand and snapping pictures of birds and seals with the other, but she wasn't sure these two were up for the added roughness. "We'll get tossed around a bit more than we are now. Are you sure?"

Pam swallowed visibly and pointed. "See those nesting murres? I want to paint them."

Tam looked at Mel for her opinion. She sighed and nodded

with the look of a martyr heading to the gallows. "Anything for the artist," she said.

Her voice was punctuated with an exaggerated, long-suffering sigh, but Tam had a feeling Mel meant those words without hesitation. The connection and love between the two women was at once awesome and sad for Tam to witness. She had never experienced anything like it herself, although admittedly she'd never hung around long enough for a real bond to form. Unattached and free. That was her motto.

She went as close to the rock as she was willing to go with Pam and Mel along for the ride. She'd have pushed the limits further on her own, but she was careful with her passengers.

"Whew," Mel said when a particularly strong wave rolled under the small sailboat. "You need to distract me, Tam. Get my mind off losing my breakfast and tell me what Pam was like as a little girl."

Tam usually hated to talk about her childhood. She, like Pam, had grown up around here with her grandparents. Pam had spent summers here, while Tam had been dropped off for unpredictable and increasingly frequent amounts of time by her freewheeling mother. Mel looked like she really needed to get her attention off the movement of the boat, however, and Tam didn't mind talking about Pam. Anyone but herself. She pointed at Pam, who was drawing with a rapt and distant expression.

"What you see is what you get, even back then," she said. "Pam was always the introspective sort, wandering the beaches with her sketch pad and a dreamy look in her eyes. We all thought she was a little loony."

Pam laughed. She continued to draw rapidly, her eyes seeming to see past the birds on the rock and onto the canvas on which she'd eventually paint them. Tam appreciated her talent but didn't share anything like it. She was connected to earth and sea, as down-to-earth as Pam was visionary and imaginative.

"I had plenty of inspiration for drawings with Tam around," Pam said. "I remember a watercolor of her clinging halfway up the side of that bluff over there while she waited for the fire department to rescue her. And I did an interesting charcoal study of her draped over the hull of a capsized rowboat before the Coast Guard arrived and hauled her ass out of the ocean. I got my first start with portrait painting by capturing the look of terror on her face."

"Exhilaration," Tam corrected with a laugh. The day on the bluff had been exciting, and she'd had her first crush on the woman firefighter who got her off the cliff. The time in the rowboat really had been frightening, but she wasn't about to admit it. She'd learned her lesson, though, and it had been pounded into her by the cold waves that had threatened to unmoor her from the hull of the boat. To this day, she might be daring, but she'd never lost her healthy respect for the ocean's power.

"Whatever," Pam said. She finally looked away from her sketchbook and at Mel. "You know what? I blame me, too. I should have remembered those incidents before agreeing to come on a boat ride with her."

"*You* asked *me* for a ride, not the other way around," Tam said with a laugh. She kept her boat moored at Newport even though she'd be in charge of the new Cannon Beach office. She knew why she had eventually applied for the position after turning it down repeatedly, but she still wasn't convinced it was a good idea to be back here. She was staying at the inn until she either ran out of money and got a place of her own, or until she quit and went back to her old job. There were too many memories here. One memory in particular—her father—had abandoned her here and now was trying to call her back. She'd needed him then, and he needed her now. He wasn't going to get what he wanted any more than she had as a child. She pushed aside the guilt she felt whenever he came to mind these days. She wasn't after revenge. She just had nothing to give.

Pam continued their joking, likely unaware of any underlying tension in Tam, who was reconsidering her return to Cannon Beach yet again. "I asked for a ride because I've been watching you sail back and forth for the past two years, in this damned cute boat with the blasted blue and white sail. It looked like fun. From the shore. My mistake."

"You'll have to give her one of the watercolors you've painted, Pam," Mel said. Now that Tam had aimed the sloop back toward the south and they were moving faster, the chop didn't have as much effect on stomachs. Mel eased herself into a more upright sitting position, let go of the death grip she'd had around her knees, and dropped her feet to the deck. "She's made a few with your boat in them, Tam. The bright colors contrast beautifully with the clouds and dark rocks."

Tam smiled and murmured something about wanting to see them, but she was startled by the idea of Pam seeing her often enough to paint her. Tam had been avoiding this place, but she realized now that her sailing trips often brought her to this area. She must have been drawn here more than she thought. The subconscious homecoming trips disconcerted her. She'd felt in control, coming here for this job as a choice and as a way to find closure and say good-bye to the past. Had she been controlled, instead, by a stubborn need to really come home? Stubborn and foolish. The past was past, and all she had to do was let it go. She turned her attention away from her troubling memories and focused instead on getting them safely back to her boat's harbor.

❖

Tam walked down the bright, shiny hallway of Seaside Hospital's new oncology ward. The unit had been in existence for decades, staffed by only two doctors and several nurses, but it had recently grown because of a sizable bequest from a wealthy local woman. She'd been forced to travel away from her beloved ocean to receive treatment in Portland, and she'd willed her entire estate to make sure others didn't have to do the same thing.

Tam had read stories about the woman's legacy in the Newport newspaper, little realizing at the time that she'd be one of the first wave of relatives coming to visit patients in the new wing. At the moment, she wasn't even sure she'd make it to his room, let alone go inside and actually visit him. She'd turned back a couple of times, almost making it to her car again. On her third attempt, she'd gotten as far as the nurses' station, but instead of getting her father's room number, she'd asked where the gift shop was located, and ended up standing in the tiny store, staring at get-well gifts she wasn't going to buy. She bought a pack of gum just to be purchasing something and to excuse her lack of willpower, and then she finally made it to her father's door.

She took a deep breath and pushed through the half-open doorway. He was lying on the bed with his eyes closed, but his gaunt hands were picking restlessly at the spotless white sheet. His color wasn't good, even though in his letter he'd told her they'd managed to ease the symptoms of jaundice by unblocking his bile duct through surgery. Minor surgery, compared to the liver transplant he'd need if he was going to survive this cancer.

Tam stepped back too quickly, ready to flee the room, and she bumped into a cart near the empty second bed. He opened his eyes at the sound and stared at her for several long moments. She saw the moment when recognition flared in his dark green eyes, mirror images of her own.

"Tamsyn. You came. I knew you would."

The first words she'd heard him speak since he'd left her and her mother over thirty years ago. Tam had been four the last time she saw him. She wondered at first how he could possibly recognize her, but she would have picked him out of a crowd with no problem.

"How did you know? I wasn't even sure until today." Not true. She had changed jobs because of this, to be close to where he was. Why? She wasn't about to sit vigil at his bedside, holding his hand and speaking soothing words of comfort and hope. She didn't want to be here.

"I can't stay," she said. He just watched her while she struggled against the unseen force that had brought her to this hospital. Finally, she won a small battle and turned around, ready to leave, when a doctor came through the door and smiled at her.

What a smile. Tam stood transfixed, confused by the beauty and light this woman brought into a room full of sickness and pain and memories too ingrained to erase or forgive. She was average height and average weight, but there wasn't anything remotely average about her. Her red hair was chin length and some scattered freckles highlighted her cheekbones. Gray flecks made her blue eyes seem like crystals.

Mostly, though, Tam was held in place by her smile. Genuine and freely given. Her entire face was transformed into something open and positive by it. Tam would put her life in this woman's hands without a second thought.

"You must be Mr. Kalburg's daughter. Tamsyn, isn't it? What a beautiful name. I'm Dr. Sherman, but call me Maggie, please."

"Tam," she said, shaking the proffered hand and not wanting to let go. She'd been feeling shaky, angry, and disoriented since receiving her dad's letter, but Maggie's touch calmed her. She cleared her throat and attempted a complete sentence. "Most people call me Tam."

"Tam. I like it. Shall we sit and talk about your dad's condition?"

Tam liked the way her name sounded coming out of Maggie's mouth and she almost let the word *dad* slide by without noticing it. She hadn't called him that ever. He had been Daddy, and then he'd been gone.

She sat on the edge of a vinyl recliner and clenched her hands on her lap. She wasn't sure where to look, torn between a fascination with the man who shared her blood—similar to the lurid way people seemed to want to stare at car accidents—and the desire to watch Maggie talk. Maggie was ahead in drawing her gaze, especially when she started to talk about his prognosis.

"How much have you told Tam about your condition, Markus?"

"Not much." Even his voice sounded hoarse and worn-out, as if every part of him was slowly dying. "I asked her to come. I wanted her here but didn't want to ask…We haven't spoken in a long time."

Maggie nodded with a sympathetic expression. "I'll fill her in on the details then, shall I?"

"Please."

Tam hadn't ever sat in a room like this one with other family members, having lost touch with all of them long ago, but she'd been in enough hospitals to recognize the respectful way Maggie treated her patient. She didn't talk down to him or act as if he wasn't even in the room and address all her comments and questions to Tam, the healthy one. She seemed ready to be his voice and advocate, without taking control away from him.

"Tam, your father has hepatocellular carcinoma. Primary liver cancer. By the time he began showing symptoms, the cancer was in an advanced stage. He needs a transplant to survive, and even though he's already on a waiting list for a donor, he might not survive long enough to be selected. If you're willing to be tested, we can ascertain if—"

"Whoa, whoa." Tam waved her hands frantically and Maggie stopped talking. "I came just to…to…I don't even know why I'm here, but I sure as hell know it wasn't to give him any part of me. How can you take my liver, anyway? What am I supposed to do after that?"

Maggie took a deep breath, and Tam found herself doing the same in spite of herself. She relaxed a fraction, but she was ready to bolt for the door if anyone came near her with a scalpel.

"A living donor can give part of a healthy liver. That portion is transplanted to the recipient, and both partial livers will grow to an adequate size fairly quickly. A donor"—she held her hand up to stop Tam's protest—"not you, necessarily, would be in the hospital for a week or so. Off work for a couple months. We don't even know if you'd be a suitable match, but if you are, you'd be his best hope for survival. Markus and I have discussed this, and I think you should know he only has two months, maybe three, to live if he doesn't get a transplant."

Tam stared at the blood pressure monitor on the wall behind Maggie. She was glad they didn't have it attached to her, because she'd probably blow it up and put a hole in the fancy new oncology ward. Give her father a piece of her liver? What the hell were he and Maggie thinking? She put a hand on her stomach as if to keep her organs from jumping ship.

"I don't…I've got to go," she said. She was off the chair and halfway down the hall when she heard Maggie calling her name. She wanted to keep running, but she turned to face her. She had to put an end to this organ quest once and for all.

"Don't even try to talk me into this," she hissed, keeping her voice low but determined in the busy hallway. "I barely know that man. He has no right to ask me for anything. You can think I'm a bad person if you want, but I'm not ready to just forgive and sacrifice part of myself because he finally sent me a letter after all these years."

"I would never judge you, Tam. The decision is yours to make, and no one else's." Maggie fidgeted with a heart-shaped locket, twisting the chain around her slender finger. Tam stared at Maggie's hands, and then shook her head, not understanding the pull Maggie had over her. How was she able to distract Tam at a time like this?

"Markus told me you two are estranged, and even though I don't know the details, I can tell you I've seen other families in a similar situation," Maggie continued. "Even a simple meeting with your dad right now would be stressful and overwhelming, let alone having his disease and prognosis added to the mix. Every situation is different, of course, but I've witnessed reunions like this before. I know it's not easy for you. Or for him."

"And I suppose all of those people cried and hugged each other and jumped right on a gurney bound for the operating room?"

"No. Some did, some didn't."

Tam looked away, wishing she'd wake up from this dream. "And the ones who said no. Did they feel guilty after?"

"I have a suggestion, Tam," Maggie said without answering her directly. "We don't even know if you're a good match, and there are several tests we'd need to perform. The first ones are relatively noninvasive, just a blood test, a health assessment, and a CT scan. We can start with those and give you time to process this information before you make a decision. If the results look good, we can reevaluate and determine whether you want to go forward from there. You can say no at any time, and we'll stop."

"I already said no."

"Promise me you'll consider it," Maggie said. "Yes, you'll be potentially saving a man's life, your father's life, but think about yourself, too. I know you believe you're doing that right now by saying no, but imagine how you'll feel in the future. You can always go through the surgery, then walk away and never see each other again. If you refuse to do it now, there's no changing your mind six months down the road."

Tam gave a sort of nod, like she was an inanimate bobblehead, and turned toward the exit. This time, Maggie didn't try to stop her, but Tam felt her gaze burning through her back as she walked away.

Once outside, Tam bent over and put her hands on her knees. She probably looked as bad as Mel and Pam had yesterday. She had a feeling Maggie was trying to protect her from something, some guilt or remorse she'd seen in other family members who had refused to help. But the thought of going through with the surgery seemed just as impossible to handle.

Tam stood up again and walked to her car. She got inside and rested her forehead on the steering wheel. Did she really have a choice? She acted as if she did, but presented in Maggie's soothing voice, her choice was clear. Go through the preliminary tests. She didn't even have to speak with her father to do it. Hopefully, she'd be a bad match and wouldn't have to face the ultimate decision.

And if she was suitable? Given her luck, she probably was. Maybe she'd say no. Or maybe she'd do what Maggie had said. Go through with the surgery and walk away from him without looking back.

Like father, like daughter.

❖

Maggie sat on a folding chair and watched the skydiving video with a growing feeling of dread. She had no doubt about what happened if *anything* went wrong. Splat. Why did she need to be told the different possibilities when the final outcome of all of them was her plummeting to earth?

She signed a release waiver with a shaking hand and sat on the bench waiting for her name to be called while she reviewed the instructions from the short film. She was supposed to have a lesson with her tandem jump instructor, but she went through the process in her mind over and over again. Arms bent and held out from her side at ninety degree angles. Knees bent between the instructor's legs. Head up. Don't panic. She added that one on her own.

What the hell was she doing here, anyway? Just because her last girlfriend had gone off to sail around the world or down the Pacific coast or wherever, why had Maggie needed to reevaluate her own life? She'd said no when Gem had asked her to come along, even though she could easily have managed at least a sabbatical for a short trip if she wasn't ready to commit to a full year of adventure. She didn't miss the girlfriend all that much, and they'd never have been able to stand each other in such close quarters for months at a time, but she'd felt like something was missing in her life once Gem was gone. Something about Maggie herself seemed off once she'd realized how fear ruled her world and dictated her choices.

She jumped out of her seat when her name was called and rubbed sweaty palms on her jeans as she walked to the side of the room and through the door. The back room was hectic, with people everywhere and brightly colored parachutes laid out on the floor. The guy who had called her introduced himself as Mike and pulled a blue jumpsuit off a rack crammed full of them.

"Put this on," he said. "And this helmet."

"Seriously?" Maggie had to laugh at the soft leather hat he thrust in her hand. It wouldn't offer adequate protection if she fell off a bike, let alone out of the fucking sky. "What is this for? To keep my brain from splattering all over the landing zone if we crash?"

He looked at her with raised eyebrows and she sighed, tucking her hair behind her ears and pulling on the helmet. Not everyone appreciated the morbid humor common among the doctors and nurses in her ward. For them, it was a survival mechanism. She stepped into the jumpsuit and zipped it closed. It was at least three sizes too big for her frame and fell to the ground in folds. Mike motioned for her to follow, and she hiked up the legs of her suit and hurried after him as he walked with quick, long strides to a Jeep waiting outside.

Maggie squeezed in between a man and a woman in the backseat. They wore equally ill-fitting suits and had the freaked-out expression she was certain was on her own face, so she guessed they were also first-timers. She'd seen the poster advertising an afternoon of introductory skydiving lessons and had expected an atmosphere of camaraderie and laughter, not the silence of people being transported to their doom. When was Mike going to give her that lesson, anyway?

He and the other instructors chatted in the front seat, and Maggie stared out the window as they drove the short distance from the skydiving base to the runway. Soon she'd be parachuting back to that base, where her sister Jocelyn would be to greet her with a hug and a bottle of champagne. She was ready to skip right to the drinking portion of the afternoon.

Still, she had made a vow to be more daring. She had been living with too much care and caution, barely getting out of her television and frozen meal rut long enough to go to lunch with Joss or to book club. She faced life and death every day at her job, and she wouldn't trade what she did for anything, but she'd felt something slip out of her grasp when she'd been immobilized by the thought of leaving with Gem.

So here she was, on some idiotic, quixotic quest. Did she really want to jump out of an airplane that wasn't on fire or experiencing some other emergency? Or was it merely the most stereotypical daredevil feat she could consider doing?

The Jeep hit a bump in the road, and Maggie gasped audibly. She felt her face flush with embarrassment, but her two seatmates didn't seem to notice anything. They were probably too busy watching their own lives flash through their own minds and couldn't be bothered with hers.

Maggie gave up pondering the steps that had gotten her here and thought instead about the proud and angry woman she had met two days ago. Tam. Striking, with her blond hair and green eyes that were as impenetrable as an old-growth forest. Hurting like a child, but strong and fiercely independent. Maggie had been dealing with Markus long enough to see the similarities between the two. Somewhat in looks, and a whole lot in bearing. Markus had stooped low enough to ask Tam to come to the hospital but wouldn't go further and ask her to be a potential donor. Tam would probably be the exact same way if their roles were reversed. Well, would Tam have even written to Markus at all? Probably not.

The Jeep stopped, interrupting Maggie's thoughts of Tam. She was a good distraction, even able to push the images of ripped parachutes and broken ripcords from Maggie's mind and replace them with ones of Tam's full lips curved in a frown or her beautifully muscled forearms when she wrapped them protectively around herself.

Maybe Maggie should get her mind back on the dangers of skydiving. Her attraction to Tam wasn't exactly taboo—Tam wasn't her patient and never would be. The transplant, were it to occur, would happen at a large hospital in Portland or Seattle. But Tam didn't seem like the average girl next door. Maggie had a feeling that dating her would be as hazardous to her heart as jumping out of this plane could be to her body.

"Put this on," Mike said, handing Maggie a nylon harness with thick straps. Were those the only words he knew? She stepped into the harness and he pulled the straps tight, bunching her baggy jumpsuit until she looked like she was wearing an extra-large Hefty bag with a snug belt.

"We'll jump at thirteen thousand feet. I'll hook our harnesses together a few thousand feet before that. Once we're out of the plane, don't grab me or any part of the harness or chute. Got it?"

Maggie nodded weakly. That was all she was getting from him? She'd expected an outlined lesson plan, some diagrams on a whiteboard, or a PowerPoint presentation. Maybe a quiz at the end to make sure she had assimilated the information. She sighed and followed him and the others as they trudged toward a teeny plane. Everything but the two front seats had been removed, leaving a small empty space for them to sit. A hole in the side of the plane, presumably where she'd be making her exit, was covered by a piece of canvas they kept insisting on calling a door. Doors, in Maggie's mind, should be solid and not flap in the breeze. She wedged herself in front of Mike's knees and scrunched in a ball.

Maggie let her mind wander back to Tam as the plane taxied to the runway. Two days, and she still hadn't heard from her. She couldn't interfere beyond giving her and Markus the facts about his prognosis and the transplant procedure, but she hoped for Tam's sake that she'd make the decision to go ahead with the initial tests. She'd witnessed it firsthand—rarely, but enough for it to make an impression on her—when long-lost relatives refused to help and then changed their minds after it was too late. She couldn't bear to have Tam go through the emotional trauma it would likely cause. Better to do what she could to keep her dad alive, even if she never moved beyond hating him to forgiveness.

Maggie's throat felt paralyzed as the plane took off, bucking in turbulence as it climbed, and she fought down panic as she tried to swallow and couldn't. She forced herself to relax, recalling her conversation with Tam. She hadn't been able to stop herself from stretching her boundary of acceptable interference just a little. Tam was pushing her away, pushing her father away, but Maggie sensed she wasn't as unmoved by his situation as she pretended to be. She seemed to be someone who felt deeply, whether it was anger or defiance, and Maggie wanted her to make a decision that would bring her peace of mind, not the opposite.

The plane gained altitude in large, lazy circles. When she thought they must certainly be high enough to jump, she checked the altimeter on Mike's wrist, where it rested on his knee. Twelve hundred feet. Only eleven thousand eight hundred to go. If she lived through this delightful adventure she'd gotten herself into, maybe she'd hear good news from Tam next week. Maybe she'd agree to start the tests. And then, Maggie would have a chance to see her again. She wanted to see her again, almost as much as she wanted to get her feet back on solid ground. She usually didn't feel this way about the people she met while on the job, no matter how attractive or interested in her they seemed to be. Tam was different somehow. She'd been on Maggie's mind since they'd met. Maggie had to keep distance between her personal life and the people she met through work. She used to pride herself on finding balance between maintaining a necessary detachment and still caring deeply about her patients, but lately she'd been listing dangerously close to an excess of the latter. The internal turbulence she'd been feeling since

Gem left had weakened her defenses, and she'd realized she had to make some changes. She had to face her personal fears before they took control. Otherwise, she'd be consumed by the fears of her patients and their families.

Maggie reached under the collar of her jumpsuit and fiddled with her locket, suddenly ready to jump and have the wind knock some of the painful memories she carried with her out of her mind. Too many sad stories for one person to bear. Sure, there were recoveries, both miraculous and expected, but sometimes the sad held more weight in her heart.

Mike tapped her on the shoulder, and Maggie moved in front of him as he buckled her to his own harness. The next minutes were a blur as one by one the other student-and-instructor pairs jumped. She was just about to say she'd changed her mind when they were out of the plane.

In the video, the skydivers had wafted through the air with upbeat background music, but in reality, Maggie was flung into chaos. The rushing sound reminded her of plunging into the ocean. Hearing and not hearing at the same time. Her cheeks lost all tension and flapped in the wind. Did she bend her arms and knees and keep her head up? She had no idea since time seemed to blur as she tried to reconcile the feeling of motionlessness with dropping out of the sky at a tremendous rate.

She yelped when the parachute opened and broke their fall with a sudden jerk on the harness between her legs and under her arms. She was going to feel that tomorrow. She caught her breath as they floated toward the ground in a more controlled manner, and she managed to enjoy the swing of her legs every time Mike corrected their course.

One last turn, and they swooped down to the gravel landing site. A whole lot of scary preparation for a few seconds of cacophony. Had she changed anything about herself, or proved anything? She didn't feel different, just a little more battered. She ran a few yards once her feet touched the ground, trying to get her balance back, and she would have fallen on her face if Mike hadn't held her upright. Once they were standing still, he unbuckled her and Jocelyn bounded over with a big grin.

"You were so tiny up there when you jumped," she said, squeezing Maggie tightly. Jocelyn's girlfriend, Ari, stepped up next to hug her.

"What did you think?" Jocelyn asked. "Was it fun? Would you do it again?"

"I'm not sure to the first, and no to the second," Maggie said, pulling off the leather helmet and running a hand through her damp, flattened hair. She felt as if her body had been put through some daunting ordeal, like running a marathon, when all she'd really done had been to dangle in the air. "I think once is enough. Where's the champagne?"

"Back at the car," Jocelyn said with a laugh. She tucked her arm in Maggie's and leaned her head on her shoulder as they walked. "I was worried about you."

"So was I," Maggie admitted. They stopped to drop off her jumpsuit and helmet before going to the car. An indifferent clerk tossed the suit on top of a pile behind her in what seemed to Maggie to be an anticlimactic ending to her afternoon. "I guess it was worth doing once."

"Can you describe what you were feeling when you were on the plane?" Ari asked, pulling a notepad and pen out of her back pocket. "What did it sound like? What were you thinking?"

Maggie wasn't about to admit she'd been thinking about Tam to her sister's author girlfriend. "Are you interviewing me for a book?"

Ari shrugged. "Maybe, or a story. I wanted to get your impressions while they're still fresh."

Maggie looked at Jocelyn for support, but she was gazing at Ari with a look of absolute adoration. Maggie rolled her eyes. "Why don't you go in and sign up? You can jump today and write your own notes."

"Are you kidding? I saw your face before you went up, and you looked even worse when you landed again. I'm staying on the ground, thanks."

Jocelyn poured them all some champagne, and they leaned against her bumper and toasted Maggie's step toward bravery. She fended off Ari's questions and watched the two of them snuggled up against each other and felt something lacking still. She'd jumped out of a plane, she'd been scuba diving, and she'd gone on a miserable spur-of-the-moment trip to a Mexican resort. She didn't feel any different, any more fulfilled. She was no closer to feeling unbound and fearless than she'd been before Gem left.

Maggie drained her paper cup and let Jocelyn pour her another. She sighed. On to the next adventure. Maybe this one would be the key to changing her life.

❖

Tam went to the hospital and stood outside her father's room, leaning against the wall and not making a move to either leave or go inside. She kind of wanted someone to call security and have her ass hauled out of the ward, but the nurses and other patients walked past her as if she belonged there.

She'd called Maggie and told her to go ahead and schedule the tests. Maggie had sounded relieved over the phone and hadn't wasted any time getting Tam's appointments set up. She was right. Tam didn't have anything to lose at this point. She could always say no before anyone started to cut her open. Besides, she needed to figure out why she had accepted the job at Cannon Beach after getting the letter about his cancer. The new field office had been created after the oil spill, and Tam was offered the job since she had ties to the community from her past and from the work she had done here in the aftermath of the disaster. She'd turned it down, preferring to stay in the more neutral town of Newport. She'd never been there as a child. But as soon as she'd heard about her father, she had applied for the new post, barely making the deadline. Why? Why hadn't she just tossed the letter in the trash and forgotten it?

Tam opened the door and walked in without knocking. Her father was lying in the same position as before, eyes closed even though the television was turned on. She hadn't made any attempt to be silent like she had the last time, and he opened his eyes as soon as she got close to his bed.

"Hello, Tam," he said. He'd always called her Tamsyn, but he must have listened when she gave her shortened name to Maggie.

"Where were you?" she asked instead of returning his greeting. What a strange question, spanning over thirty years. It might take hours to answer, and Tam wasn't going to hang around that long.

"All over the place. Nowhere important." He paused, as if those few words had worn him out. "Fishing in Alaska, oil rigs off the coast of Louisiana. Kuwait for a few years. Wherever the money was, I'd follow. I was young and foolish, Tam. Not ready to settle down and have a family. I made a mistake leaving you after your mom and I split up, but I didn't realize until too late."

"And you didn't try to contact me until you needed something." Neither of her parents had been ready for family life. Tam had been a mistake, and her dad had been the first to leave. Her mom was next, leaving Tam with her grandparents while she pursued second-rate acting and modeling jobs. At least she would visit every once in a while.

"I thought about you all the time," Markus said.

"Oh, okay. That makes it better. Is this where you pull out the scrapbook with photos of my first piano recital and my graduation and tell me you've been secretly keeping track of my life?"

He sighed and his fingers moved on the sheet again, as if he was winding a rope. Tam had a sudden flashback to her first lesson in a sailboat, a year before her capsized rowboat incident. Her dad had taken her out on the ocean, and she'd laughed at the breeze and the powerful swells. She'd forgotten that day, mistakenly remembering another time as her first sailing experience.

"I don't have a scrapbook, Tam. I don't know where you went to college or anyone you've dated or what you do for a living. Yes, I only contacted you because of this damn cancer, but it's brought us here together. We've got a second chance, no matter how it came about. I don't want to blow it again."

"Too late," Tam said. She turned and walked out of the room, leaving him there alone. She could have left the hospital, too, like she had last week, but instead she consulted a directory and found Maggie's office.

"Tam, come in," Maggie said with her wonderful smile when she saw Tam standing in her doorway. She pulled a file across her desk and opened it. "Thank you for being here today. We'll pull some blood and have you fill out this questionnaire, and then a coworker of mine will give you a physical. Nothing major, just a general health check."

Tam wondered why Maggie wasn't doing the physical, but she didn't dare ask. She wouldn't lie and say she hadn't pictured Maggie's hands on her, but she'd prefer it to happen somewhere outside of a doctor's office. She'd be less awkward having someone else see her naked and prod her stomach and glands.

"I saw my father," she said. She'd guessed Maggie wouldn't ask, but she wanted her to know.

Maggie closed the folder and rested her clasped hands on it. "How did the visit go?"

Tam shrugged. "He didn't apologize or anything. Just said he hadn't wanted to be tied down, and he told me some of the places he went after he left us."

"Do you still want to go ahead with the evaluation today?" Maggie fingered her locket and Tam watched the patterned gold reflect the light from Maggie's desk lamp.

"Yes." Tam hesitated. She wanted to talk more about her past and about her confusing feelings toward her father, but she changed the subject instead. "You play with your locket sometimes," she said, her eyes on Maggie's hand and the delicate pendant cradled in it. "Is it a family heirloom?"

"Hmm, I suppose it is," Maggie said, glancing down at the necklace. She lowered her hand to her lap. "My twin sister had cancer when we were children. Leukemia. There were times when we didn't think she'd survive the night, let alone make it through childhood, but she did. During one of those bad times, an aunt gave me this locket with a tiny braid of Jocelyn's hair in it. She said I should have something to remember her by if she died."

Tam shuddered at the misguided and callous words. She could

see the residue of young Maggie's reaction in the expression on the adult Maggie's face. "How cruel."

Maggie touched her locket again, running her thumb over the gold. "I agree. I'm sure she meant well, but what an awful thing to say to a child. I wouldn't leave Jocelyn's side for weeks after that. Whenever someone tried to get me away or put me in my own bed, I'd scream and cry, so they let me stay with her."

"And you still wear it?" Tam asked. She was amazed by Maggie. Her decision to specialize in oncology had to have roots in her sister's illness. She was helping other families through the very situation she'd experienced as a child.

"I do. It reminds me that none of us knows the future. My aunt passed away four years ago, and Jocelyn is alive and well."

"Jocelyn. The owner of the bookstore in town?" Tam had been wondering why Maggie looked vaguely familiar. She'd thought she must have been one of the volunteers after the oil spill, helping to clean the birds and animals. Tam didn't believe she would have walked past Maggie anytime, in any situation, and not notice her. "I met her when I worked at the rescue center after the spill. I was in her shop a couple of times, too."

Maggie laughed. "Did she recommend just the right book for you to read?"

"Three of them, actually. I thought it might have been a sales gimmick, but then I started reading the books and realized she was eerily accurate with her choices. She looked healthy and happy. I take it she made a full recovery?"

"Yes. After chemo, surgery, radiation, and a stem-cell transplant."

"From you." Tam didn't need to ask the question, she simply stated it as a fact. Maggie had looked away when she mentioned that aspect of Jocelyn's treatment. She had no doubt Maggie, even as a child, hadn't hesitated to offer anything her sister might have needed to survive. "Given freely, I'm sure."

"Tam, don't compare our situations. She's my twin, and we've always been close. We still are. Would I have made a different choice if I'd been older? If we'd lost touch for years, or if she'd been someone who had abandoned me? Perhaps. Every situation is different, but some things are the same in this ward. Entire families, not just the patients, experience emotional upheaval and face nearly impossible choices."

Maggie came around her desk and leaned against it near Tam's chair. "I'm here for you, Tam, if you ever need to talk. I'll explain the procedures as many times as you need and answer any questions you might have. If you just want a friend to talk to, I'm available for that, too."

Tam wanted to shift her legs an inch or two to the right and make contact with Maggie's calves. She reminded herself that Maggie was only making this offer because of her job, not because she cared about Tam in particular. She might take her up on it, though. If only because she wanted a chance to spend more time with her and learn more about her.

Tam stood, her leg gently brushing against Maggie's. The barest of touches, but the sensation coursed through Tam's nerves until she felt as if Maggie was touching her everywhere.

"Maybe, someday. I'm sure I'll have questions as we go along." Tam cleared her throat. She was trying to sound noncommittal and unaffected by Maggie's closeness. She needed to get away before she made a fool of herself and asked Maggie on a date when she was only trying to be a kind and helpful physician. Tam grabbed at the first excuse she could call to mind. "I should go. I wouldn't want to be late for my doctor's appointment."

Tam left the office and closed the door, leaning against it for a moment before walking toward the elevator. She was strong and didn't rely on anyone. Usually. Now she was forging a distant but undeniable connection with her father by agreeing to the tests, and she seemed to have a crush on his doctor. She'd get through the day and get out of this place. On her boat, on the open sea, and heading south. Away from Cannon Beach and all the complications it seemed to provoke.

❖

Maggie came through the open front door to the Sea Glass Inn and poked her head in the kitchen, looking for Mel. The room was empty, as were the dining and living rooms. She leaned against the banister of the staircase leading down to the private downstairs rooms.

"Mel? Pam? Are you here?" she called. No answer. A glance out the kitchen window let her know Pam wasn't in her art studio. Maggie sighed. She'd hoped to find her friends here and had used Jocelyn's book club as an excuse to come to the inn. Usually members came to the bookstore and bought copies of the next month's selection, but these had been delivered behind schedule, and Maggie had volunteered to bring them here.

She put the books on the kitchen counter and snagged a couple of cookies from a jar shaped like a killer whale. Mel always kept it full of something sweet for her guests, and Maggie couldn't resist a snickerdoodle. She took another for the road and was about to leave when the real reason she had come to the inn walked down the main staircase.

Tam was wearing cargo pants and a long-sleeved T-shirt with the Oregon State beaver mascot emblazoned across the chest. Her blond hair was clipped off her face and she had an army-green backpack slung over one shoulder. As one of Maggie's attempts at bravery, she had come here to casually prod Mel and Pam for information about their houseguest. She knew little about Tam except that she had a job here in town but no place to live yet. Maggie wasn't sure her fledgling courage was ready for a direct conversation outside the comfort zone of her hospital, but she didn't have a choice. Tam saw her and changed course, coming into the kitchen instead of continuing on toward the front door.

"Hi, Maggie. What brings you here? Oh no…"

Maggie's smile faded as she watched Tam move one step ahead of her to the wrong conclusion. "Your dad is fine, Tam," she hastened to assure her. "I didn't mean to frighten you."

Tam brushed off Maggie's concern with a sound of dismissal, but Maggie had seen Tam's expression change from a friendly smile of greeting to a pale look of concern in a heartbeat. "You didn't. I just didn't expect to see you here."

Maggie held up a cookie. Tam was obviously disconcerted by her own concern about her father. She kept emphasizing the distance between them, but she had been visibly shaken when she thought Maggie was here with bad news. Maggie knew her best option was to change the subject and let Tam deal with her emotions in her own time. "I'm here to deliver books and to swipe a snack. You look ready for a trek."

"I'm checking some inland ponds today. Counting birds, collecting blood samples, checking for oil residue. That sort of thing. My favorite part of my job."

Maggie leaned her hip against the counter. "I don't even know where you work."

"That's funny," Tam said with a wry grin. "Since you've learned more about my personal life and past than most people know. I'm in charge of the new Department of Fish and Wildlife field office in Cannon Beach."

"Ah," Maggie said. She wasn't sure how to keep Tam here and talking when she had work to do. Next best thing? "Can I come with you?"

Tam raised her eyebrows. "Are you sure? It involves a lot of slogging through marshy areas and the occasional dunking if you slip and fall."

"I don't mind a little pond water," Maggie said, trying to keep her mind off all the water- and mosquito-borne diseases she'd learned about in medical school. "There aren't leeches, though, are there? I'll have to draw the line at leeches."

"Don't worry. I'll pluck them off you if we encounter any."

"Comforting," Maggie said. "I'd offer to reciprocate, but no way am I touching one."

Tam laughed. "Okay. I'll be in charge of leech removal." She fished through her backpack and got out a plastic bag with a spiral-bound notebook and pen inside. "You can be the record keeper."

Tam held out the bag, but Maggie didn't take it. "You want me to be your secretary?"

"No? Well, how about you be in charge of counting lice eggs on the birds we capture." She started to return the notebook to her backpack, but Maggie reached for it.

"I have really neat penmanship," she said. "You can add lice to your list of duties."

"Cool. Come on. I have an extra pair of waders in the car."

Maggie got in Tam's white SUV and buckled her seat belt. Such normal actions, but she felt more alive than she had during her skydiving adventure. This was the feeling she had been looking for. She'd done things she thought of as brave or foolhardy or exciting, hoping to feel a rush of pride in conquering her fears. Instead, she had felt let down, as if the accomplishments meant little or nothing in her life. Somehow sitting here with Tam, about to spend some of her day off traipsing through swamps, had more meaning than anything else she'd done lately.

"Any news on my test results?" Tam asked with a seemingly feigned air of indifference. She glanced over her shoulder and backed onto the road.

"Too soon to say," Maggie said. She'd seen the preliminary results, of course, and the likelihood was good that Tam would be a suitable donor. She didn't like to speculate, though. Her instincts were usually right, but she couldn't offer them as a medical opinion. She also thought Tam might be better off with a little more time to think about the role she was willing to play in her dad's treatment.

"We've sent the packet to the surgeon in Portland who would perform the transplant. He'll either give us an answer soon, or ask for more tests to be performed."

"More needles. Great."

"Oh, do they bother you?" Maggie asked. She gently poked Tam in the ribs. "We can always use leeches to suck out your blood instead."

"Let's stick with needles." Tam laughed and grabbed Maggie's hand, holding it for a long moment before she let go. She sighed then, and her smile vanished. "You said you see people with relationship issues all the time. How do they forgive and move on? I thought my father had taken everything he could from me. My childhood, my mother, the relationships I have now. He took those from me and changed them forever. And now he wants more. What if he takes my liver and disappears from my life again? Or worse, what if he wants to barge in to my life?"

Maggie looked out at the passing scenery while she gathered her thoughts. Dark fir trees were interspersed with lighter green deciduous growth. Spring was filling in the spaces left by winter. She stared at the thick vegetation, parting now and again to give glimpses of the gray, wintery Pacific Ocean, and considered different philosophical arguments for forgiving and letting go, case studies or personal stories to help guide Tam to a decision she would be able to live with. Maggie rejected them all. She couldn't guarantee Tam's father would stick around, or that Tam would even want him back in her life.

"What if there was a person on the side of the road, wounded and bleeding," she said, condensing her philosophy to its simplest form. "Would you drive by and ignore him, or stop to help? And if you stop, would you interrogate him before you stopped the bleeding? Maybe ask him what he's done wrong in his life, or demand to know if he'll stick around and be your friend after you help him? Or do you save his life, just because it's…"

"The right thing to do." Tam finished the sentence.

"I wasn't going to say that," Maggie said. "No right or wrong, just what is most aligned with who *you* are. Not who he is, what he's done, or what he'll do in the future."

Tam turned off the main highway onto a rutted, barely paved road. She rubbed her forehead with her left hand. "You make everything seem so clear when you're talking to me. But when I'm alone, I have questions and doubts. Yes, I'd stop to help anybody who's hurt, but this is personal, not general."

Tam parked on the shoulder at a wide spot on the road, but she didn't make any move to get out of the car.

"I understand," Maggie said. "It's not like you're handing your dad a pill to take and he'll get better. You're going through an invasive procedure and giving him something that is part of your body. Your essence. Or"—she shrugged—"just think of it like you're giving him a pill that will make him better. After a short time, you won't even notice it's gone."

Tam put her hand on her belly in a gesture Maggie had seen her make several times, as if reassuring herself that she was still intact. After a moment, Tam sighed and raised her hand, brushing Maggie's cheek with her fingers. Maggie felt the roughness of outdoor work in Tam's touch and she craved more. Too soon, though, Tam moved away and opened her car door.

Maggie got out, too, and climbed into the rubber waders Tam found in the back of her car. The loose fit and unyielding material took time to get used to as she followed Tam along what must have been a deer trail. The spring day was chilly, but whenever the sun found strength to break through the clouds, the temperature inside the rubber boots rose uncomfortably high. First the baggy jumpsuit and now the too-large waders. Maggie decided she needed to find an adventurous hobby with a better-fitting wardrobe.

She imitated Tam and dropped to a crouching walk as the trees thinned. Maggie was looking ahead, trying to figure out how a pond could possibly be hidden among all these trees, when Tam reached out and grabbed her around the waist.

"Careful," she whispered, pointing at the ground. The solid dirt changed to wet muck right in front of Maggie. Tam kept her hand and led her past the thick mud and up a small incline. Once they reached the base of a huge cottonwood, the forest seemed to expand and create space for the wide, still body of water.

"Oh." Maggie exhaled softly as she looked around. Glistening red and blue dragonflies zipped past, occasionally settling on the surface of the water. Birds flitted overhead, tiny silhouettes of dark among the bright leaves. Shadows from the canopy of trees speckled the entire area. Tam sat with her back to the tree and patted the ground next to her. Maggie squeezed close beside her, awed by the small circle of magic she'd never realized existed so close to her home.

Tam gestured at the notebook, and Maggie gingerly opened the plastic bag and took it out as quietly as she could. Tam handed Maggie a pair of binoculars before she raised her own to her eyes and began to whisper types and numbers of birds. At first, Maggie merely transcribed what Tam was saying, but she soon caught on to the methodical way Tam identified and estimated bird species. Before long, Maggie was adding her own notes to the margin of the page and pointing out birds she recognized to Tam.

"Look! A heron." Maggie kept her voice low, but she pinched Tam's arm in her excitement. "They're my favorite. And there's another one, under that low-hanging branch."

"Ouch," Tam hissed. She panned across the clearing with her binoculars. "Good sighting. Watch, Maggie, he's about to catch a fish."

Maggie saw the heron make a quick lunge and come up with a thin silvery fish in its mouth. If she had blinked, she would have missed the moment. She sighed and leaned back, reveling in the sensation of having the entire length of Tam's body pressed against her own. Just like life, she thought. Blink, and it's gone. She'd missed so much by being cautious and afraid, but even when she pushed out of her comfort zone, she didn't feel like she was living better or larger than usual.

This moment, right here with Tam and the heron and the dappled shadows, was something to be treasured. This was Tam's world, though, and Maggie was only visiting. She saw lives cut short every day at her job. Relationships left unhealed and dreams left unfulfilled. She had taken her job because she believed life was precious and she wanted to help prolong and enrich it for her patients. She, of all people, should be out living her life to the fullest every day, every moment because she knew how fragile health and the future really were. Instead, she went home alone night after night and eased the tension from her day by watching TV.

Maggie reached for Tam's hand and gave it a squeeze as the heron's sharp bill flashed out of the water with another fish.

❖

Tam leaned over Maggie's shoulder and added a note about a lone cedar waxwing. Being this close to Maggie and inhaling her delicate citrusy scent with every breath was intoxicating. Tam had been cautious at first when Maggie had offered to come with her today. She barely knew Maggie outside of the realm of the hospital's oncology ward. She was attracted to her, without a doubt, but that didn't necessarily translate into an easy few hours in someone's company. Besides, Tam preferred to work alone whenever possible.

Tam usually started her field excursions with quiet observation, like they had today, watching undisturbed life in the pond or ocean take place in front of her eyes before she had to step in and disrupt it. She'd waited longer than usual today before starting actual fieldwork because she'd loved the peaceful feeling of sitting close to Maggie. The contact with Maggie's thighs and hips was arousing, but the companionable way they'd communicated through whisper and touch had been more intimate than anything Tam had experienced before. They'd shared the thrill of the heron's fishing and had laughed quietly together at the antics of a tiny nuthatch. Tam hadn't wanted the closeness to end.

Of course, closeness and intimacy always ended. Tam might be angry with her father and reluctant to assume this new role in his life, but she was definitely his daughter. She'd inherited his need to roam and his inability to stay in a relationship. She'd tried hard but had never been able to form a tight enough bond to keep her in place. She was lonely sometimes, but it was her choice and her personality.

Maggie was probably someone who forged deep and lasting connections. She and her sister sounded very close, and she seemed to have good friends within the community. Already, Tam could feel a web spreading over her and Maggie as they expanded the sphere of their relationship from a professional one at the hospital to a friendlier one out here in the woods.

Tam shouldn't lead Maggie on. She liked her, yes. Was attracted to her and interested in her life and thoughts. But she was destined to wander. To leave. Maggie deserved better. She was a nurturer, giving her attention and energy to her patients and guiding people through traumatic times with empathy and compassion. She needed someone who would be there for her forever, no matter what. Tam was reluctant to break the still and quiet sphere they'd created under the cottonwood tree, but she needed to separate from Maggie for both their sakes.

Tam pulled her backpack between her knees and gathered her supplies, stuffing the pockets of her vest and pants with vials, sample kits, and leg bands. She usually had to balance her notebook and equipment on her own, often dropping something vital in the water, and she was glad to have an extra set of hands. She wasn't sure what to expect from Maggie, though. She'd been funny when she acted squeamish about the leeches back at the inn, but once it came time to get dirty and do fieldwork, how would she react?

Maggie, of course, surprised her. She didn't hesitate or hold back no matter what Tam asked her to do. She waded through the opaque water of the pond without a peep of concern, and held whatever bird or frog or bug Tam managed to catch.

"You're great with birds," Tam said as she ruffled the feathers of a small wood duck she'd captured, checking for any sign of oil. Maggie cradled the duck against her stomach while Tam took a blood sample and attached a band to its leg. She had the right balance between handling the fragile creatures gently and being firm enough to keep the birds from flailing and hurting themselves. "Did you work at the rescue center after the spill?"

"A few times," Maggie said. "I had a lot of patients and not much time, so I did more beach cleanup than work at the center. I could be out there at sunrise and shovel dirty sand for a few hours before I had to be at the hospital. I don't think our paths crossed at all. I'd certainly have remembered you."

"Same here," Tam said, not meeting Maggie's eyes. "You can let her go. She's clean."

Maggie lowered the duck onto the surface of the pond and stepped back with a laugh as the bird skittered away with a spray of water.

"You do great work at the hospital," Tam said as she scribbled notes about the wood duck. "I admire you for volunteering on top of all you do."

Maggie shrugged. "I wish I'd done more."

Tam bent down to collect water samples from varying depths. She capped the first one and handed it to Maggie. "How do you handle it? All the emotions and loss you face every day, I mean. I'm having a hard enough time dealing with the intensity of having my father there and reliving our past relationship, but you have an entire ward full of patients. You seem to truly care about them, too."

Maggie wrapped her hands around the small stack of vials filled with murky pond water. "I do care, but I have to set limits. Even though I chose this field for emotional reasons, the only way to survive it is to remain as unemotional as possible and to support my patients by searching for solutions and evaluating options with a clear head." She hesitated. "When I was young, I felt helpless to cure Joss, and I decided really early that I wanted to become a doctor, so I'd be able to help people like her and have some control over the threat of death. Her illness frightened me to my core, but I've been able to keep that fear separate from my work. Until lately, when it's been sort of…leaking through. The suffering and sorrow I'm exposed to have been taking something out of me, piece by piece. I shouldn't let it happen."

Tam stood still, her samples and notes forgotten as she watched Maggie's expression change. Tam remembered her gorgeous smile when they'd first met. She'd seen it again today, several times during their observation session. She knew the light in Maggie was genuine, but she hadn't realized what she was going through inside and she was surprised and honored that Maggie had shared this internal struggle with her. Maggie looked as surprised by her revelations as Tam felt. Tam stuck her notebook and the vials in her pants pocket and moved closer to Maggie. She cradled Maggie's face in her hands and kissed her.

She meant it as an expression of sympathy and of gratitude. Tam and her father were two of the people who were stealing part of Maggie's soul. Her father's cancer was advanced, and they brought plenty of family drama into the hospital ward. Tam wanted to thank Maggie in some way and apologize in another. She thought a tender kiss would convey what she was feeling more than words could do.

Tam didn't expect the reaction she had to the kiss. She was

giving it away, offering it to Maggie, but she was the one who received an infusion of energy and heat. Standing thigh deep in pond water, wearing rubber waders that left her feet chilled and her legs sweaty, Tam was too uncomfortable to feel desire. Or so she thought. She opened her mouth at the gentle pressure from Maggie's tongue, and suddenly her world exploded. Her discomfort, the setting, and the reality of the hospital ward faded away as Maggie wrapped her arms around Tam's neck and pressed her body close. Tam gripped Maggie's hips and groaned at the sweet onslaught of Maggie's tongue. She broke away long enough to kiss Maggie's neck from her shoulder to a spot just behind Maggie's ear that seemed to drive her crazy.

Back to her mouth. The delicious scratch of Maggie's short nails on her scalp. A thigh pressed between her legs and resting snugly against the crotch of her pants. If they hadn't been standing in the water, they'd be on the ground now with clothes coming off. Tam stepped back too fast and slipped, almost falling on her ass in the pond.

Maggie reached out to steady her, with a hand under each of Tam's elbows. Even the non-intimate touch rubbed Tam's nerves raw.

"I didn't expect..." Tam hadn't expected any of this. Her father's letter, his revelations, her own crazy relocation to be near him, or her conflicting refusal to spend time with him. Even more bewildering was Maggie. From the moment Tam had seen her smile, she'd been hooked. Their situation had forced a closeness Tam had welcomed at first, but now it was moving too fast.

Tam shook her head. She and Maggie had shared personal information because of their circumstances—Maggie was helping her work through the issues with her father and the transplant process. But Tam had a feeling she'd have melted into Maggie's kiss the same way if they'd met casually at a bar or mall. Sickness and doubts and guilt surrounded them, but the only reality that mattered was taking place between the two of them. Separate from everything and everyone else.

The realization struck Tam as hard as the kiss had. She'd be better able to cope if she could explain away her feelings for Maggie as the by-product of her emotional reunion with her father, but she couldn't.

Tam stepped away again, more carefully this time. She wondered if Maggie could somehow read her thoughts, because her expression seemed to grow distant while Tam's mind was trying to do the same thing.

"The situation between us is complex," Maggie said slowly, as if choosing her words carefully. "I think this would be a good time to take a step back. Put some space between us while we sort through our feelings. Separately." Maggie paused. "On our own."

"Yeah, I got that," Tam said. Why was she annoyed by the *I need space* speech when she had been about to give the same one to Maggie? "Look, I've got enough samples from this location. Why don't I drive you back to your car and you can have all the separation you need."

"Tam, wait," Maggie said, splashing after her as she walked away. "The kiss was wonderful. You are wonderful. I'm just not ready—"

Tam stopped and held up her hand. "I get it, Maggie. I don't want to get too involved any more than you do. Just spare me the clichés."

Maggie nodded, her eyes red as if she was holding back tears. Tears of what? Pity for Tam? Regret over the kiss? Or sadness because neither of them had been ready for the fire they ignited between them? Tam wasn't sure. She turned and walked back to her car.

❖

Maggie tapped on the plate-glass window of the Beachcomber Bookstore and waved at her twin sister Jocelyn, who was setting up a display in the front case. Jocelyn smiled and extricated herself from the book-filled dormer while Maggie opened the door and went inside. Jocelyn came over and gave her a big hug. She had been kneeling in the cramped window space, baked by the heat of the sun coming through the glass, but she somehow looked as if she'd just hopped out of the shower and into a designer outfit. Her pinstripe oxford shirt was neatly pressed and unbuttoned enough at the neck to show the curved neckline of a perfectly white tank. Her beige slacks were creased and tidy. In comparison, Maggie felt like something that had recently crawled out of a swamp. Which she had. Her jeans felt glued to her legs after hours in rubber waders, and she'd barely managed to make her red curls look presentable after Tam's hands had been tangled in them.

The thought of their kiss brought flames to Maggie's cheeks and she fanned herself with her hand, hoping to throw her too-perceptive sister off the scent of a juicy story.

"It's warm out there in the sun. It feels good to be inside."

Jocelyn wrinkled her brow. "Yeah, it must be at least…what? Sixty-five degrees out there? A real heat wave."

"Mm-hmm." Maggie wandered toward the counter where her sister always kept a full pot of coffee. "The store looks great, by the way. Ready for the tourist season."

She poured herself a cup of coffee and dumped heaping scoops of sugar and creamer in it before wandering to one of the endcap displays. She avoided looking over at her silent sister and instead studied the display. Stacks of Jocelyn's girlfriend's books were pleasingly arranged, and each one had an autographed-by-author sticker on it. "You must keep Ari busy every night signing books."

"Among other things," Jocelyn said in a self-satisfied voice. Maggie looked at her in surprise and Jocelyn shrugged with a big grin. "What? Haven't you seen someone in love before?"

"Never you and never this much love," Maggie said. She put down her coffee and went over to hug Jocelyn again. "I love knowing you're happy."

"Deliriously." Jocelyn put her hands on Maggie's shoulders and held her at arm's length. "Now stop changing the subject and tell me what's going on with you. You look different somehow. Have you been on another of your adventures? What was it this time—spelunking? Swimming with the sharks?"

"Of course not," Maggie said. She tried to move away but

Jocelyn held her in place. "If I'd done anything like that I would have had you waiting for me with a bottle of champagne if I survived."

"I'm left with only one explanation," Jocelyn said with a smug smile. "Who is she?"

"She? There is no she."

Jocelyn's gaze dropped to Maggie's neck. "Do you have a hickey?"

Crap. Maggie clutched her throat with her hand. She hadn't checked herself carefully enough in the rearview mirror of her car. "No...I mean, I think I'm allergic to something. I've had these hives and—"

Jocelyn pushed her playfully. "I was kidding, Mags. But obviously you were doing something with someone and there was a possibility of a hickey. Tell me about her."

"There's nothing to tell," Maggie said. She walked back to the counter where she'd left her coffee and took a sip. "We kissed, but it's over now. I don't want to talk about it."

"Right. So you came here, to see me. The one person you know will be able to read you and know something's going on. But you don't want to talk about it."

Maggie paused with her cup partway to her mouth. Joss was right, of course. Maggie could have gone directly home after Tam dropped her off at the inn. She could have waited until she was back in control of herself before she saw her sister. What happened between her and Tam was a fluke—emotions were running high because of Tam's situation and Maggie's own internal conflicts. They'd fallen into each other's arms, but they had managed to get away unscathed. Or had they?

"Start with an easy one," Jocelyn said. "Tell me her name."

Maggie waved her hand. "She's no one."

"Okay. What you really mean is she's someone I know. Do you want me to start listing all the residents of Cannon Beach in alphabetical order? I'll see it in your face when I say the right name." Jocelyn headed toward the back of her store where she kept her file cabinet. Of course there'd be a folder in there with Tam's name on it. Could Maggie escape before Jocelyn got to the *K*s?

"Fine. Tamsyn Kalburg." Even saying Tam's name gave Maggie a prickle of delight.

"No way. The Viking goddess? Good job, Mags."

Maggie laughed at the nickname. She hadn't heard it before, but it fit Tam's strong and beautiful appearance. "I guess we're talking about the same woman, but don't congratulate me on anything. We shared one kiss, and now it's over."

But what a kiss it had been. Maggie wouldn't forget it anytime soon, if ever.

"Let me guess. You got scared and pulled back." Jocelyn didn't wait for Maggie's response. "What have we done to you?"

"We?" Maggie asked with a frown.

"Me. Gem. You've been afraid of life since my illness, and Gem pushed you over the edge when she left. You've imploded."

"First of all, don't lump yourself in with her. Yes, maybe I worry about you a little, but I'm getting better." Maggie couldn't lie to Jocelyn. "Well, at least I'm trying. And Gem…well, you never liked her. You should be glad she left."

Jocelyn shook her head. "I'm not glad you got hurt. But no, I didn't think Gem was right for you. She never seemed to make you feel cherished, and a partner should do that for you. She wanted you to change, and you let her convince you that you aren't good enough as you are. Ask me, ask anyone in this town or anyone you've treated at the hospital. You're more than good enough as you are. You're exceptional."

Maggie turned away and stood in silence for a few moments, staring at the books surrounding her. The main displays were for the tourists now. Best sellers and local travel guides. Mass appeal. A veneer of banality similar to what the rest of Cannon Beach's stores showed on the surface. In the background were the books that nourished the people who came to Jocelyn's store. So much of this community was coursing beneath the surface, available only to those who looked deeply for it. Jocelyn fed Maggie the same way she did her regular customers. By reaching inside her and giving her exactly what she needed.

"Tam didn't think I was missing anything," she said. On the

contrary, Tam had seemed to see inside her soul and to like what she saw there. "But it's complicated. She's going through some family things…"

"Then take it slow, Mags, but don't give up completely." Jocelyn came up behind her and put a hand on her shoulder. "You don't need to leap out of a plane or fly to another country to make changes. Sometimes the small steps are the ones that eventually take you farthest."

Maggie sighed and leaned toward Jocelyn's hand. She'd have to jump out of a hundred planes before she'd feel anything close to the emotions Tam's kiss had stirred in her. Jocelyn was right. Maggie really had come here, subconsciously at least, for advice and comfort. Maggie had to accept the former if she wanted the latter. She'd tried to shut out any possibility for her and Tam to repeat today's kiss, but she wouldn't close the door completely. Even the thought of another chance to touch Tam made her terrified and exhilarated at the same time. "Sometimes the small steps are the scariest."

❖

Tam got to the hospital two hours before her scheduled appointment with Maggie. They hadn't spoken in over four days, since their glorious and heartbreaking kiss in the middle of the pond. Maggie had been silent during the car ride back to the inn, not speaking after Tam told her to stop with the typical breakup platitudes. Apparently, she didn't have anything more profound to say to Tam than *I need my space*. Maybe the kiss hadn't meant anything to her.

Tam couldn't get it off her mind. Or out of her dreams and fantasies. Her heart had raced when she'd heard Maggie's voice on the phone yesterday, but all she'd said was that Tam's test results were in and she wanted to discuss them with her.

Without wavering, Tam walked directly to her father's room and opened the door. He was really sleeping this time, his hands still and his face relaxed and sagging slightly. Tam stood by the bed for a few minutes and watched him sleep. Her life had been defined by him leaving. What power he had had over her, even in his absence. Or, rather, because of his absence. He looked very human to her all of a sudden. A man who was sick and asleep.

Tam sighed and pulled the gray chair a little closer to his bed. She sat and curled her feet beneath her, then got out her book and started to read.

She stayed in the same position for over an hour, turning pages with a quiet rustle, and occasionally glancing at her father. When she looked at him the next time, his eyes were open and he was watching her.

"He's one of my favorite authors. Patrick O'Brien," he said, gesturing at her book.

Tam took her time placing a bookmark between pages. "I've never read him before. Jocelyn, Maggie's sister, recommended it to me when I went to her bookstore."

"Ah, the Book Witch," he said with a weak smile. He leaned his head back on the pillow. "That's her nickname around here, because she always seems to know exactly the right title to recommend. She's the one who got me reading him in the first place."

Like father, like daughter. Would the similarities never end? "Why'd you come back here?" she asked. "You left when I was here and came back when I wasn't. I think I'll have to take it personally."

"Not you. Your mother. It was never about you."

Tam opened her mouth to respond, but shut it again. She'd never really thought about their marriage beyond how it affected her. When he'd initially left, she'd been too young to see them as individuals and not just her parents, and the pattern of thinking had stuck. It didn't excuse him, but she felt an odd sensation of stepping off center stage for a brief moment. Her parents' lives would probably have played out the same way whether or not she'd been born. Remembering their fights, sending herself back in time as an observer and not the star, was an interesting experience.

"You're a lot like her, you know," her father said.

Tam laughed without humor. "Again, I'll take that personally. You just said you couldn't be in the same town with her."

Markus waved his hand. "We weren't good for each other. We learned that soon after we got married and had you, but we tried to make it work. By the end, we couldn't be in the same state, let alone city. But I'll always love her, just like I love you. You should have seen her when we first met. Feisty and smart. She had the same way of arching her eyebrow, just like you do, when she was about to say something sarcastic. You take after me more, though."

Tam was wondering whether she'd ever in her life heard her father say so many words at once, but his last sentence jarred her because she'd been thinking the same thing, in a negative way. "I know I do. I'm a roamer, never satisfied to stay in one place. I'm incapable of maintaining relationships and I only think of myself."

"Oh, Tamsyn. Don't imitate my mistakes. You're better than that."

Tam's voice rose and she struggled to keep it from disturbing anyone beyond this room. "Am I? I don't think so. You can't beat genetics." She stood, ready to leave. She didn't want to wait around until Maggie came in and said her liver was the perfect match. Her father held out a hand to stop her. She didn't touch him, but she stayed.

"Do you want to know what parts of myself I see in you? You love books and nature, and you probably spend most of your time alone. You're not a roamer. You're an explorer, an adventurer. And when the right person comes along, you'll be more capable of love and loyalty than you ever dreamed possible."

Tam frowned. The last sentence sounded personal—for her father, not for her. Of course he had found someone else during those three decades, but Tam had assumed he'd had numerous companions, not someone special. The image of him with another family constricted her throat until she could barely breathe, let alone rasp out the questions tumbling through her mind. Where was this mystery woman? Had she died or left or been abandoned like Tam and her mother? And God forbid, did Tam have siblings? The questions might be answered at some point, but right now Tam could only manage to ask a simple one. "Who was she?"

Markus shook his head and looked away. "I'll tell you about

her sometime, if you really want to hear. I wish I'd had that kind of relationship with your mother, but I didn't. And when she found out I was with someone new, she told me never to come back. I should have tried harder to see you."

Tam sighed and sat at the foot of the bed, as weary as her father sounded. "Yes, you should have," she said, but the venom was gone from her voice.

Maggie tapped on the door. "Am I interrupting?"

Tam got to her feet and looked at Maggie. Her face was pale, making her freckles stand out more than usual, and her usually bright smile was dimmed. Had the past four days been hard on her, too?

"No. We were just talking," Tam said.

Maggie looked from her to her father and grinned with more of her usual cheerfulness. "Good to hear. I'm going to steal you away for just a moment, Tam. Then we can come back here and chat."

Tam followed her out the door, unsure where the conversation would lead. Once they were in Maggie's office again, she didn't keep Tam waiting any longer.

"You're a good match, Tam. The surgeon in Portland believes the chance of a successful transplant is quite high. I wanted to tell you in private, to let you think about what you want to do now. This is your medical information, and I'll only share it with your dad if you say I can."

"What's the next step? Provided I say yes, of course."

"You'll need to go to Portland for a procedure to map your liver's blood vessels. They'll most likely do another CT scan as well. Things get more invasive from this point forward, and I think it might be best if you make your decision now, before proceeding."

Tam was silent, and Maggie came around her desk again. Just like the first time they'd met in this office, Maggie stood close enough to touch.

"I'll give you as much time as you need to think this through, Tam. I just want to add that I think you're very brave to have come this far. I know none of this has been easy for you, and I admire what you've done. I think you're an amazing person." Maggie's voice snagged on the last sentence, but she cleared her throat and stood upright. "I can let you have some privacy."

Tam stood as well. She didn't need any more time to think about her decision. She had to make the choice she could live with forever, regardless of the outcome.

"You can tell him I'm a match," she said. "And I guess I'll go back to the inn and pack for a trip to the city."

Maggie's hug nearly knocked the breath out of her. Tam barely had time to squeeze her in return before Maggie moved away and disappeared out the door.

❖

Tam haphazardly threw some clothes and toiletries into a canvas bag. She would only be in Portland for a few nights, and she had a feeling she'd be wearing a hospital gown for most of her stay. Besides, she already had tons of emotional baggage packed and ready to go wherever she went. She'd have plenty of downtime to unpack it and dwell on every aspect of her relationship with her father over the next week.

She zipped the suitcase shut and went outside. She walked past the studio and waved at Aspen, who was working on a new, life-sized sculpture. Aspen returned the wave with a clay-covered hand and a happy smile on her face. Tam wished she had some sort of outlet for her emotions. She'd like to sculpt her pain and emotional upheaval away like Aspen, or write it out like Ari. She didn't even have anyone to talk to about the uncertainty she felt inside.

Except Maggie. Tam turned when she heard someone calling her name and saw Maggie jogging toward her along the backyard path. Maggie was the only one who really understood all sides of Tam's situation.

"Hey. I'm glad I caught you before you left," Maggie said when she reached her. She handed Tam a cloth bag with the Beachcomber logo on the side. "Jocelyn sent these for you to read while you're sitting in waiting rooms in Portland. You are still going, aren't you?"

Tam laughed without humor. "Of course I am. Once I make up my mind, I stick to it." True, but even she had wondered if she'd be as faithful to her word as she usually was. "I just wanted to walk on the beach once more before I go."

"Do you mind some company?"

Tam remembered all too well the last time Maggie had asked to come along with her. The afternoon had been one of the best in Tam's life, and it had ended with a tsunami of a kiss. She cleared her throat and hoped to clear her mind of the memory as well. "Are you keeping an eye on me, making sure I'll really follow through with this?"

Maggie laughed as they started to walk down the staircase leading to the shore. Tam loved the sound, especially when it mingled with the splash of waves. "No. Every step is your decision to make, not mine to force. I just wanted to…to be here if you need to talk."

What had Maggie been about to say? That she just wanted to be with Tam? Tam pushed the thought away and peered into the bag. "What did Jocelyn send? I'm guessing titles like *Fathers and Daughters: Healing Complicated Relationships* or *Know Your Enemy: How to Face and Beat Cancer.*"

Maggie bumped her shoulder into Tam's as they walked along the sand. "Don't worry. I asked her what they were just to make sure she wasn't sending anything like that, but they're fantasy novels. She said sometimes you just need to escape."

Tam folded the bag around the books and held them to her chest. "Tell her thank you. They'll be perfect."

Maggie was silent for a moment. "Speaking of complicated relationships, how is yours? I saw you in his room the other day, but I didn't want to disturb the two of you. You seemed to be…talking."

"As opposed to me snarling at him, as usual?" Tam asked with a wry smile. She was getting accustomed to seeing her father now and could stay in the same room with him without losing control of her voice or feelings. It didn't mean she'd forgiven him or was ready to bond, but it was something. "He was telling me about his second wife. My mom knew he was with someone else, but she never told me. She let me believe he was a player, moving from one relationship to the next."

"Does this change how you see him?" Maggie asked quietly.

Tam thought for a long minute. "No. I mean, it doesn't help me understand why he abandoned me or make it any easier to remember growing up fatherless, but in a way it changes how I see myself."

"Ah."

This time, Tam was the one to bump into Maggie. "What do you mean by that, oh, wise one?"

Maggie looped her arm through Tam's. "*Ah* means I've noticed you relate to your father, even though you're angry with him. You've grown up believing you're just like him, including his alleged philandering ways. When you found out he really wasn't a player, it made you rethink your own need to avoid relationships. Am I close?"

"Uncomfortably so," Tam said. She tightened her hold on Maggie's arm and pulled her a little closer. She should be pushing her away now, getting distance from her and from the conversation, but Maggie was right. Tam had fallen into a life of transient relationships because she figured either she or her partner would be a repeat version of her father. One of them would eventually leave, so it might as well be her. Her father had left her mother, but he'd stayed with his true love. What did that mean for her?

"Nature versus nurture," Maggie said. "You're wrestling with one of the biggies."

"I guess. It's complicated, but at the same time it's simple. If I try to let myself commit to a relationship, will I be like he was with me and my mom, or like he was with his real love?"

Maggie pulled Tam to a stop and faced her. "Or maybe you'll be *you*. If you're with someone you truly love, you won't want to go."

Tam caressed Maggie's cheek with the back of her hand. Maggie wasn't necessarily offering herself as that person, but Tam allowed her own mind to consider the possibility. Would she ever want to walk away from Maggie? Surprising, smart, funny, kind Maggie? Not likely, but she still couldn't be sure. She saw her own conflict and doubt reflected in Maggie's expression. Not for the same reasons, but with the same outcome.

She let her fingers trail down Maggie's neck and saw her breathing increase at the touch. Tam smiled and tugged Maggie back into a walk. "You know my deepest fears now," she said, only half joking. Maggie really did understand her better than anyone ever had. "So tell me, what's yours?"

"I always thought it was death," Maggie admitted. "When Jocelyn was sick, I was so afraid to lose her. I feel something similar, but less personal, with my patients. And when I went skydiving, I was definitely afraid of the parachute not opening and me plunging to my death."

"You went skydiving?" Tam asked. "You'll have to tell me the whole story sometime."

"Okay. It makes my palms sweat to talk about it, but someday I will."

Tam turned her imagination away from the arousing picture of windblown Maggie in a jumpsuit and returned to the topic. "Have you changed your mind about your fear?"

Maggie shrugged and her arm rubbed against Tam's. Tam gave in to the screaming request of her nerve endings and put her arm around Maggie's waist, pulling them closer.

"I see it differently now. Dying is a fact of life. I've seen it met with dignity and acceptance, or with fear, but either way it's something that happens to us. Living is the harder part because we make it happen. It's the choices we make and the dreams we choose. The way we think and act and love. I'm more afraid of not living well and fully than anything else."

Tam walked without speaking, enjoying the feel of Maggie's steps matching hers. Synchronized in movement and thought. Had she ever had a conversation like this with another person? She'd remember if she had. Thoughts openly expressed and minds connecting. "I guess it's a good fear to have. It makes you aware of the choices you make and what they mean. It makes you question assumptions, especially if they're holding you back from living fully."

"Like the assumption that you're incapable of staying in a relationship?"

Tam had to laugh at Maggie's ability to turn her comments back on her. "I suppose so."

Maggie halted again and pulled Tam into one of her warm hugs. She released her and stepped back. "This is going to be a huge week for you. You have a lot going on with your dad and your procedures, and you'll have a lot of time to be alone with your thoughts. You can call me anytime, and turn to Jocelyn's books for an escape, but don't shortchange yourself on these topics. They deserve time and reflection from both of us."

Tam nodded and gave Maggie a kiss on the cheek. Even the brief touch of lips on skin made her want more, but she realized they needed to move apart and let this conversation sink in. She watched Maggie walk back toward the inn without attempting to follow her. This wasn't the same as the way they'd separated at the pond after their kiss. Then there'd been too much left unspoken and too much fear holding them apart. Now there was only the promise of coming together again. Tam turned away from the inn and continued along the beach.

❖

Maggie drove through the dark, winding along the Highway 101 curves she knew by heart. Even though she couldn't see the ocean, she knew when the trees would open and expose breathtaking views. Every passing lane, every roadside scenic view. Gem had criticized her for being a homebody and returning to the town where she and Jocelyn had grown up, but Maggie felt a reassuring completeness in her familiarity.

She'd struggled with her lack of devil-may-care attitude and quiet routines and somehow had let Gem's decision to sail around the world—and her corresponding decision *not* to—make her feel inadequate and boring. She'd jumped out of a plane trying to escape what she saw as a meaningless existence, but she hadn't found a magical solution on the way down.

She'd found it in Tam. She'd felt complete sitting by her on the edge of the pond, watching dragonflies buzz by. She'd definitely found passion and excitement in Tam's kiss. Somehow, when she'd been rocked from the top of her red head to the bottom of her wader-clad toes, she'd discovered an adventure more terrifying than any skydive. If she yielded to her feelings for Tam and allowed herself to feel the full brunt of her growing desire for her, Maggie would have to be present in her life. Not displaced into the drama and sadness belonging to her patients and their families, and not numbing herself in front of the TV with a plastic bowl of fake food.

When was the last time Maggie had been fully and unabashedly herself? She couldn't even remember. She'd been Jocelyn's sister and her stem-cell donor. She'd never regret the way she'd lost her childhood to Jocelyn's illness—each of them had been refined and defined by the experience. Maggie had turned her attention to the more general population of cancer patients. Now she often felt she lived her patients' lives more than her own.

Loving Tam would change all that. A small, but growing flame of courage inside Maggie said she was ready for the change.

Maggie took one of the Newport exits and drove toward the pier where Mel had told her she'd find Tam tonight, after her return from testing at the hospital in Portland. She had food with her, filling the car with delicious aromas. A chocolate tart from Helen's bakery, and a meal Maggie and Jocelyn had prepared. While they'd been cooking, Ari had sat at the kitchen island working on her new book and tasting everything they offered her. Maggie had felt the last of her stubbornly lingering fears vanish as she watched her sister and Ari interact. They were happy and settling together. They had trips and vacations planned—a research trip to Canada for Ari and a booksellers convention in England for Joss. But they didn't need to prove anything with risks or gambles or massive upheavals in their lifestyles. They kissed and touched and laughed about small, inconsequential things. The revolution occurred in barely discernable increments. They didn't need to throw away jobs, friends, and homes and sail the seven seas. They found meaning together, in daily life. Present with each other.

Maggie's hands shook as she put her car in park and climbed out. The decision to stay in her life, but add Tam to it, required more bravery than she'd ever realized.

She let herself through the chain-link gate and walked along the wooden dock, hearing the suction-like sound of waves lapping against hulls and pylons. She counted boats to find the right one but stopped when the silhouette of Tam made it unnecessary. Tam was sitting lengthwise on a bench, staring out to sea with an expression of calm. Was the calm coming from peace or resignation? She held a glass of wine in one hand and the other rested on the metal railing. Maggie could guess at some of the thoughts in her mind, given the impending surgeries and her experience being near her father again. Were any of Tam's thoughts about her? Maggie hoped so.

"Permission to come aboard?" Maggie asked in a voice loud enough to carry across the wind and waves.

Tam turned toward her with a ghost of a smile. "Sure. Watch your step, though." She put her wineglass down and came over to the railing.

Maggie took Tam's hand and climbed off the dock and onto the unsteady boat. She wavered for a moment, balancing the cardboard box of food on her hip, but soon she felt the rhythm of the waves and she felt more stable.

"I brought dinner and dessert," she said, holding out the box. "If you don't mind company, that is."

Tam took the box from her and carried it to the stern where she set it on a round plastic table. "Wine?"

"Yes, please," Maggie said. She walked around the little sailboat—a tour lasting less than a minute—and then settled on the red bench. "Thanks," she said, taking the glass Tam offered. "How did it go in Portland?"

Tam leaned against the railing and stared out at the harbor. "The surgeon said I'm a perfect match, which you already knew. Then he scheduled the transplant and explained everything that would happen, which you'd already told me."

Maggie nodded even though Tam wasn't looking at her. Tam was right—Maggie had all the details about the medical side of

Tam's life. Tonight wasn't meant to be about Tam's father. Maggie wanted it to be only about her and Tam. She changed the subject to one close at hand, hoping to bring them both here, to the present. "This is a cute boat."

Tam laughed and sat next to her. "Cute? Too tame. This sleek beauty and I have braved the rough ocean and raced whales together. *Cute*," she repeated with a snort.

Maggie laughed. "What I meant to say was what a fiercely intimidating little boat you have."

"Drop the *little* and we're good." She took a sip of her wine. "Have you sailed before?"

"Not much. We went once or twice before Joss got sick, but not after. My dad's boat was one of the many things he had to sell to help cover the deductibles from her medical bills."

"I'm sorry," Tam said.

Maggie shrugged. The years had been tough, but her family had stuck together so tightly they didn't need possessions or elaborate times together to be happy. The contrast between her experience with a sick family member and Tam's was vast. Maggie wanted to be someone stable for Tam to rely on through this ordeal. She had been there for her, as Markus's doctor, but now he had been transferred to a different surgeon and hospital. Maggie's only responsibility now was Tam.

"My ex-girlfriend bought a sailboat. She wanted to leave everything behind and sail around the world, or through the Panama Canal. I don't know. She changed her mind every other day."

Tam raised one eyebrow. "Sounds like a responsible way to plan a serious sailing venture."

"Yeah. I think her main goal was to live without obligations or time schedules, not to be a responsible sailor."

Tam shook her head with a stern expression. "Sailing, especially on the ocean, is a dangerous activity. Without careful planning and the right skills and equipment, she'd be putting herself in danger as well as the lives of those who eventually had to try to rescue her...Sorry. I'll stop my lecture. You apparently weren't party to her irresponsible behavior. Were you one of the things she wanted to leave behind? If so, she was dumber than I originally thought."

Maggie grinned at Tam's quiet addendum to her question. She rested her arm on the railing so her hand was next to Tam's shoulder. "No. She asked me to go with her, and she had some brutally expressed opinions about my character when I said no."

"Aargh," Tam said with a visible shudder. "The thought of you out there with her, clutching the mast while she tried to sail through an ocean storm, makes me sick." She grabbed Maggie's hand off the railing and kissed it. "You made the right decision."

"I doubted myself at first. Not really about going with her, because it would have been a disaster, even without the mast-clutching and the storm. But a lot of the criticisms she threw at me really hit home. Jocelyn's sickness scared me. Facing the loss of my twin sister was overwhelming when I was little—of course, it would be at any time in life, but I was old enough to be aware of death and too young to really understand it on an intellectual level. I got scared, and the fear never went away. I'm still protective of Jocelyn, even though she's better now and old enough to take care of herself. Even more, though, I shelter myself from any chance of loss. It was easy to let go of Gem, and I realized how little I truly cared about her or the other women I've dated. But you? I'd give up my career and my home and sail to the end of the world with you. That scares the hell out of me."

"But you're here anyway, aren't you, brave Maggie?" Tam cradled Maggie's hand against her cheek.

Maggie shrugged. "I'm here. Hoping you'll let me stay." The expression on Tam's face was glowing with what Maggie suspected was a mix of loving and being loved. She had to look away and get her breath back again, but she didn't make any move to pull away. "I'm here, but I have one request."

"Anything."

Maggie scooted across the bench and into Tam's arms when she heard the utter truth behind Tam's single word. "Well, if we do decide to drop everything and sail away, can we get a bigger boat?

As cute…er, fierce as this one is, it looks like it might break into splinters if the swells got too high."

Tam gave an indignant gasp and then held Maggie against her and tickled her side until she breathlessly begged her to stop.

"Say you're sorry first," Tam said, wrapping her arms around Maggie's waist.

"Fine, I'm sorry I called your boat—"

"Not to me. To my boat."

"Okay, okay," Maggie said with a laugh. "I'm sorry, tiny boat…"

Tam laughed along with her and settled Maggie between her legs, with Maggie's back pressed against her chest. "We'll need to work on your respect for this craft," she said. "But we're both willing to forgive you and bring you aboard as first mate."

Maggie turned her head and kissed Tam, lingering as their joking and playfulness subsided and her arousal grew. "First your secretary and now your first mate? We'll need to discuss a role reversal before this relationship goes any further."

Tam rested her hand on the side of Maggie's face and kissed her again. "Then, in the interest of moving this relationship into the cabin, I'll give you an immediate promotion."

Maggie twisted around and rested her body flush against Tam's. "As long as the boat has a bed, it's big enough for me." She kissed Tam with all the passion they'd shared in the pond, but without the need to push her away and force distance between them. Never again. She broke away from the kiss with all the willpower she could muster. "I'd like a tour of the cabin right now, please."

"Aye, aye, Captain," Tam said with a grin.

EPILOGUE

Mel rearranged some bottles of liquor on the small mahogany table to make room for the covered containers of cherries and lime wedges. She flipped through the thick stack of papers on her clipboard until she came to the page labeled *Bar* and crossed off the two items. Then she went over to the long folding tables lining the back wall of the studio and mumbled to herself as she made sure everything was in place. Stainless-steel chafing dishes and decorative glass dishes stood on the sea-foam green linens, ready to be filled with either hot or refrigerated food. Everything Mel could leave on the table during the ceremony was already there— pale peach plates and napkins, freshly baked rolls, and big bowls of early-summer fruit.

She went over her to-do lists one more time before looking up from her clipboard with a huge sigh. Hosting weddings at the inn was one of the most time-consuming and stressful parts of her job, but also her very favorite. She agonized over every detail even though she'd done so many weddings by now, she had the routine down cold. The responsibility of caring for a couple's most important day was overwhelming, especially when the brides were her close friends.

Mel looked around the studio. The artwork usually took center stage here, but for this day it was relegated to a back corner. The task of moving the fragile items used to be easy, but now that Aspen was working here with Pam, there were large sculptures to move as well as Pam's easels and canvases. Mel walked among the pieces, making certain any interested guests could move among them without jostling anything. She noticed a few new student sculptures and drawings in the mix. Heather was taking her role as Pam's new partner seriously, and she'd kept a steady flow of visiting artists coming through the studio. The blend of ideas and approaches was exciting to Mel, both because the studio was a popular place for the inn's guests to visit and mostly because she could see how much the fresh input invigorated Pam.

Mel turned away from Aspen's recent work, a stunning life-sized nude female. The woman was twisting away from the viewer, and a curtain of hair and a raised hand kept the form general and not recognizable as a specific person, but Mel was pretty sure the model was Heather. She shook her head. TMI. The finished sculpture would be a gorgeous addition to any home or gallery, but Mel felt a little awkward looking at it too directly when she spent so many evenings sitting across a dinner table from Heather herself, either here at the inn or in Pam's old beachside bungalow where Heather and Aspen now lived.

"Anyone order a cake?" A familiar voice interrupted Mel's musings. "Oh, hi, Heather. I didn't see you there."

Mel came out from behind an easel and laughed when she saw Helen pretending to address Aspen's statue. Helen and Jenny were carrying a piece of plywood with an enormous sheet cake on it.

Jenny gave a loud wolf whistle. "Looking good, Heather. But when the invitation said casual attire I don't think it meant stark naked."

"You two have to stop or I won't be able to look the real Heather in the eye when I see her today," Mel said. She looked at the cake Helen had made in the shape of a large open book. Beautiful cursive writing in icing spelled out the phrase *The story of my life began the day I met you* on the pastel fondant. "Helen, it's lovely. What a perfect design for them."

"It's lovely and heavy," Jenny commented with an exaggerated sigh.

Mel took one edge of the plywood and helped them carry the cake over to a table near the dance floor. She was more than delighted to hand over the job of cake baking to Helen these days. Before the Sand Dollar Bakery had become a fixture at Cannon Beach, Mel had made most of the cakes for weddings at the inn. The tiers were a nightmare to assemble, and the most intricate decorations she could make were frosting roses. Once they set the cake in place she leaned over and examined it more closely. "You do such marvelous design work."

"Maybe you can ice a blouse onto Heather over there," Jenny said, wrapping her arm around Helen's shoulders as soon as her hands were free.

"I have an extra apron in the car. She can wear it during the reception."

"Come on, you two." Mel put her hands on her hips and tried to speak with mock severity, although her laughter betrayed her. "Aspen's just expressing her love. It's sweet."

Jenny tilted her head and regarded Mel for a few moments. "Did Pam express her love through oil paintings when the two of you first got together?"

"Of course not," Mel said. She felt her cheeks burn and knew she must be bright red. "Well, there might have been some sketches, but nothing we'd put on display."

Helen turned to Jenny. "I'll bet they're in her bedroom. You distract her and I'll go search."

"What's so funny?" Heather joined their trio. She still dressed in tailored and pressed clothes as if she was heading back to her old banking job, but Mel saw the transformation in Heather's face. Her expression was soft and happy, a far cry from the tension and uncertainty she'd shown when she'd first arrived at the ocean.

"We were talking about Naked Heather," Jenny said, gesturing toward the statue. "We're debating whether to frost her or cover her with an apron."

"Jenny!" Mel exclaimed at the same time that Helen punched Jenny lightly on the arm.

"Neither one," Heather said indignantly. She looked at the statue and grinned. "I like her just the way she is."

Mel excused herself from the laughing group when she saw

Maggie and Tam entering the studio. As she left, she overheard Helen making a comment about some risqué drawings Pam had allegedly made. She wrote a quick note on her clipboard to lock the door leading down to the bedroom she shared with Pam in case one of the three went searching for them.

"How are you feeling, Tam?" Mel asked, giving her and Maggie a hug. Maggie's gold locket gleamed against her simple ivory dress and her red hair was clipped off her face. She looked as radiant as her twin had when Mel saw her this morning. Tam, in contrast, was too pale and she leaned against Maggie for support.

"I'm fine," Tam said, then she shrugged. "To be honest, I feel about as ill as you and Pam looked when I took you sailing. But in another week or two I'll be back to normal."

"And your father?"

Tam and Maggie exchanged glances. "His prognosis is good," Maggie said. She rested her hand on Tam's chest, just above her heart. "Thanks to Tam."

Mel nodded and didn't pry. She had never been told the details of Tam's relationship with her dad, but she knew enough to realize it was a touchy subject. Tam had made it through her surgery and she had saved a life, and that was all Mel needed to know.

"I'm very glad to hear it." She held out her arm. "Why don't we find you a seat in the garden, Tam? Jocelyn is upstairs getting dressed and probably wants Maggie's help."

Maggie kissed Tam and left to find her sister. Mel thought Tam might brush off her offer of support, but she linked her arm with Mel's and they walked slowly out to the garden.

"Did you hear how she proposed?" Tam asked.

Mel stopped in surprise. "Maggie proposed to you? How wonderful!"

Tam laughed. "Yikes, no. Not yet. I mean we haven't…I meant Ariana."

Mel smiled. Tam wasn't nearly as pale anymore. "Oh, my mistake. No, I haven't heard the story yet."

"She told Jocelyn it wasn't fair that she always recommended books to other people, but no one did the same for her. So Ari gave her one to read. She'd bound a collection of her journal entries starting from the first day she met Joss. The last entry apparently was all about how much she loved Jocelyn and wanted them to spend the rest of their lives together."

Mel sighed and started walking again. "How beautiful."

"I know," Tam agreed.

Mel stopped by a chair near the spot where Maggie would be standing during the ceremony and helped Tam settle in it. "I'd never have pegged you as a romantic."

"Me either," Tam said. She rested her hand on her lower abdomen and winced slightly as she shifted in her chair. "Until I met Maggie. She changed everything. They wanted to postpone the wedding in case I wasn't well enough to come. I told Jocelyn I couldn't think of a better place to recuperate than here, celebrating with them."

Mel heard the wonder in Tam's voice. Had Tam ever before experienced anything like the sense of family Maggie had brought into her life? She brushed her hand over Tam's shoulder. Whatever healing Tam needed after her surgery, both emotional and physical, Mel was certain Maggie would help her through it.

❖

Almost an hour later, Mel had finally laid aside her clipboard and was sitting next to Pam in the garden. The cry of a lone seagull whirling overhead blended with the pure scent of salt and enveloped them in the ocean's distinct atmosphere. An old sailboat and some flowering shrubs decorated the small alcove, but Mel never had to add decorating to the myriad details she oversaw before a wedding. The curve of Haystack Rock, defined by sharp edges of basalt, and the thump and swoosh of the waves hitting the beach and then receding made this area more special than cut flowers or streamers could ever do.

Ariana and Jocelyn stood in front of everyone and recited the vows they had written. While Jocelyn was speaking, a soft breeze teased a few strands of her auburn hair free from their tidy coil, and

Ari brushed them back in place with one gentle finger. Mel sighed and squeezed Pam's hand. This ceremony was a formal declaration of their commitment, but small gestures like Ari's seemed to show real love even more clearly.

Mel glanced at Pam and saw her watching the gull soaring on invisible currents. It was nearly a year to the day after the oil spill had threatened to strangle the life out of their home. Mel hadn't been certain their business or town would survive the disaster, but here they were in a garden, at a wedding, surrounded by friends and love. The community hadn't let the spill destroy them. Instead, the tragedy had opened hearts and lives in unexpected ways.

Pam looked at Mel and gave her a smile tinged with the depth of the past year. Sadness and hope mixed together. She lifted Mel's hand to her lips and kissed it before cradling it on her lap.

Mel smiled, too, and returned her attention to the ceremony. The little gestures meant the whole world.

About the Author

Karis Walsh is a native of the Pacific Northwest and an adopted citizen of Texas. When she isn't wrapped up in a book—either reading or writing one—she spends her time with her animals, playing music on her viola or violin, or hiking among the prickly pears.

Books Available From Bold Strokes Books

Best Laid Plans by Jan Gayle. Nicky and Lauren are meant for each other, but Nicky's haunting past and Lauren's societal fears threaten to derail all possibilities of a relationship. (978-1-62639-658-6)

Exchange by CF Frizzell. When Shay Maguire rode into rural Montana, she never expected to meet the woman of her dreams—or to learn Mel Baker was held hostage by legal agreement to her right-wing father. (978-1-62639-679-1)

Just Enough Light by AJ Quinn. Will a serial killer's return to Colorado destroy Kellen Ryan and Dana Kingston's chance at love, or can the search-and-rescue team save themselves? (978-1-62639-685-2)

Rise of the Rain Queen by Fiona Zedde. Nyandoro is nobody's princess. She fights, curses, fornicates, and gets into as much trouble as her brothers. But the path to a throne is not always the one we expect. (978-1-62639-592-3)

Tales from Sea Glass Inn by Karis Walsh. Over the course of a year at Cannon Beach, tourists and locals alike find solace and passion at the Sea Glass Inn. (978-1-62639-643-2)

The Color of Love by Radclyffe. Black sheep Derian Winfield needs to convince literary agent Emily May to marry her to save the Winfield Agency and solve Emily's green card problem, but Derian didn't count on falling in love. (978-1-62639-716-3)

A Reluctant Enterprise by Gun Brooke. When two women grow up learning nothing but distrust, unworthiness, and abandonment, it's no wonder they are apprehensive and fearful when an overwhelming love just won't be denied. (978-1-62639-500-8)

Above the Law by Carsen Taite. Love is the last thing on Agent Dale Nelson's mind, but reporter Lindsey Ryan's investigation could change the way she sees everything—her career, her past, and her future. (978-1-62639-558-9)

Actual Stop by Kara A. McLeod. When Special Agent Ryan O'Connor's present collides abruptly with her past, shots are fired, and the course of her life is irrevocably altered. (978-1-62639-675-3)

Embracing the Dawn by Jeannie Levig. When ex-con Jinx Tanner and business executive E. J. Bastien awaken after a one-night stand to find their lives inextricably entangled, love has its work cut out for it. (978-1-62639-576-3)

Love's Redemption by Donna K. Ford. For ex-convict Rhea Daniels and ex-priest Morgan Scott, redemption lies in the thin line between right and wrong. (978-1-62639-673-9)

The Shewstone by Jane Fletcher. The prophetic Shewstone is in Eawynn's care, but unfortunately for her, Matt is coming to steal it. (978-1-62639-554-1)

Jane's World by Paige Braddock. Jane's PayBuddy account gets hacked and she inadvertently purchases a mail order bride from the Eastern Bloc. (978-1-62639-494-0)

A Touch of Temptation by Julie Blair. Recent law school graduate Kate Dawson's ordained path to the perfect life gets thrown off course when handsome butch top Chris Brent initiates her to sexual pleasure. (978-1-62639-488-9)

Beneath the Waves by Ali Vali. Kai Merlin and Vivien Palmer love the water and the secrets trapped in the depths, but if Kai gives in to her feelings, it might come at a cost to her entire realm. (978-1-62639-609-8)

Girls on Campus, edited by Sandy Lowe and Stacia Seaman. College: four years when rules are made to be broken. This collection is required reading for anyone looking to earn an A in sex ed. (978-1-62639-733-0)

Miss Match by Fiona Riley. Matchmaker Samantha Monteiro makes the impossible possible for everyone but herself. Is mysterious dancer Lucinda Moss her perfect match? (978-1-62639-574-9)